"Oh, you're going to pay, Olivia. Now lift up that skirt and show me your panties."

Olivia blinked. "Excuse me?"

"Your panties," Deacon repeated. "I want to see them." He watched a blush stain her cheeks and her breasts lift in a quick inhalation of breath.

"B-but why?"

"Let's just say that your lingerie designs intrigued me, and I've been wondering what style you chose as your own."

She glanced at the door and then whispered, "Someone could walk in."

The fact that she was even considering it excited him even more. "Don't tell me you're too bashful."

There was a moment's hesitation before she spoke so softly that he had to tip his head closer just to hear. "What with everything, I haven't had a chance to do laundry." She swallowed and blushed even brighter. "So…"

Her words trailed off, taking all the oxygen in the air with them. He couldn't think past one thing. Olivia wasn't wearing any panties. What had started out as an attempt to get a little peek escalated to an overwhelming desire to touch. And sure enough, above the tops of the sheer, silky, thigh-high stockings was nothing but sweet, warm, welcoming flesh…

TROUBLE IN TEXAS

"Sizzles with raunchy fun...[Elizabeth and Brant's] dynamic provides the drama to complete this fast-paced novel's neatly assembled package of sex, humor, and mystery."

—Publishers Weekly

"Lots of fun and games, enticing intrigues with tidbits of wisdom here and there make *Trouble in Texas* a tantalizing tale...Katie Lane's writing style keeps the reader turning pages."

—LongandShortReviews.com

CATCH ME A COWBOY

"Lane gives readers a rip-roaring good time while making what could feel like a farce insightful and real, just like the characters themselves."

—Booklist

"Katie Lane is quickly becoming a must-buy author if one is looking for humorous country romance! This story is an absolute hoot to read! The characters are real and endearing...the situations are believable (especially if one has ever lived in a small town) and sometimes hilarious, and the romance is hot as a June bug in July!

—Affaire de Coeur

MAKE MINE A BAD BOY

GOING COWBOY CRAZY

ACCLAIM FOR THE HUNK FOR THE HOLIDAYS SERIES

RING IN THE HOLIDAYS

"A return visit to the headstrong McPherson family for another year of holiday high jinks...Lane's trademark brand of humor will keep the pages turning."

—RT Book Reviews

"Fans will enjoy this sexy and humorous story."

—Publishers Weekly

"*Ring in the Holidays* is all at once extremely sexy, intense, and a compelling story."

—FreshFiction.com

HUNK FOR THE HOLIDAYS

"4½ stars! Sharp, witty dialogue, a solid sense of humor, and a dab hand at sizzling sex is going to push Lane far, if this is an example."

—RT Book Reviews

"Lane's contemporary series launch sizzles from the moment Cassie McPherson's hired escort appears to accompany her to the company Christmas party...The romance is inevitable, but Lane makes the couple work for it, writing with warmth and humor. [Readers will] adore James, Cassie, and the affectionately jocular McPhersons."

—*Publishers Weekly*

"I was interested from the first page to the last...There was enough chemistry between Cassie and James to set the place on fire."

—Romancing-the-Book.com

A BILLIONAIRE
between the sheets

Also by Katie Lane

Deep in the Heart of Texas series

Going Cowboy Crazy
Make Mine a Bad Boy
Small Town Christmas (anthology)
Catch Me a Cowboy
Trouble in Texas
Flirting with Texas
A Match Made in Texas
The Last Cowboy in Texas

Other novels

Hunk for the Holidays
Ring in the Holidays
Unwrapped

A BILLIONAIRE
between the sheets

KATIE LANE

FOREVER

NEW YORK   BOSTON

Forever
Hachette Book Group
1290 Avenue of the Americas
New York, NY 10104

HachetteBookGroup.com

Printed in the United States of America

First Edition: November 2015
10 9 8 7 6 5 4 3 2 1

OPM

Forever is an imprint of Grand Central Publishing.
The Forever name and logo are trademarks of Hachette Book Group, Inc.

The Hachette Speakers Bureau provides a wide range of authors for speaking events. To find out more, go to www.hachettespeakersbureau.com or call (866) 376-6591.

The publisher is not responsible for websites (or their content) that are not owned by the publisher.

To Jamie, the author of my happily ever after

CHAPTER ONE

Did I close the garage door before I left the house? Slap!
Is that moss dripping from those trees or some type of vine?
Slap! *Can you die from too many mosquito bites?* Slap!

Olivia Harrington reached around to the side pocket of
her backpack and pulled out the bug repellent. Not that it
seemed to help. The bloodsuckers didn't even wait for the
mist to settle before they were back biting.

"Got DEET."

She glanced at the man behind her. He stood in the
back of the pirogue, the sinewy muscles in his saggy-
skinned arms flexing as he used a long pole to propel
the boat through the murky water. She wondered if that
type of pole had a name. Then she wondered if the man
was too old for such exercise. He looked to be about as
ancient as her neighbors Mr. and Mrs. Huckabee, who
had waved at her from their balcony that morning when
she left for the airport. She had waved back, but averted
her eyes. The Huckabees were nudists who, at well over

seventy, completely ignored the city ordinances about flaunting private parts. Thinking about leaving San Francisco brought Olivia full circle to wondering whether she'd closed the garage door.

"DEET," the old man repeated in his mumbled Cajun accent as he continued to lift the pole and press it against the bottom of the swamp in a slow and steady rhythm that would've been soothing if she were in Venice on vacation. But she wasn't in Venice. She was in Louisiana on a business trip. The most important business trip of her life. Which meant she needed to get a handle on her easily distracted brain and focus.

Smiling politely, she tried to motivate him—not that she had ever been good at motivating people. "Do you think you could...umm...pole a little faster?"

The old man lifted the pole and repositioned it. "Skeeter spray got DEET?"

"Oh!" She squinted at the ingredients on the bottle of insect repellent. She had bought it from REI, along with a backpack, a wide-brimmed hat, a T-shirt, khaki shorts, and an ugly pair of hiking boots that laced around her ankles. As a non-traveler, she'd been thinking more African safari than Louisiana bayou. What she really needed was a pair of night goggles, a fan, and, apparently, DEET.

A splash drew her attention to the left bank. With very little sunlight filtering in through the thick branches of the moss-covered trees, it was hard to tell what had made the sound. Probably one of those long-legged birds. The thought of birds had her thinking of her own bird problem. Jonathan Livingston was an annoying seagull who had taken to landing on her balcony, eating whatever garbage he had collected, and leaving his calling card on her Pottery Barn outdoor rug. It was truly disgusting, and she had bought more carpet cleaner in the last month than she'd bought coffee. And she bought a lot of coffee. It was the only thing that seemed to keep her mind on track—

"Gator."

The word focused her brain better than a double shot of espresso. She scanned the water between the bank and the boat as she inched back on the seat. "As in alligator? Where?"

"Just yonder."

Yonder? How did that translate? Fifteen feet? Ten? Two? Olivia tried to stay composed, but it was hard to be composed when you were traveling in "gator"-infested waters in a banana peel of a boat.

"Can they jump?" she asked.

The man kept lifting and pushing, taking his sweet time in answering. Figuring that his nonchalant demeanor was a good sign, she relaxed her shoulders. Her calm was short-lived when the man spoke.

"Up until last year, would've said no." Lift. Push. Lift. Push. "Damned gator knocked Cousin Pip right out of the boat and death-rolled him."

"Death roll? What's a—" A thump had the boat wobbling and her composure completely deserting her. "Ohmygod!" She jumped to her feet and attempted to join the man in the back of the boat. Unfortunately, she was more agile in high heels than in awkward hiking boots. She stumbled and fell headfirst over the side.

The water was colder than she'd thought it would be. Or maybe it was just cold in comparison to the hot, humid air. Air she now struggled to find. Being a northern California girl, she wasn't that good a swimmer to begin with, and the heavy backpack didn't help matters. It weighed her down like a pair of cement shoes, quickly taking her to the mushy bottom. As much as she wanted to hang on to the backpack and her dreams, she realized she would have to make a choice. She had just slipped off one strap when strong jaws clamped her waist and pulled her through the murky water like a rag doll. She kicked and fought against the death roll, but it was no use.

It took her breaking the surface of the water and air rushing into her empty lungs for her to realize that she wasn't locked in an alligator's grip as much as a man's. At first she thought that it was the old man she'd paid to bring her into the swamp, and she marveled at his strength and agility. But then a deep voice spoke next to her ear that sounded nothing like the pirogue gondolier's. This voice was silky Southern and used pronouns.

"You need to be still or I'll leave you to the gator."

Olivia stopped struggling and relaxed in his hold, and with just a few strong kicks, he had her on the bank. Exhausted, she lay in the thick grass, too weak to even push her slime-coated hair from her face. With the backpack still attached, she no doubt looked like a beached turtle as she listened to the conversation between the men.

"What were you thinking bringing a little bit of a helpless girl out here, Coon?" the man who'd saved her asked.

Olivia bristled at the demeaning reference. She might not be able to reach the top items on a grocery shelf, but she was not helpless. But before she could defend herself, Coon spoke.

"Deliver my granny to the devil for a hundred."

"A hundred? She paid you a hundred dollars?"

Another long pause. "Yep." There was a creak of wood and the swish of displaced water.

"Coon, you are *not* leaving her here," the man said

with authority. His statement was quickly followed by an exasperated "Shee-it."

It took a moment for Olivia to realize what was happening. By the time she sat up and swiped the hair from her face, the pirogue was already heading back the way it had come.

"Wait!" She wobbled to her feet, weaving like her mother after one of her social events. "I gave you a hundred dollars to take me to the Beaumonts'."

Coon lifted the pole and pushed, then did it again before answering. "Done it."

Surprised, she glanced back at the man who stood on the bank not more than ten feet away. He looked like some kind of hairy swamp creature. Lichen slime streaked his dark, shoulder-length hair and his thick beard.

Even with the beard and the passage of sixteen years, Olivia had no trouble recognizing the oldest Beaumont brother. Although Deacon Valentino had filled out since she'd last seen him. His shoulders were broader and the muscles of his chest more defined. But he still had the same arrogant stance and hard features.

"Who are you?" he demanded.

Suddenly alligators weren't the only threats in the swamp. But having grown up with the owner of the most successful lingerie company in the world, she had learned how to show no fear—even to intimidating men who studied her with an intensity that was as palpable as the humidity. Holding Deacon's direct gaze, she squished her way closer and held out a hand.

"You probably don't remember me, but I'm—" A strange tingling sensation had her slapping at her neck. But instead of a mosquito, she encountered a glob of goo. "What in the world?"

"Leech."

Her tough-businesswoman act vanished, and she released a high-pitched squeal that had birds taking flight. She clawed at her neck, but the plump, slimy leech held tight, which turned her squeal into more of a hysterical scream. "Get it off me!" She slapped and spun in circles.

"Stand still," he ordered, and grabbed her arm. Her squeals lowered to breathy whimpers as he tipped up her chin and examined her neck. She felt the scrape of his nail against her skin before he tossed something over his shoulder and it plopped into the swamp. Then he ran his fingers along the collar of her shirt, behind her ears, and through her hair. And she had to admire his competent thoroughness...and the heat of his skin. After the cold dip in the swamp, the contrast took her breath away—as did his eyes.

The Beaumont brothers all had deep indigo eyes that bordered on violet—a color she had tried to duplicate more than once in satins and silks. Now she realized she had failed miserably. Deacon's eyes were more intense— an almost Technicolor vibrant. As she studied them, there was a flicker of something in their depths.

"What?" she said. "Are there more leeches?"

Without a word he released her and turned away. She watched as he picked up a cell phone that was lying on the ground. He glanced at the screen with a long, spidery crack and frowned.

"It should still work," she said. "I dropped mine once and it cracked, but it worked fine until I could get a new one."

His frown deepened before he grabbed his fishing pole and tackle box and headed along a path that led into the trees.

"Wait!" She hurried after him to explain why she was there. But it was hard to explain while dodging the tree branches Deacon released in her face. She batted them away and then got distracted by the good three inches of underwear that showed above the waistband of his wet camouflage pants.

Having spent the last year studying men's underwear, Olivia knew they weren't designer. Probably discount store. Boxer briefs. Cotton with a touch of polyester. Still, she liked the way the wide band hugged his trim waist and the white—almost transparent—cotton conformed to the top muscles of his butt. If she hadn't been on a mission, she would've asked him the brand. But she was on a mission. A mission that involved getting his signature. Not the brand name of his undies.

He led her farther into the trees to a ramshackle house on stilts that looked like it had come straight out of Critter Country in Disneyland. It was made of rustic, bleached-out boards with a sagging roof and porch. A rocking chair sat on the porch, along with a rusty antique washing machine. Not the kind that you plugged in, but the kind with two tubs and crank rollers that wrung out water.

"You live here?" she asked.

Instead of answering he set the fishing pole and tackle box down by the stairs and reached for a coiled garden hose. A part of her felt a little guilty that this was his home. The other part—the business part—jumped for joy. If he and his brothers lived in the run-down shack in an alligator- and leech-infested swamp, her proposition would be all the more appealing. Which would make the harrowing past few moments well worth it. Now all she had to do was convince the Beaumont brothers.

But right when she started to speak, he turned on the hose. Green slime was quickly washed away to reveal tanned skin and hard muscle. One would think that, after spending the last week looking at male underwear models, she would be difficult to impress. But Olivia was more than impressed. The boyish models with their overdeveloped stomach muscles and hairless chests didn't hold a candle to the image of virile masculinity before her. Deacon had a man's body. Broad shoulders and sculpted muscles that didn't look like they had been formed by protein shakes and hours spent at the gym, but rather by a carnivorous diet and hard work. A line of dark hair ran from the waistband of his boxers up a flat stomach with just the right amount of abdominal definition before it fanned out between his pectoral muscles. Two perfectly formed pectoral muscles that made Olivia's palms tingle.

She had always had fine-tuned tactile perception. And this heightened sense of touch had made her extremely good at picking out the perfect fabrics for lingerie designs. She wanted to touch now. To cup each pec in her hands and test the hardness of the muscle and the rigidness of each puckered nipple. But before she could do something really stupid, he shook his hair, sending water flying. The feel of the ice-cold droplets snapped her back to reality.

He scraped his hair off his high forehead and directed those indigo eyes at her. "What do you want?"

Since touching was out of the question, she swallowed and got straight to the point. "I'm here to offer you a proposition."

"Really?" He took a step closer. Then another. His bare, narrow feet stopped a mere inch from the toes of her hiking boots. "You came clear out here to proposition me?"

She ignored the innuendo. "Not just you, but also your brothers." The water droplets in his thick beard caught her attention. "Does it itch?"

His brow knotted in puzzlement before he turned and walked away. "Sorry. Not interested in any proposition." He climbed the long row of rickety steps to the porch.

"You haven't even heard what it is."

"Don't need to." He shimmied out of his jeans and underwear, jerked opened the screen door, and disappeared inside the house with a flash of virile manhood—followed by a longer look of pale, well-defined butt. A well-defined butt that would look great in an underwear ad. But as great as his ass was, his penis was the thing that held her attention long after the screen door slammed. She'd thought that cold water caused shrinkage, but he hadn't looked shrunk. And if his penis was that big after a dousing in cold water, what would it look like fully aroused?

Usually it took plenty of foreplay to get her aroused, and even then an orgasm wasn't a given. Yet with just a flash of flesh, this Beaumont brother had her primed and ready. Obviously the stress of the last six months was causing weird bodily reactions.

Taking two deep breaths, she climbed the stairs, stopping to remove her muddy boots and socks before she stepped inside. She expected a typical bachelor's pad—clutter, dirty dishes in the sink, empty bottles of beer and pizza boxes. But although the furniture was old, the inside was neat and clean. The main room had a fireplace, a dilapidated couch with a rolled-up sleeping bag and pillow stacked on one end, a card table with a laptop and four nylon-strapped aluminum lawn chairs around it, and a small kitchenette with a refrigerator and stove as ancient as the washing machine on the porch.

Deacon was nowhere in sight. But there were three closed doors off the main room that she didn't hesitate to open. The first room held a neatly made bed, a nightstand with a stack of books and magazines, and a scarred dresser. The second room was much messier. Clothes were strewn across the floor, the twin bed was unmade, and acrylic paint and paintbrushes cluttered the top of the dresser. Next to the dresser, an easel sat in front of the window, holding a painting of a naked woman reclining on a faded quilt. With a minor in graphic design, Olivia knew that whoever had painted this was good. Very good.

The squeak of water pulled her attention away from the painting and had her checking the last door. It was a small bathroom with a sink, toilet, and bathtub shower. Through the plastic curtain, she could see the shadowy outline of a man lathering his body. Limbs lifted and hands glided, causing the tingle of sexual awareness to return. She ignored it and cleared her throat. The shadowy figure halted in mid-lather.

"I just need a few minutes," she said. "Two tops. And believe me, it will be well worth your while."

After only a second, the infuriating man started to sing Barry Manilow's "Copacabana" in a loud baritone. Olivia groaned in exasperation and turned to the mirror over the sink.

Talk about a swamp creature. She looked like she'd been slimed by the kids on Nickelodeon. Her normally shiny blond hair was tinted green with bits of bark and whatever else lived in the bayou. Besides the leech suction mark on her neck, she had numerous mosquito bites on her arms, and her clothes were just plain disgusting. For a brief moment, she considered hopping in the shower with Deacon, clothes and all, and joining in on the chorus. Instead she took off her backpack and reached for the bar of Dial soap on the side of the sink. She had just finished washing her hands and face when the screen door slammed, the sound followed by the loud clomp of boots and unidentifiable clicks. By the time she'd dried with the towel on the rack, two bearded men and a big dog had appeared in the doorway.

The dog gave one deep-throated woof. Olivia might've been scared if the animal with the droopy face hadn't had the most soulful eyes she'd ever seen.

"Don't mind Blue," the taller of the two men said in a Southern drawl that slipped from his lips like the finest satin. "That's just his way of saying hello. He loves the ladies." He flashed a lazy smile that, even disguised by a full beard, dripped with sex appeal. "Nash Beaumont at your service, ma'am."

The water shut off, and the plastic shower curtain jerked back so hard that it tore from two of the metal hooks. Standing there with water cascading down his naked body, Deacon looked at his brother.

"No need to introduce yourself, Nash. You and Grayson should remember Uncle Michael's brat."

CHAPTER TWO

Deacon Beaumont had pictured his second meeting with Olivia Harrington much differently. In his fantasies he was always dressed in an expensive designer suit and either helping a supermodel out of his brand-new Maserati or sitting behind a massive desk in his penthouse office. Olivia was always dressed in hand-me-downs and begging for money...and mercy. Of course in the fantasy he gave her neither. Money and mercy were for people who deserved them. And as far as he was concerned, Olivia didn't deserve anything but his strong dislike.

His hatred was reserved for her stepfather.

Nash took a towel off the rack and handed it to him. "I'm going to make a guess and say that you and our cousin decided to take a swim. And while I would love to hear the story, I think it can wait until after we show Olivia some Southern hospitality and let her get out of those wet clothes."

Olivia's clothes were soaked. Her white T-shirt was completely transparent, showing every detail of the lacy bra beneath. And when Nash's gaze lowered, Deacon had to squelch the desire to wrap the towel around her. Fortunately, his brother had never been much of a gawker and quickly averted his gaze.

Grayson, on the other hand, was out-and-out gawking. He had always had an almost reverent fixation on women. He had trouble talking to them, but he loved to look at them. And paint them. It didn't matter if they were beautiful or plain. Skinny or fat. Young or old. Or covered in bug bites and lichen. If you were a woman, Grayson wanted you as one of his subjects. For some reason—his brother's pretty-boy good looks or his innocent blushes—women didn't mind posing for him, usually with their clothes off.

Well, it wasn't happening with Olivia. She wasn't staying long enough for Grayson to paint her, or for Nash to show off his Southern hospitality. And Deacon made that perfectly clear when he shoved both his brothers out of the bathroom and slammed the door behind him.

"She's not staying," he said as he strode into his bedroom.

Nash and Blue followed, Nash flopping down on the bed Deacon had painstakingly made that morning and Blue dropping to the floor in a puddle of loose bloodhound skin. "We can't just throw her out, Deke," Nash said. "Especially when she came all the way here to visit her Louisiana cousins."

Deacon glanced back to see Grayson standing in front of the closed bathroom door, his hand twitching as if he were sketching Olivia. "Jesus." He walked into the hallway and grabbed his brother by the collar of his shirt and pulled him into the bedroom before closing the door. "There is no way prissy Miss Olivia Harrington trekked from California just for a visit. Especially after the way she treated us the first time we met. And we're not her cousins. Her gold-digging mother just happened to marry our filthy-rich asshole of an uncle."

"I don't remember being treated that badly." Nash stretched out on the bed and tucked a pillow behind his head. "If Donny John had shown up at my California mansion begging for money with his three urchin sons in tow, I would've called the cops too."

Deacon pointed a finger at him. "Get your dirty boots off my bed." After Nash rolled his eyes and complied, Deacon pulled open the top dresser drawer and took a clean pair of boxers from the neatly folded stack. "No, instead good-hearted Uncle Michael took pity on his poor hillbilly relatives and invited us to stay the night before kicking us out the following morning."

"Only after you molested his stepdaughter." Grayson finally pulled his head out of the clouds and entered the conversation.

Deacon slammed the drawer. "I did not molest Olivia!"

Grayson raised his hands. "I believe you, Deke. But you have to admit that the evidence was pretty damning."

"Damning evidence seems to be the bane of the Beaumont brothers," Nash said dryly. And if anyone knew about damning evidence, it was Nash. He had spent months in jail after being falsely accused of a crime.

Olivia hadn't accused Deacon, but she hadn't spoken up for him either. She had just stood on the balcony like a spoiled Juliet and watched as the neighborhood security officers escorted him and his family off the property. Now she wanted to offer him and his brothers some kind of proposition. Well, as far as he was concerned, she'd had her chance to talk.

"One of you can take her back to town." He pulled on the boxers. "I need to head out to the work site."

"What work site?" Nash asked. "I thought you couldn't break ground until you reeled in a new investor. Did you find one?"

Deacon had. Unfortunately, the one investor he had on the line was the one he didn't want to reel in. Francesca Devereux had made it very clear what she wanted from the deal. And it wasn't a return on her investment. She wanted a cougar cub—a man she could parade around her social events like her froufrou pet poodle. Deacon had never been pet material. But he wasn't the type of guy to give up either. The project had taken him years to pull together, and he was convinced the lakeside condos would make money. If he had to prove it by becoming some rich woman's arm candy, then so be it.

He pulled open another drawer. "Speaking of catching, you need to catch a job, Nash—instead of living here for free."

"Free? I cook all the meals, and I believe Grandpa willed this house to all of us. Besides, I'm working on an idea that could make us filthy rich."

"Is that what you've been doing on your laptop? And here I thought you'd been playing games."

Nash grinned. "Maybe a few. But I'm telling you, big brother, that apps are the wave of the future. And I have this idea for a great app that will work in conjunction with all the new electronic sensors they have out. With just a tap of your phone, you can dim your lights, turn on music, and start up your gas logs."

"Dim your lights, turn on music, and start a fire? Are we talking business or seduction, Nash?"

Nash laughed. "Why can't we talk both? And I don't need an app to seduce women, Deke."

It was the truth. Nash didn't need anything to seduce women. There was something in his DNA that made women do things they would never do with another man.

"And when will this app be ready to make money?"

Nash got to his feet. "Unfortunately, I find myself in the same boat as you're in. In order to start making money, I'll need an investor."

Great. Maybe Francesca wouldn't mind three pet poodles.

Grayson, on the other hand, wasn't thinking about needing money or making it. As if he were sleepwalking, he opened the bedroom door and moved out into the hallway. "I need to paint her. Now. While the afternoon light is still good."

Nash laughed. "I don't blame you, baby brother. Despite the bug bites, she looked pretty hot in that wet T-shirt. Of course I'm interested in doing something other than painting her...now, while the light is good." He glanced at Deacon. "Or would that be considered incestuous?"

"She's not our damned cousin!" Deacon snapped just as the door to the bathroom opened and Olivia's head peeked out. She looked much cleaner. Almost squeaky-clean with her wet hair and steam-flushed skin. Her eyes were as green as he remembered them and still seemed to cover half her face.

"Do you think I could get something to wear until my clothes dry?" she asked. "A robe? Or a T-shirt, perhaps?" Her gaze drifted over to Deacon and then sizzled down his bare chest to his boxers. "Ahh, I was right. Cotton boxer briefs mid-cut." She tipped her head to the side and the door cracked open a little more, revealing a naked shoulder. "Nice fit in the butt, although they're a little too snug in the crotch area."

Before those innocent eyes could make his crotch area even snugger, Deacon grabbed a pair of jeans from the drawer and held them in front of himself. "Grayson, find Olivia something to wear."

While Grayson went to do his bidding, her gaze finally lifted to Deacon's eyes. "You're right. I'm not your flesh-and-blood cousin." She looked at Nash, who now stood next to Deacon. "But alas, I still can't have sex with you, Nash. I'm in a relationship." Grayson returned with a stack of clothes, and she gave him a soft smile as she took them. "And yes, you may paint me. But only if you bring me a comb." With that she pulled her head in and closed the door.

While Deacon's features hardened, Nash laughed.

"I think I like her better now that she's all grown up."

*   *   *

Deacon had always thought of California girls as having long, straight, bleach-blond hair and tanned, leathery skin. Olivia had neither. Her hair was shoulder-length, but a deep golden wheat color and wavy, and her skin was pale and smooth. She wasn't what he would call a stunner, especially in the baggy T-shirt and jeans Grayson had loaned her. Which didn't explain why he couldn't seem to look away.

"Thank you," she said as Nash handed her a glass of sweet tea before sitting down at the table across from her.

Grayson sat on the couch, flicking a nubby piece of charcoal over his sketchpad. Deacon preferred to stand. He leaned against the old stove with his arms crossed, trying to look bored and uninterested. It was difficult when every cell in his body seemed to be on high alert.

The shower had helped Olivia's hair, but only agitated the leech hickey on her neck and the bug bites on her arms. Deacon didn't doubt for a second that they itched like hell. Or that she was sweating her butt off in the humid heat. But Olivia showed no signs of discomfort. She sat with a placid smile on her face as she took a sip of her tea.

"So the reason I'm here is because—"

"Don't move," Grayson said as his hand flew over the sketchpad. "Stay right where you are for just a second."

"I apologize for my baby brother," Nash said. "He's so busy thinking with the right side of his brain that he doesn't know how to socialize."

"Because we all know which brain you think with, Nash," Deacon cut in. "Now if you'll excuse me, I'm going to work." He took a step toward the door, but she stopped him.

"Please, Deacon. Just give me five minutes."

The *please* had him taking his cell phone from his back pocket and glancing at the time. With the crack running down the center, it wasn't easy to read. "You've got two."

Taking another sip of her tea, Olivia cleared her throat as if preparing for a long speech. "I'm sure you were surprised by Uncle Michael's death and the details of his—"

Nash cut her off before Deacon could get his mouth closed. "Uncle Michael is dead?"

Her eyes widened in surprise. "Michael's lawyers haven't contacted you?" She glanced around, and then answered the question herself. "I guess it makes sense, seeing how hard it was for me to find you." She looked back at Nash, and tears flooded her eyes. "I'm sorry. Michael died two weeks ago after a severe stroke had hospitalized him."

Deacon waited to feel something. Hurt. Pain. But all he felt was disappointment. Disappointment that he hadn't been able to achieve success before Michael died. Disappointment that he could never rub that success in his uncle's face.

"So if lawyers were supposed to tell us about Uncle Michael, why are you here?" he asked.

She turned her gaze on him. "Michael put you in his will."

And there it was. After all the years Deacon had waited to be recognized by Michael, the man had waited until he was dead to do it. There was a moment when Deacon wanted to hit something. Instead he shoved down the anger and spoke in a deceptively calm voice. "Now why would he do that?"

Olivia shrugged. "Believe me when I tell you that I don't have a clue. I can only guess that with you being his blood relatives, he thought it was the right thing to do."

"The right thing to do?" His anger flared. "Your step-father wouldn't have known the right thing to do if it bit him in the ass. He disowned his family and never looked back—even when they needed him most. And I will never forgive him for that."

"Stop it, Deacon." Nash got up from his chair. "The man is dead. You don't need to point out his flaws now. And you certainly don't need to take it out on Olivia."

But that's exactly what Deacon wanted to do. Now that he could no longer confront his uncle, there was only one person to take his anger out on. He glared at her, but she only stared right back with those deceptively innocent eyes.

"I don't know what happened between my stepfather and your father," she said, "but Michael must've felt badly about it because he put you in his will."

"I have no use for guilt money," he said. "So you can take the will and go to hell." He strode to the door, but again she stopped him.

"Not even for fifty million dollars?"

Olivia's words had his hand freezing on the worn wood of the screen door. He slowly turned. "Fifty million dollars? Uncle Michael willed me fifty million?"

She shook her head. "Not just you, but your brothers as well. And he didn't will you money. He willed you shares of his lingerie company."

"How does that equate to fifty million?"

Instead of answering she reached for the backpack by her feet. The same one that had been strapped to her back when he'd pulled her from the swamp. It was soaked, so it took her a while to get it unzipped. Once she had it open, she pulled out a damp file folder. She unhooked the loop and opened it, taking out a stack of legal papers that were surprisingly dry.

"I'm willing to offer you and your brothers fifty million dollars each for your shares." She set the stack of papers on the table before pulling out a pen. "All you have to do is sign these contracts, and then once the will goes through probate and the shares transfer, I'll give you the money."

"Fifty million dollars?" Nash's chair creaked as he sat back. "This is a joke, right?" He glanced around. "There has to be a hidden camera somewhere around here."

"It's no joke." Olivia held out the pen. "With a simple signature, you could be a millionaire."

"So what's the catch?" Deacon asked.

"No catch." Her innocent eyes stared back at him. "I want your shares of the company."

It was rumored that the Beaumont men had an uncanny ability to read women's minds. Deacon didn't believe in such hocus-pocus. He believed in General Patton's theory of knowing your enemies. He'd done his research on Michael...and Olivia. In numerous interviews she had made no bones about the fact that she ate, slept, and breathed her job. She loved the company. Loved it enough that she wouldn't want three men who knew nothing about the lingerie business having any kind of control over it.

He should be elated. This was what he'd dreamed of, wasn't it? To make his first million before he turned thirty-five? And even with Francesca's backing, it was unlikely that he would achieve the goal in three years. Now fifty million had landed on his doorstep. It was just unfortunate that the windfall had come from the same family he wanted nothing from.

He glanced at the contracts. "I'll need to read through it and then talk to my brothers before we sign anything."

She nodded and got up, picking up her glass of tea. "I'll be on the front porch." She paused on her way out the door and looked at Deacon. "Do you think I could use your cell phone? Mine got wet and isn't working."

Deacon took his phone from his pocket, swiped the touch screen, and tapped in his passcode before handing it to her. Then, because he couldn't seem to help himself, he held open the screen door. She stopped on her way out. So close that he could smell the scent of his shampoo that she'd used and see the splash of gold that lined the pupils of her green eyes.

"I know you don't like me, Deacon," she said, "but please don't let that keep you from getting money you obviously need."

The word *need* annoyed the hell out of him. He didn't *need* anything from Olivia. But he kept his cool and waited for her to walk out onto the porch before he let the screen door slam and closed the heavy wood door with a decisive click. When he turned, he found his brothers staring at the legitimate-looking documents on the table as if they were a pot of gold at the end of a life that had been anything but rainbows.

Unfortunately, Deacon didn't believe in pots of gold, rainbows, or women with innocent green eyes. He believed that you worked for everything you got, and life was a bitch and then you died. Walking over, he picked up the contracts and handed one to each of his brothers.

"Let's not count our chickens before they hatch."

$\mathscr{C}$HAPTER THREE

$\mathscr{O}$nce on the porch, Olivia would've moved over to the open window and tried to listen in on the Beaumont brothers' conversation if not for the dog who lay sprawled in front of it. With his floppy ears and droopy face, he didn't look vicious, but she wasn't willing to take the chance. So instead she did some snooping on Deacon's phone. Despite the crack, it was a newer version of hers with twice as many apps, and she had to wonder if he needed money as badly as she'd thought. Her question was answered when she scrolled through his recent text exchanges with his brothers. It appeared that Deacon did need money and was having trouble getting it. Numerous banks had turned him down for a loan.

Relieved, Olivia started to close the message screen when she noticed a woman's name in the list. The name Francesca brought with it an image of a lush, full-figured woman who enjoyed stomping grapes with her bare feet and seducing men with her deep-throated laugh. It turned out that the mental image wasn't too far off. Francesca's text about meeting for lunch was filled with sexual innuendo.

Olivia wasn't surprised. Not only was Deacon extremely good-looking but he also had a sexual aura around him that could make any woman think naughty thoughts. Olivia's brain still clung to the image of Deacon in all his naked glory and was now trying to insert her into a fantasy that involved lots and lots of touching.

Not wanting to go down that dead-end road, she clicked over to the phone app and dialed the French Kiss corporate office. Setting the glass of tea on the railing next to her drying clothes, she moved off the porch and around the corner of the house. She sidestepped an anthill where an industrious ant was trying to get a Cheez-It into the small hole. Olivia couldn't help sympathizing. Since Michael's stroke she'd felt like she carried the weight of saving the company on her shoulders, and the window of opportunity was getting smaller and smaller.

Three trucks were parked at the side of the house. One older and mud-splattered, one dinged up and splotched with gray primer, and the last newer and sparkling clean. She didn't wonder whose was whose as much as how they had gotten there. Obviously there was a road to the house. Which meant that the old gondolier had cheated her out of a hundred dollars. While she was fuming over this, her assistant Kelly Wang finally answered.

"Okay, so I'll have sex with you. But don't think that it's going to lead to anything permanent. I'm way too young to be tied down to one man...or one penis. And no kinky stuff—well, maybe a little kinky is okay. But I'm not dressing up like your mother or letting you lick my shoes."

Once again Olivia wished she'd hired the gray-haired, Nazi-looking woman instead of a twenty-two-year-old nympho who thought that working at French Kiss would get her free lingerie and a wider selection of sexual partners. Of course the gray-haired lady had been scary, while the plump, talkative young woman had seemed more willing to take orders from a non-confrontational boss. Boy, had Olivia been wrong. Kelly spent her days reading *Cosmo* and talking inappropriately to the male employees.

"It's me, Kelly," Olivia said.

"Ms. Harrington? I thought you were doing a spa day with your mom."

Olivia didn't like lying to her assistant, but Kelly was a notorious gossip, and Olivia didn't want anyone finding out about Michael's will or her plans to buy the Beaumonts' shares until things were settled.

"I just called to check in," she said, "and to let you know that my cell phone got wet so you can't reach me by that number."

"What happened? Did you drop it in one of those sea salt soaks? I dropped my cell phone once when I was in the bathtub. It scared the shit out of me. I thought I was either going to be electrocuted or start reading women's thoughts like Mel Gibson in that movie—what was the title?"

"I don't know. I really don't have time to watch movies."

"You don't have time for anything. All you do is work, work, work. Which makes absolutely no sense to me. Especially when you're the boss. If I were you, I'd be going to the spa twice a week. And not with my mother. I'd be taking my hot boyfriend for one of those couples' massages. And speaking of hot boyfriends, Mr. Calloway came by looking for you and seemed kinda annoyed when I told him you weren't here."

Olivia was shocked that Kelly knew about her relationship with Parker. Not that she would call it a relationship. They were more FWOB—Friends with Occasional Benefits. Still, she didn't want anyone from work knowing about it.

"It's probably not any of my business," Kelly continued, "but you need to be careful with clingy guys. I mean, this isn't the Dark Ages or *Fifty Shades*. If you want to spend the day with your mom at the spa, or with some other guy, then that shouldn't be any of his—"

Olivia cut her off. "If Mr. Calloway should come back by, would you please tell him that I'll call him later. And if there's nothing else…"

There was a long pause. "Well, I did sorta spill my Diet Coke on the computer, and it sorta quit working. But that lawyer guy you just hired who always has the food stains on his tie—Jason something or other—came by and got it running. I hate to say this, but I think he wants to have sex with me. He got a major hard-on when I bent over to flip the power off. For a second I thought he was going to boink me right there on the desk. Not that I would've gone along with it—although he does have pretty eyes."

Olivia massaged her temples. "Okay, then. If there's not anything else, I'll talk to you when I get back."

"Sure. Don't do anything I wouldn't do."

Olivia felt that left things wide open. "I'll try not to." As soon as she hung up with Kelly, she called her mother. The voice was less friendly, but the morals pretty much the same. Deirdre Beaumont looked at sex as a way to a man's heart...and his wallet. And for her it had been true. Her beauty and sex appeal had captured the attention of three wealthy husbands in her lifetime. Which was a good thing, since her mother went through money as quickly as she had gone through husbands. Michael had been the one exception. The one man her mother had actually loved. When Michael met her, Deirdre had been in her late forties. Well past her gold-digging prime. Her last husband, Olivia's father, had disappeared without a trace after bankrupting his company. With no prospect of a rich husband in sight, she and Olivia had been living off credit cards and close friends. Michael had arrived like a knight in shining armor. Something Olivia would always be grateful for.

"Hello, Mother," Olivia said.

"Olivia? Whose phone are you calling from?" Deirdre didn't even wait for an answer before she started in. "I cannot tell you the hell I've been in since you left. That Frenchwoman you convinced me to invite into my home is nothing but a foulmouthed guttersnipe who will no doubt kill me and the entire staff in our sleep."

"Stop being dramatic, Mother. Babette is not going to kill anyone. She's just creative and high-strung."

"High-strung, yes. Creative, no. I don't have a clue why you brought her from Paris. You are much more talented than she is."

Olivia smiled. For all Deirdre's flaws, she had always been a proud, protective mother. "Thank you, but if I was that good, Michael would've had me designing. Babette is considered one of the best lingerie designers in the world."

"I find that hard to believe. And Michael was always selfish. Even if he liked your designs, he would've wanted you helping him, instead of helping Samuel in the design studio. Does Samuel know about Babette?"

"No, not yet. But I plan to tell him soon."

"I doubt that he'll be happy. He's extremely sensitive about his work."

The head designer wouldn't be happy that Olivia had hired someone else to design the new line. But she had to do what was best for the company. With sales declining, French Kiss needed fresh blood and new ideas. Babette seemed to have both and had convinced Olivia that adding a collection of men's underwear was the way to save the company from the brink of bankruptcy.

"Samuel will go along with what's best for the company," Olivia said.

Her mother released an exasperated huff. "I cannot understand why you continue to care about the business. And now you've talked me into selling the house and investing in your crazy scheme when I should sell it and retire to the French Riviera. And just so you know, I hate having complete strangers trooping through my home at all hours of the day and night."

"They're called real estate brokers and prospective buyers, Mother," Olivia said, "and you don't have to be there when the house is shown. The broker selling my house calls beforehand."

"And just where are we going to live if the houses sell at the same time?"

"We'll rent an apartment downtown. And it won't be for long. I'm going to get the money from the sale of the house back to you as soon as Babette's new line starts selling." Unless it didn't sell, in which case they would both be in big trouble. "So has Babette been working?"

Deirdre snorted. "Not that I can tell. She spends most

of her time in the guest wing eating my imported Swiss chocolate and watching the past seasons of *Downton Abbey* on demand."

Olivia really wanted to yell at her mother to light a fire under Babette's tight French ass. But it wasn't her mother's job to keep Babette on task. Olivia was lucky that Deirdre had been willing to keep an eye on the annoying Frenchwoman while she was in Louisiana. Until the new line was finished, Olivia didn't want anyone knowing about her plans.

"So did you find the Beaumont brothers?" Deirdre asked.

"Yes." She glanced at the house. "And I don't think that they're doing much better than they were when they came to visit years ago."

"That was certainly a surprise. I didn't even know Michael had a brother until the ghastly man showed up with his three delinquent sons. Of course Michael never talked about his past…or talked much period."

Olivia's stepfather had been a man of few words. Which had worked nicely for an introverted nine-year-old afraid of her own shadow. Michael's silence and stability had been a welcome relief from her mother's constant chatter and unreliability. After her father ran off without a word, Michael was the strong, reliable father figure Olivia craved, and he didn't seem to mind her tagging along behind him, or spending every possible second she could at the corporate offices of French Kiss. She had always struggled in school with her attention deficit disorder, and the company and Michael became her entire world. And when she went off to college, she followed in Michael's footsteps, majoring in business and marketing, even though she was more interested in design. After college she'd worked side by side with Michael on every new line, marketing idea, and store opening.

Michael was the one person who had known how much French Kiss meant to her. Which was why she couldn't understand how he could have willed it to three men who had never set foot inside French Kiss's doors. Three men he didn't know or love. And maybe he hadn't loved her either. Maybe it had all been wishful thinking.

The slam of a screen door pulled her out of her thoughts, and she quickly finished the call. "Listen, I have to go. Try not to kill Babette."

"You ask too much," her mother said dryly.

Olivia hung up just as Deacon came around the corner of the house. After his shower he had changed into a blue T-shirt that hugged his muscles and a pair of faded jeans that hugged his...

"Do you always stare at men's crotches?"

Her gaze lifted to Deacon's annoyed eyes. Between the sapphire-blue shirt and azure sky, they looked even more purple. "What color would you say your eyes are?"

He squinted. "Is something wrong with you? Do you have a hearing problem? I ask you if you always stare at men's crotches and you answer by talking about the color of my eyes."

"I'd say indigo—somewhere between a deep blue and dark purple." She pulled her gaze away from his eyes and looked down. "And me looking at your crotch is strictly business. I'm planning on starting a new line of men's underwear."

"Right." He held out his hand. "I'm assuming you're done with my phone."

She handed him the phone. "It's slimmer than mine. Did you just buy it?"

"Let me guess. You thought my cell phone would be the size of a sneaker." He slipped the phone into his back pocket. "Obviously you're still the same stuck-up little rich girl you were at fourteen."

She had never been stuck up, just terrified and jealous of the three brothers who had shown up on her doorstep. They had come into Michael's mansion like a whirlwind of burping, roughhousing, cussing testosterone, and Olivia had been completely unprepared. Like her mother, she hadn't known that Michael had family. She'd thought she was the only child in his life—the only one vying for his attention. Suddenly there were three boys who shared his blood. And no matter how hard she'd tried to be a perfect little stepdaughter, she couldn't compete with that.

Her fear of losing Michael's love had kept her from being a good hostess. She'd tried to avoid the Beaumonts, until…the one afternoon she'd discovered Deacon in the garden. His resemblance to Michael surprised her and made her even more jealous, which led to her doing something completely out of character. Now all she could hope was that Deacon wouldn't hold the incident against her.

"So did you read the contract?" she asked.

"Most of it."

"And?"

Instead of answering he headed back to the house, leaving her no choice but to follow. Once on the porch, he sat down in the rocker and scratched the dog's ears, rocking slowly back and forth. It was a stall tactic if ever there was one, and she tried to push down her apprehension and act like it didn't matter.

Climbing the steps, she checked to see if her clothes were drying. She had just lifted her panties from the railing when he spoke.

"I'm assuming those are from French Kiss's latest collection?" When she turned he was looking at the panties she held in her hand with a hot-eyed intensity that made her feel all flushed and needy. Since flushed and needy wouldn't get her what she wanted, she set the panties back on the railing.

"Actually they're last year's. Since Michael's stroke we haven't produced a new collection."

He picked up her glass of sweet tea and took a long drink from the same spot her lips had been only moments before. When he was finished, he set it back on the railing. "That doesn't seem very smart."

It wasn't, and she hated his pointing it out. Her eyes zeroed in on the droplet of sweet tea that clung to his beard just below his full bottom lip. "So are you going to sign the contract or not?"

He studied her with his intense eyes, allowing the seconds to tick by while sweat beaded at her temples. Finally, he got up from the chair and answered. "Only an idiot wouldn't."

Olivia's shoulders relaxed. "You won't be sorry. It's a good deal for everyone involved." Without thought she reached out and brushed the droplet of tea from his beard, her finger grazing his lip.

As quick as a snake's strike, he grabbed her wrist, his fingers curling around her thumping pulse. His gaze locked with hers, and all the oxygen seemed to evaporate from the humid air as he tugged her closer. So close she could feel the heat of his words against her lips when he spoke.

"Don't screw with me, Olivia." He released her and walked into the house.

As the screen door slammed behind him, one thought paraded through Olivia's mind.

His beard had been soft.

As soft as Deacon was hard.

CHAPTER FOUR

"Sometimes you are such an ass, Deke," Nash said. "Grayson and I would've taken Olivia back to her rental car so she wouldn't have had to call a car service. It's the least we could do for fifty million."

Deacon stood at the window watching the SUV bounce down the dirt road. He waited until the last of the dust had settled before he released the curtain and turned to his brothers. Nash was sprawled out on the couch, tossing darts at the dart board above the fireplace, while Grayson sketched on his sketchpad. "The Beaumont brothers aren't chauffeurs. Besides, the deal isn't final yet."

"You're so skeptical, Deke," Grayson said. "It will go through. I trust Olivia."

"You don't even know Olivia."

"I don't have to know her. Honesty is etched in the lines of her face." Grayson continued to draw. "Damn, I wish I could've painted her."

"Once you have millions, you can hire any woman you

want to be your model." Nash threw a dart, and it hit the bull's-eye dead center.

Grayson stopped sketching and smiled. "I can, can't I?"

"And while you're at it, you might want to buy some whiskers to fill in that sparse beard of yours." Nash changed his aim. The sharp point of the next dart stuck in the back of Grayson's sketchpad with a soft *thunk*.

Grayson hopped to his feet. "What the fuck, Nash? You could've put my eye out."

Nash laughed. "Not likely. I always hit what I aim at." To prove it, he tossed another dart. This one whizzed past Deacon's cheek and embedded in the window frame.

Deacon lifted an eyebrow. "It seems that you've been away from home a little too long, Nash. You've forgotten the order of the food chain."

"Maybe I'm just challenging it." Nash got to his feet.

"You think you're ready for that?"

"Only one way to find out." He grinned. "Beaumont test?"

While most brothers' test of strength consists of a little playful wrestling, the Beaumont brothers tested their prowess in the boxing ring. For some reason their father thought boxing a gentleman's sport. Where he had gotten the idea, Deacon didn't know. Probably from the same place he'd gotten the idea that it was a man's duty to pleasure the women of the world. And while Deacon had refused to follow in his father's womanizing footsteps, he had always enjoyed fighting—either in the ring or in a barroom brawl. There was something cathartic about the feel of a fist hitting flesh and bone. Not that he and his brothers ever punched each other with the intent to permanently damage. Although there had been a few accidental broken noses and knockouts.

Being the oldest, Deacon probably should've put an end to the idea. But since Olivia arrived, he'd been filled with a restless energy that needed an outlet. And punching his brothers in the face seemed like as good an outlet as any. Of course, with no gloves or protective sparring helmets, they needed rules.

"One round only," he said.

Nash unbuttoned his shirt. "One round is all I'll need."

"You mean all I'll need." Grayson jerked off his shirt. The youngest Beaumont would've started swinging if Deacon hadn't stopped him.

"Outside. I'm not going to have Grandpa's house busted up."

Nash smiled. "You sound just like Mom when we started roughhousing. You're as persnickety as a girl."

"Then you should be able to win easily." He led his brothers out the door and around to the side of the house, where he traced a ring in the dirt with the heel of his boot. Blue had awoken from his nap and sniffed along behind Deacon's boot, no doubt wondering if the new game involved tracking. His bloodshot eyes looked thoroughly disappointed when Deacon made him sit in a spot out of the way. "First person to connect wins," Deacon said as he pulled off his shirt.

Grayson and Nash squared off first. Nash was a technical boxer, dodging and hedging until an opening appeared for his wicked right hook. Grayson, on the other hand, was more of a rapid-fire boxer. He threw jab after jab while Nash danced around him. And Deacon had to wonder if, despite his smack talk, Nash hadn't gotten a little soft during his time away from home. When he had the openings to connect with Grayson's chin, he didn't take them. Instead he ducked and wove until Grayson finally slipped a fist through his guard and sent him stumbling back.

"And the winner is the great Grayson Beaumont!" Grayson jogged around the line dug in the dirt with his hands in the air. He dropped them and pointed at Deacon. "You're up, big brother."

Having always been protective of his littlest brother, Deacon shook his head. "I think it's only fair to let Nash get a chance to redeem himself."

It turned out to be a bad idea. While Nash had held back with Grayson, he didn't waste any time swinging at Deacon's jaw. Deacon ducked and came around with a one-two body jab, but Nash was too quick. They continued to dance around the ring for what felt like hours before Nash got in a hook that grazed Deacon's cheek and hurt like hell.

"Now this is a sight that warms a father's heart."

With a hand cradling his face, Deacon turned to see their father coming around the corner of the house. As always, Don Juan Beaumont was dressed like a pirate version of Don Johnson in *Miami Vice*. He wore a white button-down shirt, linen pants, and loafers without socks, while his long gray hair was pulled back in a ponytail and a gold hoop hung from one ear.

Don Juan, or Donny John as most folks called him, lived up to his name in every way. He loved women with the same passion with which he loved life. It was unfortunate that neither passion involved earning money.

As he watched his father saunter toward them, Deacon tested his cheek with two fingers. "Please don't tell me that you already spent the money I gave you."

Donny John held up his hands. "What good is money unless you enjoy it, Valentino?"

The use of his middle name never failed to piss Deacon off. "It's Deacon."

Donny John released an exasperated sigh. "I don't know why you boys insist on being referred to by the ordinary names your mother gave you. Being named for legendary lovers is part of the Beaumont heritage. And Valentino, Lothario, and Romeo are names that get people's attention."

"And get your ass kicked on the playground," Nash said dryly.

"Which is why I taught you to box," Donny John said. "Although it looks like Val...Deacon could use a refresher course." He pointed a finger at Deacon. "You forget defense always comes before offense and timing is everything." He demonstrated by lifting his fists in front of his face. "That's why Nash always gets the upper hand. You've never learned how to close the hole after a jab."

No, Deacon had never learned how to close the hole. Whenever life had thrown him a jab, he had always been open to the pain that followed. His father's inability to provide for his family. His mother's death from cancer. His true paternity. The wounds were still there and unhealed. Which might've explained his sharpness.

"If you want money, I'm tapped. If you want to fish, the poles are on the porch. And if you want something to eat, there's hot dogs in the fridge."

His father looked wounded. "Why, I just wanted to spend a little time with my sons." He tipped his head. "Of course, now I am a little curious about Olivia Harrington. When she passed me in that big ol' Suburban, she looked in quite a hurry."

Damn. It figured that his father would run into Olivia and recognize her immediately. Of course Deacon had known her as soon as he'd looked into those big innocent-looking eyes that seemed to take up half her face.

"So I'm going to assume that she was here to tell you about her father dying?" Donny John said.

"How did you find out?"

"I ran into Francesca."

Deacon didn't have to ask how Francesca knew. Wealthy people kept track of wealthy people, and Francesca had always been overly curious about Michael Beaumont.

Donny John shook his head. "Poor Michael Casanova. I never thought he would go first." His father's eyes were sad. Donny John might have his faults, but he loved his family.

"I'm sorry, Dad," Deacon said.

After only a few moments, Donny John shrugged. "I had hoped that we could reconcile before he died, but I guess that's what this is about." He pulled one of the contracts Olivia had left from his back pocket. "I found this on the kitchen table. Now I'm not good at deciphering legal jargon, but it seems to me that Michael decided to do his forgiving through my sons."

Deacon released his breath. Now that Donny John knew about the money there would be no getting rid of him until he got his share. A share he would no doubt blow at the crap tables.

"Nothing is final yet," Nash said.

"Nor will it be." Donny John unfolded the contract and flipped to the back page. "Especially when Deacon has yet to sign."

His brothers turned on him.

"You didn't sign?" Grayson said. "But I saw you."

Nash grabbed the contract from his father and studied

the signatures at the bottom before his gaze narrowed on Deacon. "Are you fuckin' crazy?"

It was a good question. One he'd been asking himself since Olivia had driven away. A sane person would've signed the papers and celebrated all the way to the bank. Instead Deacon had not just kept himself from realizing his dream of being a millionaire, he'd kept his brothers from realizing theirs. And he wasn't sure why. One minute he was bent over the contract with pen in hand, and the next he was air-writing. Since only a fool would screw up a deal for one hundred and fifty million, Olivia hadn't even glanced at the signatures before putting two of the contracts back in the folder and heading out the door to wait for her ride.

He had little doubt that his stupidity had to do with the fantasy he'd clung to for all these years. When he met Olivia again, he'd wanted to be a self-made man with all the power. Instead Olivia was still the powerful one, handing out charity to the hillbilly Beaumonts. And it just hadn't sat well. Not well at all.

Unfortunately, his damned pride wasn't worth losing millions over.

"Look, I'm sorry," he said. "I'll sign this copy and send it to her. I'm sure it won't change the deal."

Donny John slapped him on the back. "Now, that's my boy." He rubbed his hands together. "So what say we head into town for a steak dinner?" He smiled. "My millionaire sons' treat, of course."

"No one is celebrating yet," Deacon said. "Not until I see the will for myself and we have the money in the bank."

He should've taken the contract from Nash and signed it right then. Instead he turned and headed for the front porch.

He needed some time to think. And since he did his best thinking alone, he grabbed his fishing pole and headed to the same fishing spot he'd been in when Olivia had taken the plunge into the water.

An evening mist had settled around the swamp and the moss-draped cedars, giving them an almost surreal look. Some folks found the bayou beautiful. Deacon just found it sad. After his mother died, Donny John had moved them here to live with their grandfather, and Deacon had spent many an afternoon in the secluded spot, grieving for the woman who had been the center of his universe.

Althea Beaumont had been a beautiful, vivacious woman who saw the best in everyone and everything. While Donny John had been taught that boys didn't need hugs, Althea handed them out freely to her sons. Along with kisses on each cheek. An amazing seamstress, she had been the main breadwinner in the family. She made choir robes for churches, ballet recital costumes for dance studios, and cheerleading uniforms for high schools. But regardless of how much sewing she had to do, she would always make time for her boys. She played catch with them, read to them, tickled them, and tucked them in each night.

They had all adored her, but none more than Deacon. She was everything to him. And when she died, it was like all the joy in the world died with her. Gone were the hugs, the two-cheek kisses, and the love. All that was left was a father who seemed as lost as his sons. Donny John lost his job, lost their house, and lost his desire to be a father to three boys with eyes just like their mother's. So, at thirteen, Deacon took charge. He worked at odd jobs to help his grandfather with the bills and budgeted the money so there was enough for food and school supplies.

When Donny John had finally come out of his grieving, he hadn't gotten a job. Instead he'd dragged his sons to California to get a handout from his big brother. Donny John had been convinced that Michael would help them and had been oblivious to how pathetic they had looked standing in Michael's huge entryway like the poor hillbillies they were. But, at sixteen, Deacon had been very aware. He'd been aware of the look of disgust on the face of the butler who answered the door. The look of shock on Olivia's mother's face when she learned they were relatives. And the look of resignation on his uncle's face when he offered them the guest rooms.

But even from their first meeting, Olivia's face had given nothing away. Not when his uncle had asked her to show them around the large house. And not when Grayson and Nash had raced down the hallways whooping with delight.

Deacon hadn't raced around or whooped with delight. Not wanting to show his embarrassment over his brothers' reaction, he'd stood with his arms crossed over his chest and glared with pure teenage belligerence. In fact he'd held on to the belligerence the entire next day, refusing to enjoy the huge game and media rooms. Instead he borrowed a bestselling thriller from the shelf in the library and headed for the garden. That was where Olivia found him.

"Michael doesn't want you here."

Startled, Deacon dropped the book. He turned to see her standing there in a prim and proper sundress. She had a pimple on her chin, and braces puffed out her full lips.

"Who cares what your uncle wants?" he said as he

picked up the book and went back to reading. But her hurtful words made it impossible. As much as he tried to act like he didn't care what his uncle thought, he did. He cared more than anyone would ever know.

"Then why did you come?" She moved closer, the heels of her sandals clicking on the paving stones. "I overheard my mother say that you came for money."

He jumped to his feet. "I don't want shit from you or your stepfather. I think he's an arrogant ass."

"Is not!" she snapped. "Michael's a kind, caring man—"

"Who makes his money off selling cheap, sleazy under-wear!"

Her eyes turned hard and angry. "They are not cheap or sleazy!"

To his surprise she jerked up her dress. Not just to her waist, but all the way over her head. And she was right. The lacy bra and panties didn't look cheap...or sleazy. Barely covering her petite body with its small breasts, they looked hot. Especially to a sixteen-year-old who got a boner just by climbing a rope in gym class. His penis came to full attention, something his uncle couldn't help but notice when he arrived on the scene.

"Deacon!"

Deacon snapped out of his daydream to see his little brother barreling down the path through the trees like the hounds of hell were chasing him.

Deacon got to his feet. "What happened?"

Grayson took a moment to catch his breath. "Some guys in a black SUV arrived."

"Shit." He left his fishing pole and tackle box and started toward the cabin. "Who are they? Federal agents who have come to arrest Donny John for illegal gambling? Or did Nash get himself in trouble again?"

"Neither." Grayson followed behind him. "They aren't feds or cops. They're lawyers."

He stopped and turned. "Lawyers?"

Grayson nodded, grinning from ear to ear. "Olivia was telling the truth. Uncle Michael left us shares in the company. We're millionaires, Deke." He slapped him on the arm. "At least we will be as soon as you sign Olivia's contract. And I figure since they're Uncle Michael's lawyers, they can take the contract back to her."

Deacon should have been overjoyed. His dream was about to become true. But it was hard to be overjoyed when the daydream had left a bitter taste in his mouth. Which might explain why he wasn't friendly to the lawyers who sat at the card table with glasses of sweet tea in front of them. Both got to their feet as soon as he entered the cabin, but it was the older of the two who spoke.

"Deacon Valentino Beaumont?" When Deacon merely nodded, he continued the introduction. "I'm Jeffrey Connors, a lawyer for the late Michael Casanova Beaumont." He nodded at the younger man, who looked like he was about to faint from heatstroke. "This is my colleague Dave Johnson." Both men held out hands and Deacon shook them before heading to the refrigerator. He pulled out a bottle of beer, twisted off the cap, and took a deep drink before finally speaking.

"So Michael put me and my brothers in his will." It was a statement rather than a question, but Mr. Connors answered it anyway.

"Yes." He sat back down and removed some papers from his briefcase. "We would've had these to you sooner, but it wasn't easy locating you and your brothers." He smiled. "Although I understand. Just this past year, I went salmon fishing with my brothers in a remote spot in Canada. Most enjoyable two weeks I've had in a long time."

It annoyed Deacon that the man would think this was just a vacation spot. He scowled as the lawyer took a pair of glasses from his shirt pocket. He put them on before he started reading the will.

Mr. Connors had a low, soothing voice, one that would've put Deacon to sleep if the stakes hadn't been so high. He, his brothers, and Donny John all listened intently as the man read. It wasn't until he reached the details of the shares Uncle Michael had left them that Deacon interrupted.

"Excuse me. Did you say controlling shares?"

Mr. Connors glanced up. "I did."

"Controlling as in majority shareholders?"

The lawyer smiled. "Correct. Your uncle left you all of his shares."

Nash got up from the couch. "Does that mean what I think it means, Deacon?"

Since Deacon couldn't seem to find his voice, Mr. Connors answered the question for him. "It means that you and your brothers are now the owners of French Kiss, Incorporated."

CHAPTER FIVE

Olivia was running late...again. No matter how early she got up, she just couldn't seem to keep from being late. This morning she'd been distracted by the pretty hummingbird that fluttered by her kitchen window, Mr. Huckabee watering his flowers in the nude, and her trash and recycling bins sitting by the curb. Not that there was anything unusual about her trash bins being out. Especially on trash day. At least there wouldn't have been if she had been the one to roll them out to the curb. But until she saw them, she'd forgotten that it was trash day. Which meant that someone else had put her trash and recycling bins out. Just as they had the week before. And the week before that.

Late or not, she couldn't help opening the balcony doors and calling to Mr. Huckabee, whose dangling parts were thankfully covered by the large watering can he held, "Good morning, Mr. Huckabee."

He squinted over at her. "Is that you, Britney?"

Britney had been the former owner of Olivia's house. And even after five years, Mr. Huckabee still thought she lived there. Olivia had corrected him numerous times and had finally given up.

"I wanted to thank you for putting out my trash," she said.

"I didn't. And you left your garage door open again." Mr. Huckabee lifted the can to water his geraniums, displaying his private parts.

She averted her eyes. "Yes, I know. I guess I need to tie a string on my penis—I mean finger." With a heated face, she backed toward the doors. "Well, have a good day." On her way inside, she noticed Jonathan Livingston Seagull standing in the corner of her balcony, eating what looked like a piece of moldy banana peel. "Shoo!" she yelled, and waved her arms. The bird stared her down with a beady-eyed look before he picked up the banana peel and took flight, leaving his calling card on her rug.

She usually took the trolley to work, but after cleaning up Jonathan's mess she was running too late to wait for public transportation, so she decided to take the Porsche Michael had given her for her thirtieth birthday. It was a nice car—fast, sleek, and a pretty French Kiss silver. Which didn't explain why she felt so uncomfortable driving it.

Backing out of her garage, she ground the gears and almost ran over her trash bins. The sight of them at the curb had her glancing around to see if any neighbors were waiting to be thanked for putting out her trash. But the only person she saw was the guy who sold lemon juicers to the tourists on Fisherman's Wharf. He hurried down the street, pulling his roller suitcase of juicers behind him.

He had to live somewhere close by because she saw

him almost every day, although she couldn't see him
making enough on lemon juicers to afford to live in the
wealthy neighborhood. She would think he was a street
person if not for the quality of his coat and pants. Even his
Nikes looked new. When she drove past and waved, he
ducked his head and ignored her. She should really buy a
juicer from him. Maybe she would get one for her mother
as well. Deirdre loved kitchen gadgets. Thinking of her
mother, Olivia tapped the screen on the dashboard.

After a few trilling rings, her mother's voice came
through the Bose speakers.

"When are you coming to get this woman?"

"Today." Olivia stifled a yawn. Her sleep the last two
nights had been plagued by nightmares. Not about being
eaten alive by mosquitoes or death-rolled by an alligator,
but about showing her panties to Deacon Beaumont and
him laughing hysterically. Of course the nightmares
weren't any worse than the daydreams that kept popping
up since she left Louisiana. Daydreams about Deacon's
body. Even now it was hard to blink the image of his
manly muscles and lightly furred chest away. "So how is
Babette this morning?" Olivia asked. "Has she gotten any
work done?"

"It appears so. She spent all day yesterday scribbling
on some design or another."

"That's great." Olivia passed a Starbucks and struggled
with the strong desire to turn in. But since she was already late, her caffeine hit would have to wait until she
got to work. "Tell her I'll send a car to pick her up this
afternoon. And as soon as I call a board meeting and present her designs, she can start working with the designers
at French Kiss."

"As if the woman can work with anyone," her mother

said. "And instead of sending a car for her, why don't you come and pick her up yourself? I'd like to see you."

"I'd love to, Mother, but now that the Beaumonts have signed over their shares of the company, there's just too much to get done. What about if we have lunch this weekend?"

"Fine. And afterwards you can help me go through some of Michael's things. If the house sells quickly, we'll need to have it done. Although it's a shame to sell the house when it would be a perfect home for you to start a family."

The comment took Olivia completely by surprise. "A family?"

"Don't act like you don't know what a family is, Olivia. Yours wasn't conventional—what with your father running off and you having a workaholic stepfather who ran the largest lingerie company in the world—but you certainly don't want to end up like Regina Longley's daughter, who has to hire men to escort her to social events. You need a husband. Even if for nothing more than arm decoration."

"I have a boyfriend, Mother."

"That young man who works at French Kiss? Does he have money?"

"I don't have a clue. I don't plan to marry for money." In fact Olivia didn't plan to marry at all. She had enough complications in her life.

"Don't be ridiculous, Olivia Harrington. I won't have you marrying some yuppie businessman with nothing more than a 401(k). Do you know anything about this Parker's family?"

Olivia opened her mouth and then closed it when she realized that she didn't know anything about Parker's family. Not one thing. She didn't know if his parents were living. If he had siblings. Or even a dog.

A faint stream of French words came through the speakers before her mother spoke. "I think you owe me more than lunch for putting up with this French tyrant." Her mouth moved away from the receiver. "Yes, yes, I hear you, Marie Antoinette! And your chocolate chip crepes are coming!" She lowered her voice. "Along with a little arsenic."

Olivia laughed. "Hang tough, Mother. She'll be gone by this afternoon."

After ending the call, Olivia concentrated on taking the fastest route to work. But due to heavy traffic and a missed turn caused by admiring the haircut of the woman in the car next to her, she still arrived late.

French Kiss's corporate headquarters were located in a high-rise office building just a block away from the flagship store on Union Square. Michael had spared no expense in remodeling the historic building. While the outside kept its Gothic look, the inside had been totally gutted and refurbished, using plenty of French Kiss's trademark colors—lavender and silver. The lavish decor of the lobby included purple variegated marble floors, plush furniture upholstered in gray and purple velvet, and a huge crystal chandelier hanging over the receptionist's desk.

The corporate office employed both men and women, but front desk receptionists were always attractive women who wore business attire and lavender high heels. The high heels had been Michael's idea, and he'd expected every female employee to wear them. The men were to wear suits and lavender ties.

Olivia waved a greeting to the receptionist on her way

to the elevators. Her office was located on the top executive floor in the corner opposite Michael's. Before his stroke she had always started her day in his suite. Over coffee and pastry, they would discuss new designs and marketing plans, or laugh over something her mother had said or done. But those days were gone. And had been gone since the morning she'd discovered him slumped in his chair, unable to move the right side of his body. She had hoped that with rehabilitation he would recover. But the second stroke had removed that hope. And the final one had taken Michael's life.

The hard punch of grief came from nowhere, and needing to find some remnant of his presence, she bypassed the empty secretary's desk and pushed open the door of his office. The scent of espresso and his expensive cologne was still there, as were the photographs of Olivia and her mother on his desk and the paintings of Paris on the walls.

Michael had loved Paris, and Olivia had never understood why he hadn't located the corporate offices there. Especially when the idea for the company had come from a small Paris lingerie shop. She had asked him once, and he'd simply said, "Paris is in my past." Since he had never liked to talk about his past, she'd left it at that.

"Oh, it's you."

The clipped tone had her turning to the doorway.

Anastasia Bradley was the vice-president of marketing and an organized, punctual overachiever who would never be distracted by a hummingbird, a naked neighbor, or a hot manly Beaumont brother. While the rest of the executive board treated Olivia like an annoying relative of Michael's whom they had to put up with, Ana treated her like the village idiot.

"So nice of you to join us, Miss Harrington." She repositioned the box she carried and glanced at her watch. "Let me guess, you missed the trolley or traffic was bad?"

"As a matter of fact . . ." She let the words trail off when Ana carried the box to the desk and started unpacking it. "What are you doing?"

"I think it's pretty obvious. I'm moving into Michael's office."

"By whose authority?"

Anastasia turned and sent her a wicked-witch smile. "Imagine the board's surprise when we learned that Michael hadn't left you the company after all. Instead he gave it to his nephews. Nephews who will more than likely sell first chance they get. But until they do, I think I have just as much right to this office as anyone. Especially since you already have a big office."

Olivia wanted to take the contracts out of her briefcase and wave them in front of Ana's broad nose along with a big nanny-nanny-boo-boo. Two things stopped her: The will had yet to be probated. And, bitch or not, Ana was good at her job. If Olivia was going to keep French Kiss from going bankrupt, she needed all the help she could get.

"Fine," she said, "you may use the office for now." She tipped up her chin and swept from the room, then almost ran over Parker in the hallway. He was as meticulously groomed as he always was. Shoes polished, suit pressed, purple tie perfectly knotted in a Windsor, and not one blond-highlighted hair out of place. But what Olivia noticed more than anything was his clean-shaven face. Probably because she'd spent the entire weekend thinking about a bearded one.

"Where have you been?" he asked. "I tried calling you, but you didn't answer one of my texts or messages."

"I'm sorry. My phone broke."

"And you couldn't have used another phone and called me?"

She had thought about it, but then hadn't wanted a Louisiana area code showing up on his cell phone. Which was weird. If she was dating Parker, she should trust him—and know a little more about him.

"Do you have a dog?" she asked. His mouth opened in mute surprise, drawing Olivia's gaze to his jaw. It was not just clean-shaven but baby-smooth, and she had to wonder if he could even grow a beard.

"No," he said. "I don't have a dog."

"A sister or brother? And are your parents alive?"

He looked confused. "Are you okay? Did the doctor prescribe tranquilizers after Michael died?"

She shook her head. "No, I was curious. We don't get to talk much about our life outside of work."

"Because we don't have a life outside of work, and I thought that we were both quite happy with that."

"Right." She backed away. "I'll call you later."

Before she headed to her office, Olivia dropped the contracts by to Jason Melvin. Jason was a young company lawyer who, unlike Parker, always looked like a wrinkled mess. His hair needed a cut, his shirt an iron, and his pants an extra inch of length. Not to mention that his purple ties always had some sort of stain on them. And yet Olivia trusted him more than anyone in the company. Probably because he had chosen loyalty over confidentiality. He was the one who had alerted her about Michael's will. The one who had helped her write up the contract to buy back French Kiss.

As soon as she stepped into his office, he dropped the jelly doughnut he'd been eating and jumped to his feet. "So did they sign?" Before she could answer, he continued. "Of course, why wouldn't they? That's a lot of money."

She set her briefcase on the desk and opened it. "It wasn't as easy as I thought. Deacon Beaumont gave me a little trouble." She handed him the contracts. "Have you heard anything from your snitch at Michael's law firm?"

"They found the Beaumonts. And with the ironclad will Michael set up, it shouldn't take any time at all for you to get their shares. I'm thinking that by this time next week, you'll be the new CEO. Won't that surprise the board?"

"I don't know about that. Someone already leaked the information about the will to Anastasia."

Jason held up his hands. "It wasn't me. I'm terrified of the woman."

"That makes two of us." She nodded at the contracts. "Guard those with your life."

"Will do"—he winked—"boss lady."

Rather than make her happy, the two words made her feel slightly ill. Thankfully, Kelly was waiting at the door of her office with a cup of coffee. As usual she wore totally inappropriate clothing for work. Her blue-jean skirt was too short, her shirt too tight, and her Hello Kitty pink glitter belt too...weird. But she had caffeine, so Olivia chose to ignore her outfit. "You're a saint," she said as she reached for the cup.

Kelly pulled it back. "Sorry, but this isn't for you." She nodded at the closed door of Olivia's office. "It's for him."

"Him? Him who?"

Kelly flipped her waist-length black hair over her shoulder. "I didn't catch his name, but I think I'm going to call him Stud Muffin."

Olivia rolled her eyes. "I'm assuming he wants to have sex with you."

"No. But I damned well want to have sex with him."

Olivia looked at the door. "So why is he here?"

Kelly shrugged. "I didn't get that either."

As soon as her life became less hectic, Olivia was going to have to fire Kelly...or have someone else do it. "So you just let some man into my office without finding out his name or why he's here?"

"Pretty much. And when you see him, you'll understand why." Kelly turned the door handle.

Olivia had a corner office the same size as Michael's. There was a sitting area with wet bar, a bathroom with a steam shower, and floor-to-ceiling windows with a view of the bay and the Golden Gate Bridge. The man was standing at those windows. And if his front looked as good as his back, Olivia understood Kelly's lust. He wore faded jeans that hugged his nice rear and a white dress shirt that she would bet had never seen the inside of a dry cleaner. The soft, un-starched cotton cuddled broad shoulders and a muscled back, then hung loose to his waist. Since few businessmen wore starchless dress shirts and worn jeans, Olivia figured she knew who he was.

"I'm sorry, but I think there's been a misunderstanding." She headed toward the man, who didn't appear to be in a hurry to turn around. "I don't interview models in my office. In fact the final interviews for the fashion show runway models aren't until next week." She stopped directly behind him, and her gaze drifted over his dark brown hair. It was nice hair. Thick and rich, without a hint of salon highlights. It looked as if it had been recently cut, the layers falling in textured waves that just reached the limp collar of his shirt. He lifted a hand and ran his fingers through the strands almost self-consciously before he slowly turned around.

Olivia was impressed. Now here was a face that could make her reschedule an interview. It was a face that could launch a thousand ships, inflame millions of women... and sell billions of pairs of men's underwear. A tanned throat peeked from the open collar of his shirt and rose to a square chin and angular jaw. A serious mouth, with a full bottom lip and perfectly matched top, sat beneath a strong Roman nose. Long dark lashes surrounded eyes the color of crushed pansies—

"Deacon." The word came out of her mouth like a gasp for air.

One corner of his mouth hiked up for a brief second before dropping back into a flat line. He tipped his head at the window. "Nice view."

She blinked a couple of times and then stared at his face like a kid who had discovered a man in the gorilla exhibit at the zoo. "You shaved your beard."

He brushed a finger along the sleeve of her lavender jacket. His heat seemed to scorch right through the material. "You covered your bug bites." His gaze lowered to her neck. "But not your hickey."

"Hickey?"

Kelly's voice pulled Olivia out of her shock, and she turned to her assistant. "I've got this, Kelly. Thank you." Kelly nodded and would've stepped out the door if Deacon hadn't stopped her.

"Coffee?"

"Oh!" Kelly stumbled over her platform heels to get the cup of coffee to him.

"Thank you. I'm sure it's perfect." He gave her a smile that had Olivia doing a double take, and Kelly looking like she was about to reach orgasm. Her dark eyes glazed over as she just stood there fidgeting with her Betty Boop necklace.

"That's all, Kelly," Olivia said a little too sharply. And even after her assistant had left the room, her voice still held an edge that could slice tomatoes. "So I assume that you're here for the money."

He took a sip of coffee. Coffee that Olivia desperately needed. She thought about buzzing Kelly, but she couldn't put up with any more giddy gawking. She was doing enough of that herself. But it was hard to look away from a smooth-shaven Deacon. Not that he was completely devoid of facial hair. Dark stubble covered his lower face and seemed to be growing before her eyes. As if reading her thoughts, he stroked his jawbone as he glanced around the room.

"Do you really need all this space?"

As she had never thought about it before, it took her a moment to answer. "Probably not, but it came with the position."

"And that is?"

"Vice-president of sales." She paused. "And soon-to-be CEO."

"Hmm?" His eyebrows lifted, and he took another sip.

Since she had about a zillion things to do, Olivia sat down behind her desk. "Once all the *t*'s are crossed, I planned to have the money transferred into the bank account of your choice." She opened her briefcase and took out her checkbook. "But I'll be more than happy to write you a check to tide you and your brothers over. I don't know why I didn't think of it before." She had just finished signing the check for ten thousand when a hand covered hers. While most people had a body temperature of ninety-eight point six, it seemed that Deacon's was well above.

"There's no need for that, Olivia," he said.

She studied his long-fingered hand and the dark hair on his muscled forearm. "Then why are you here?"

Before he could answer, there was a tap on the door, and Jason stuck his head in. "Sorry to interrupt, Ms. Harrington"—he glanced at Deacon—"but I need to speak with you right away."

Thankful to get away from his mind-altering heat, she pulled her hand from Deacon and excused herself. "Pardon me. I'll be right back." As soon as she got in the hallway, Jason held out the contracts.

"There seems to be a problem." He flipped through the pages until he got to the last one. "One of the signatures is missing."

"What?" She grabbed the contracts from him. "You have to be mistaken. I was there when all three brothers signed—" She stopped and looked back at the closed door, then at the empty line beneath the two other signatures. Her heart tumbled all the way down to her feet. Without saying a word to Jason, she strode back into the office.

Deacon was sitting in her chair. He looked at the contract she held in her hand and smiled. Not the smile he'd given Kelly, but a sinister smile, like a cat that had just cornered a mouse. "Problems?"

Olivia tried not to show her fear, but it wasn't easy. "It seems that you forgot to sign the contract."

"Hmm? That is a dilemma." He picked up the pen she'd been using to write the check. "Of course it's easily solved."

She'd been in the business world long enough to know

when she was being toyed with. She stepped closer to the desk and placed the contract on the top. "But you aren't going to sign it, are you?"

He twirled the pen through his fingers a few times before he spoke. "The Beaumonts have done their share of begging, don't you think? Now it's your turn, Olivia."

CHAPTER SIX

Deacon was playing a game he had no business playing. Especially when the money he was playing it with wasn't his own. It was his brothers' as well. And both Nash and Grayson wanted him to sign the contract and make them millionaires as quickly as possible. They had no desire to be owners of their uncle's lingerie company. And Deacon didn't want that either. Which didn't explain why he'd refused to send the contract back with his uncle's lawyers. Or why he had shaved his beard, cut his hair, and traveled all the way to California to deliver it in person.

Obviously something had gone a little haywire in his brain. Something that had gotten even worse when he'd seen Olivia's opulent office, stood looking at the spectacular view, and finally turned to find a spoiled executive in a suit that probably cost more than his entire wardrobe. And now, whether he had a right or not, he wasn't through making Olivia sweat.

Although she didn't appear to be sweating too much.

"So I guess you want me to beg," she said. When he didn't reply, she shrugged. "Okay. You want me on my knees or will a couple of *pretty please*s do?"

He stopped twirling the pen through his fingers and called her bluff. "Knees would be nice." He expected her to tell him to go to hell. Instead she walked around the desk and, without the slightest hesitation, lifted her sexy-as-hell skirt just enough to flash him a peek of pretty pink garter belt fasteners and thigh-high stockings before kneeling in front of him.

Her piercing green eyes pinned him as she spoke in a voice that was anything but humble. "Please, Deacon. Please sign the contract."

It was his fantasy all over again. Technically, the desk and office were his. And while Olivia wasn't exactly in rags, she was on her knees. Which didn't explain why all the fun had drained right out of the game. Probably because he knew what it felt like to be forced to beg. Knew exactly the feeling of humiliation that came with needing something someone else had.

"Get up," he said.

"Why?" She gave him a wide-eyed look. "Did I do it wrong, Deacon? Sorry, but I'm not as good at begging as the Beaumonts."

The pen slipped from his fingers, and the leather chair creaked as he sat up, bringing his face inches from hers. "Shut up."

"Or what? You won't sign the contract?" She laughed, her breath coming out in a puff of heat. "We both know that you won't walk away from fifty million."

Her condescending attitude took Deacon from angry to flat-out pissed. So pissed that he couldn't even put to-

gether a reply that would wipe the smartassed smirk off
her face. That being the case, he chose a nonverbal way
to do it.

He kissed her.

Not a soft kiss, but a hard, forceful one that ended with
him sucking her plump bottom lip between his teeth and
giving it a nip. When he pulled back, Olivia was staring at
him with shocked eyes. He expected her anger and didn't
even tense when she lifted her hand. But instead of de-
livering a stinging, much-deserved slap she slid her hand
over the stubble on his jaw before pulling him back for
another kiss.

She kissed much better than she begged. He actually
believed that she was enjoying it. He sure as hell was. Her
lips were hungry and aggressive, her mouth hot and wet,
and her tongue slick and teasing.

Deacon opened his legs, and she moved right into the
space like a moored ship. Her hands curled around his
neck while his curved over her ass, lifting her knees off
the plush carpeting. As he squeezed the firm cheeks, his
mind ran through the list of things he would need to ac-
complish before he could be surrounded by the heat of
her body. Lift skirt. Remove panties. Unzip jeans. Pull out
cock. Get condom—damn.

He pulled away from those scorching lips. Then, just
to make sure he didn't succumb to a pair of desire-
drugged eyes, he shoved the caster chair back a good
three feet. But even with the added space, it took a while
for him to get ahold of his raging hormones.

Olivia didn't take quite as long.

After only a few blinks, she got to her feet, took two
wobbly steps toward him, then hauled off and gave him
the stinging slap he'd expected earlier. By the time his

ears stopped ringing, she had the pen and contract in hand.

"I did what you asked," she said through gritted teeth. "Now you sign."

It was difficult to keep up the smiling-asshole part with a hard-on that could easily have been used as a battering ram, but he did his best. "I didn't force you to beg. I merely asked. And you deserved it when you weren't exactly honest about how many shares Uncle Michael left us."

"The number of shares was in the contract."

"True. But you didn't explain that we owned the company."

"You don't own it. You own controlling interest."

"Which we both know is the same thing." He glanced around. "So this would be my office?"

Her eyes narrowed as she enunciated every word. "This. Is. My. Office."

Now that he was back in control, he asked the questions that had been circling his brain. "So what horrible thing did you do to get cut out of Uncle Michael's will completely? Forget to put your napkin on your lap? Burp at a dinner party? Get caught showing someone your panties?"

The look that entered her eyes was a combination of anger and hurt. "I didn't do anything. And I wasn't cut out completely."

Deacon already knew this. After his father had gotten the lawyers high on the moonshine he always carried in his trunk, they had become loose-lipped. He knew exactly what his uncle had left Olivia and her mother. According to the lawyers, the value of the estate was the same amount she was willing to give Deacon and his brothers.

He studied her. "Sorry, but I just don't get it. If you were Uncle Michael's beloved stepdaughter, why wouldn't he just leave you the shares in the company? Didn't he know how much you love French Kiss?"

She turned away. "He knew." A buzzer went off, and Olivia reached out and pressed a button on the phone. "Yes?"

"Sorry to interrupt." Kelly's voice came through the speaker. "But your mother is on line one and says that it's an emergency."

Olivia's shoulders tightened. "Thank you, Kelly." She glanced back at Deacon. "Do you mind getting out of my chair?"

"Not at all." He got up and slid the chair over.

If looks could kill, he would be six feet under. Which made his smile even broader. He liked this feisty Olivia much better than he liked the poised businesswoman. Or maybe he just liked knowing that he could get under her skin.

He moved to the sitting area and sat down on the couch. It was as hard and uncomfortable as it looked. He picked up a French Kiss catalog from the coffee table and thumbed through it. It wasn't the first time. He was on their mailing list—under an alias, of course. An exasperated grunt had him looking up from the hot model in a lacy bra and panties to the ticked-off woman in a business suit. It didn't sit well that he found Olivia almost as hot.

"So I guess you're not leaving," she said.

He shrugged. "I don't have anywhere to go. This poor Beaumont only had enough money for the plane ticket." It was an out-and-out lie. He might not have had enough money to build his condos, but he had enough to cover a plane ticket and hotel. But damned if he wasn't enjoying toying with Olivia. However, the kiss had been a mistake. One that wouldn't be repeated.

She sent him a glare before pressing a button and picking up the phone. "I'm sorry I kept you waiting, Mother, but I'm kind of busy right now. So what's the emergency? Did…" Her gaze met his before she swiveled the chair around and lowered her voice. "Did she throw another temper tantrum?" She paused for only a second before speaking in a voice at least three octaves higher. "Jail? She's in jail!"

Although he continued to thumb through the catalog, Deacon was all ears.

"What happened? Oh, good Lord." With the phone cradled to her ear, Olivia swiveled back around and placed her checkbook in the briefcase. "No, we can't leave her there, Mother." Another pause. "No, I don't have a clue how to bail someone out of jail, but I'm sure I'll figure it out." Hanging up the phone, she stood and grabbed her briefcase.

Deacon flipped down the catalog and got to his feet. "You'll probably need a bail bondsman."

She stopped on her way to the door and turned to him. "Excuse me?"

"That's what you'll need if you want to bail your friend out of jail."

"Oh." She nodded. "Thank you."

He flashed her a smile. "Anytime."

She studied him for a long moment before heading for the door. As soon as she had it open, she spoke to her assistant. But not as to an employee as much as to a friend she didn't want to offend. "Umm, Kelly, do you think you could reschedule my morning meetings? I need to drop…something off at my house and won't be back until the afternoon. And once Mr. Beaumont signs the paperwork on my desk, would you mind making him a reservation at a nice hotel and taking care of anything else he might need before he leaves town?" She glanced over her shoulder, her eyes almost daring him to contradict what she'd just told her assistant. "Goodbye, Deacon. Have a safe trip home."

Then, with the twitch of shapely hips and the click of purple high heels, she strode toward the elevators. Once she had disappeared around the corner, Kelly spoke.

"Is there a hotel you prefer?" She gave him a slow once-over, followed by the flirtatious bat of her overly long eyelashes. "Or if you like cozy, you could sleep on my couch, Mr...."

"Beaumont. And whatever hotel you choose is fine."

Kelly's eyes widened. "Beaumont? Are you related to Michael Beaumont?"

"He was my uncle."

"So you're his nephew? The one he willed the company to?"

Deacon nodded. "That would be me. But you don't have to worry. I don't have any plans to take over."

Her excitement dimmed. "That's too bad. What French Kiss needs is someone to take charge. Ms. Harrington is nice and all, but she's a bit of a pushover. Which might explain why we're going bankrupt."

"Bankrupt? French Kiss is going bankrupt?"

She glanced in both directions before she leaned in. "Since I've only worked here a few months, I don't have all the details. But rumor has it that, once you find out about the company's problems, you're going to sell it to the highest bidder. Which is going to suck for me since my roommate moved out with her rat bastard of a boyfriend and left me with the lease. And do you have a clue how expensive it is to live in San Francisco? Not that I'm hinting for a raise or anything. I would just like to keep my job."

Deacon was stunned. Last he'd heard, French Kiss was pulling in billions a year. Now it was going bankrupt? It didn't make sense. And why would Olivia spend all her money on a company that was going under?

As if reading his mind, Kelly continued. "Although I think Ms. Harrington has something up her sleeve to save the company. I overheard her talking to her mother about a secret weapon."

"A secret weapon?"

She nodded. "Some Paris designer. Unfortunately, now that person is in jail for sexual assault." Obviously Olivia's assistant didn't mind eavesdropping on phone calls.

"Do you know what jail Ms. Harrington went to?"

"No, but I do know that once she bails the designer out of jail, she's taking her back to her house." She turned to her computer. "And I have that address."

* * *

Olivia didn't live in a mansion as her stepfather had, but Deacon didn't doubt for a second that the three-story house had cost a pretty penny. Property values in San Francisco were higher than a cat's ass, which explained why the houses were snugged together like toes in a tight boot. He'd planned on waiting in front for Olivia to return and was surprised when he pulled up and found the garage door wide open. Had Olivia gotten the secret weapon out of jail that quickly? Or had Kelly given him the wrong address?

He got out of the rental car and slammed the door, taking note of the *For Sale* sign stuck in a huge flowerpot of bright-red geraniums by the steps that led to the front door. Olivia was selling her house?

"You there! What's your business?"

Deacon glanced up to see a bare-chested old guy on the balcony of the house next door pointing a watering pot at him. "I'm looking for my cousin," he called up. "Is this Olivia Harrington's house?"

The man called back over his shoulder. "Doris! Isn't the young girl next door named Britney? There's a guy looking for Olivia."

A woman's voice came out the open sliding glass door. "Good grief, Hammond, that was the woman who lived there five years ago. This one is Olivia."

"Well, whatever her name is," the old guy said, "she left her garage door open again and there's a man lurking around who claims he's her cousin."

An old woman's head appeared above the balcony, followed by a pair of saggy, wrinkled breasts. "You're Olivia's cousin?"

Deacon lowered his gaze to the geraniums and tried to clear the image from his brain. "Yes, ma'am."

"You don't look like her."

"We're step-cousins."

"Remember my step-cousin, Doris?" the man said. "Unbelievable chef, but the meanest bastard I ever had the misfortune of knowing."

"Hush up, Hammond. He doesn't want to hear your life story." She spoke to Deacon. "I guess it's okay for you to go in when she's not home, but be warned that we're going to get your license plate number." He thought she pointed a finger, but he refused to look up to be sure.

"And if anything is missing," she continued, "we'll know where to send the police."

"Yes, ma'am." It was a relief to walk into the garage. The inside of the garage looked like a girl's. No tool-boxes, athletic equipment, or grease. Just a bicycle with a silly basket on the front, a pair of purple galoshes, and two cases of bottled water.

He wiped his feet on the mat before he pushed open the door.

The lower level of the house had a bedroom and en suite bath, no doubt a guest room since there were no signs of inhabitance. On the second level, he found two more bedrooms. One was as neat as the one downstairs, and the other held an unmade bed and enough high heels spread across the thick carpet to start a shoe store—if the buyers liked purple. Four half-empty coffee mugs were on the nightstand, along with a stack of fashion maga-zines, some colored pencils, and a sketchpad. He lifted the sketchpad and flipped through the pages. They were all lingerie designs. And damned sexy ones. Obviously Olivia was in the right business.

After replacing the sketchpad, he climbed the stairs to the third level. The living space was decorated in a contemporary style. A white leather sofa and aqua chairs were positioned around a modern gas fireplace. A break-fast bar divided the space from a kitchen with gray granite counters and high-end stainless steel appliances. It was a unique floor plan. One he found himself envisioning for his condos. Unlike the two-story design he had now, in-creasing to three levels would give more square footage and the higher balcony a better view of the lake.

Once the will went through, he could start work on the condos. Of course, first he had to sign the contract. Something he'd forgotten to do in his haste to discover Olivia's secret weapon. But there was time. And since the only thing he'd eaten that day was the bagel he'd grabbed at the airport, he walked into the kitchen and opened the refrigerator.

Besides the jars of condiments and bottles of water, there was a withered-looking apple, an expired carton of orange juice, and some bad-smelling, yellow broccoli. He tossed the broccoli in the trash, then went to the cupboards, where he found a jar of all-natural almond butter and a bag of flaxseed tortilla chips. After grabbing a bottle of water, he opened up the accordion glass door that led to the balcony.

A seagull greeted him. The good-size bird was snacking on the remnants of a burrito. Rather than shoo it away, Deacon took a seat on the lounge sofa and dipped the chips in the almond butter while he had a stare-down with the bird. After a few minutes, he started tossing it chips. The audacious bird came within inches of Deacon's boots before it took a crap on the rug and, in a loud flap of wings, flew away. After he was gone, Deacon stretched out on the couch and closed his eyes. Since his flight had left at the crack of dawn, it wasn't surprising that he nodded off.

He awoke to a door slamming. Sitting up, he blinked the sleep from his eyes and listened to the sound of high heels clicking up the flights of stairs.

"You weren't supposed to leave my mother's house, Babette," Olivia said. "That was part of the deal. Until I get control of the company, you were to stay out of sight."

"Creativity cannot be held prisoner," a woman said in a thick French accent. "Especially with a tyrant who refused to meet my creative needs."

"She took the television remote away, Babette." Olivia's heels clicked to a stop just feet away from the balcony door. "And only when you refused to work on the new line. The new line that I'd planned to present to the board in just a few days."

"Zee new line is almost ready and exquisite. Now make me an omelet."

"I'm not making you an omelet," Olivia said. "I'm going back to work so we have a company to sell your exquisite line."

A string of French followed. Having grown up with a French-speaking Cajun father, Deacon understood most of it. He got up and stepped through the balcony doorway. Olivia stood at the refrigerator. When she saw him, she dropped the carton of orange juice she'd been taking out of the refrigerator, and it splattered all over the floor.

He shrugged. "Sorry, but it's probably for the best. It was expired." Then he turned to the petite, dark-haired woman and spoke to her in her native language.

"I agree that, at times, Olivia can be a little bitchy," he said. "But fat?"

CHAPTER SEVEN

The discovery that Deacon spoke French affected Babette much differently than it did Olivia. Babette released a sob and fell into Deacon's arms as if he were there to save her from the barbarian Americans, while Olivia wanted to pick up the ten-pound glass vase her mother had given her and bludgeon him with it. Instead she stepped away from the vase and reached for the roll of paper towels.

"What are you doing here?" she asked as she started cleaning up the spilled orange juice. "And how did you get in my house?"

He patted Babette's back and whispered a few French words that sounded soothing...and annoyingly sexy. Babette whimpered like a homeless puppy and cuddled closer as Deacon lifted his gaze to Olivia. "You left the garage door open. Something Hammond and Doris say you do a lot?"

"Hammond and Doris?"

"The naked couple next door." He shook his head sadly. "What is it with you Californians? Don't you know your neighbors' names?"

She started to jump into an argument, then reminded herself to stay focused on a much more important issue. "So did you sign it? Did you sign the contract?"

"So this is your secret weapon that is going to save French Kiss?" As Babette continued to sob, he thumped her back a little harder. "What is she developing? A new Wonderbra that grows breasts? Panties that give you a J. Lo butt? A nightie that will give men orgasms just by looking at it?"

Olivia's eyes widened. "Who told you?" When he didn't say anything, she answered the question herself. "Kelly."

"So what's the secret weapon?"

"That's none of your business."

One of his eyebrows arched. "Considering the fact that I own the company, I think it is." But instead of asking her again, he spoke to Babette in French. Between loud sniffs and dramatic hand gestures, she answered him. And there was little doubt that she'd spilled the beans when Deacon's eyes widened and he spoke in English. "Men's lingerie?" When Babette nodded triumphantly, he looked at Olivia. "That's it? That's your big secret weapon to save the company from bankruptcy?" He disengaged himself from Babette. "Lacy panties for men?"

Olivia tipped up her chin. "Don't be ridiculous. Of course we're not going to use lace on men's underwear."

"Perhaps," Babette cut in, "just a wee bit." She demonstrated a wee bit with her thumb and forefinger. "Not on zee waistband of course, but right around zee genitalia area would be very, very sexy—no?"

"No!" Olivia said. "It would not be sexy. We've talked about this before, Babette. I'll go along with the vibrant colors, but you can't put lace on men's—"

"Just on zee thongs." Babette picked up her tote bag and pulled out a stack of designs. She spread them out on the breakfast counter, then waved a hand in the air. "*Voilà*! These are my masterpieces."

Olivia looked at the drawings and felt her stomach drop to her feet. These weren't the designs she'd gone over with Babette. These were drawings of costumes for Cirque du Soleil performers. The thick Egyptian cotton robes they'd discussed had become long satin dressing gowns with feathered lapels that looked like they belonged on a Mardi Gras float. The satin pajamas were right, but the pink and purple colors were all wrong, as was the sagging M.C. Hammer crotch that draped to the knees. The spandex-blend, tummy-tucking T-shirts had been replaced with racerback tanks made of flimsy silk that wouldn't hold in a cube of Jell-O, let alone a beer belly. Instead of boxer briefs made in the new soft laser-sculpted fabric their engineers had developed, the briefs were made with see-through mesh that showed all the manly bits and pieces—and from the drawings, it looked like Babette knew her manly bits and pieces extremely well. The final straw was the drawings of thong underwear in hot pink, lime green, and bright purple. Each page was divided in half, showing both bulging frontal view and bare-butted rear.

Olivia was struck speechless. Obviously, while she'd been in Louisiana, Babette had gone completely off track. Or completely off her rocker. Even now the French designer looked a little wild-eyed as she pulled rhinestone-studded thongs from her tote.

"Magnificent, no?" She stretched them around Deacon's manly bits and pieces. "I can only imagine how...how you say in English...awesome these will look on you." She sent him a seductive look from beneath her eyelashes. "Shall we go see?"

Deacon looked as if she'd just asked him to murder one of his brothers. "Have you lost your mind, woman?" He jerked the thongs away from her and held them up, the rhinestones flashing in the sunlight that spilled in through the balcony doors. "I wouldn't be caught dead in these. Nor would any man I know." He glanced at Olivia. "I would expect some confusion from a foreigner about what American men want, but not from a woman who has been in the business for as long as you have. What were you thinking?"

No matter how much she might agree with him, his condescending tone had Olivia's shoulders stiffening and her defending something that had no defense.

"This coming from a backwoods hillbilly who wouldn't know style if it smacked him in the face."

He held out the underwear. "You don't have to know style to know shit when you see it. Who would buy these?"

Olivia sniffed. "Cosmopolitan men who are much more open-minded than you."

"And just what percentage of the men in the world do you think are cosmopolitan, Olivia? Fifty percent? Forty? Thirty? How about under ten percent? And of those ten percent of cosmopolitan men, how many do you think are going to like walking around with a strip of diamonds stuck up their ass?"

They were good questions—questions someone with a knowledge of marketing would ask. Which made Olivia wonder if Deacon was more educated than she thought.

"Women wear thongs all the time," she pointed out.

"They also wear painful high heels, tight uncomfortable clothes, and carry purses that weigh a good thirty pounds," he said. "All because they want to look good. Men aren't interested in looking good as much as they are in feeling good. And I don't have to try these on to know that these aren't going to feel good."

"He's r-r-right." Babette's French tongue rolled over the *r*'s. "He's absolutely correct. I completely forgot that, for men, zee ultimate thing isn't fashion as much as comfort." Without any warning she grabbed the designs off the counter and started ripping them to shreds. "Garbage. Trash. Poo-poo." Olivia tried to stop her, but when Babette got on a roll, there was no chance of that happening. She tore up every design, then grabbed the mock-up thongs from Deacon, raced to the balcony, and sent them sailing over the railing.

When the last twinkle of rhinestones had vanished, she turned with a dramatic wail and flounced from the room. Once she was gone, Olivia looked down at the ripped designs and couldn't keep the tears from her eyes.

Not because she had liked them, but because Babette had wasted weeks on something that would never sell. Weeks that Olivia didn't have. In less than two days, she had a board meeting at which she'd promised to present a new line that would pull French Kiss out of bankruptcy. And now she had nothing but a pile of ripped-up drawings. She flopped down at the breakfast bar and cradled her head in her hands.

A handkerchief appeared in front of her.

"If you're going to start crying, use this," Deacon said as he pulled out the chair next to hers. "My shirt can't take any more tears."

Olivia wanted to do more than cry. She wanted to put her head down on the breakfast bar and sob her eyes out. She just refused to do it in front of this man. She stared at the handkerchief and willed her tears into submission. "You carry around a flower-embroidered hankie?"

"It was my mother's."

Feeling guilty for being so rude, she lifted her head and looked into eyes that were the same color as the flowers. "It's very pretty."

He studied the handkerchief. "She loved purple flowers. She put them on handkerchiefs, pillowcases, our mailbox." He carefully folded the hankie, then shifted closer as he placed it in the back pocket of his jeans. So close that his face was only inches away.

Olivia had spent the better part of the drive to get Babette out of jail trying to forget the kiss they'd shared in the office. Now suddenly it came flooding back. The possessive slide of his lips against hers. The heated pull of his mouth. The teasing swirl of his tongue.

"Olivia?"

Her gaze lifted from his mouth to his questioning eyes.

"Where do you go?" he asked.

"Go?" She blinked his face into focus.

"You mean you don't realize that you drift off when people are talking with you?"

She slipped off the stool and walked over to the cupboard to see if she could locate anything that would help her focus... and not on Deacon. "I realize it."

"Attention deficit?"

"Probably. I was never tested for it. My father just thought I had a creative mind. I just think it's screwed up. Which would explain why I put my faith in Babette."

"So where did you find her, anyway? Never mind, stupid

question. Obviously you found her in France. The better question would be…why did you hire her? Especially when her specialty seems to be burlesque costumes."

She searched through the teas her mother had given her. *Herbal* obviously meant no caffeine. "Babette has talent. Some of her lingerie designs are amazing." She closed the cupboard and turned around to find Deacon studying a ripped piece of one of Babette's pages.

"I wouldn't go that far." He crumpled the piece in his hand and tossed it at the trash can. It hit dead center, of course. "So what did she do to get arrested?"

"She walked to the high school by my mother's house and started talking underwear with a group of young boys. Thankfully, once I got there and confirmed her story about working for French Kiss, they released her with a warning to stay away from underage kids."

"That sucks," he said. "Almost as much as her idea for men's lingerie."

She bristled. "It isn't such a bad idea. And the statistics support that men are spending more and more money on clothes these days. Why wouldn't they want their own lingerie line?" She glanced down at the sketches. "No, not thongs or see-through boxers, but I think men would buy nice robes, tummy-tucking T-shirts, and sexy—but comfortable—briefs. And why can't men look as sexy in their underwear as women?"

Deacon smiled, a sensuous smile that made Olivia's tummy do a cartwheel. "Because men's bodies aren't as beautiful as women's. Although I'll admit that the premise isn't such a bad idea. I have trouble finding underwear that fits, doesn't shrink up, and is comfortable. And I wouldn't mind a nice, thick bathrobe. But, regardless of how good the idea is, men are creatures of habit.

It's going to take a while for men's... 'lingerie' to catch on. Too long to save the company if it's that close to bankruptcy. So what happened? I thought French Kiss pulled in seven point one billion a year."

She stared at him. "How do you know our sales figures?"

He shrugged. "It's not like they're a secret."

The sales figures weren't a secret, but they weren't exactly common knowledge either. A person would have to do some research to find out the exact amounts. And she was surprised that Deacon had been interested enough to look them up. Especially when he acted like he couldn't care less about his uncle's business.

"What does it matter to you?" she asked. "All you have to do is sign the contract to get your money. Then you never have to worry about French Kiss again. Speaking of which, do you have the signed contract with you?"

"I'm afraid not. I left it at the office."

"Signed?"

Before he could answer, Mr. Huckabee's voice came through the open balcony doors. "Doris, get out here! Britney's houseguest just jumped off the roof!"

While Olivia tried to process the words, Deacon headed for the balcony doors. His "Holy shit" had her hurrying after him. When she got outside, she saw what had caused his disbelief. Babette dangled from the roof by a rope of daisy-chained thong underwear. It looked like she had tried to fashion a noose, but instead of putting the lime-green thong around her neck, she'd put it around her waist. Which was par for the course with the dramatic woman.

"My life is over," she wailed. "I don't deserve to live. Not when no man will ever wear my creations."

Deacon looked at Olivia. "You want me to get her or let her swing for a while?"

After all the trouble Babette had put her through, Olivia really wanted to let her swing. But the sound of ripping stitches changed her mind.

"Go get her, please."

While Deacon headed for the stairs that led to the roof, Olivia leaned over the railing. "Hang on, Babette. Help is on the way."

"I don't want help. I don't want to live." A loud tearing sound finally got Babette's attention. "What was that?" She looked up. "Zee material is tearing? Help! Help me! Please, someone help me!" Deacon appeared, and within seconds Babette was in his arms, sobbing a mixture of French and English.

"So is your houseguest trippin', Britney?"

Olivia glanced at the house next door and saw Mr. Huckabee standing on the balcony wearing nothing but gardening gloves. Mrs. Huckabee stood next to him, sporting a wide-brimmed visor. She jabbed her husband with her elbow, causing her unfettered breasts to swing.

"It's Olivia, Hammond." She looked at Olivia. "So what's she on, dear? LSD? Quaaludes? Magic brownies?"

Olivia tried to keep her eyes off the Huckabees' dangling parts. "Actually she's just a little overdramatic. But thank you so much for alerting us." She paused. "And for the pot of beautiful geraniums by the front door."

"I didn't give you geraniums." Doris looked at her husband. "Did you, Hammond?"

"No. Maybe her cousin did. He seems like a helpful fellow." He directed his next comment at Olivia. "I hope you don't sell your house to old farts who have a problem with loud rock and roll. It would be nice to have a couple living next door who are up for a little swinging."

The mental picture that popped into Olivia's head had her cringing. "I'll try to keep that in mind," she said. "Well, thanks again. Now I better get inside and check on Babette." She turned for the door only to stop when she saw Jonathan Livingston standing on the back of her chair.

"Scat!" She flung out her arms, but this time the bird didn't take flight. Instead he hopped to the table and picked up a flaxseed tortilla chip and ate it whole. And since Olivia had lost all control over her life, she let him.

CHAPTER EIGHT

What the hell are you doing, Deke?" Nash's voice came through the phone receiver before Deacon could even say hello. "And don't give me the crap you gave Grayson and Dad about wanting to make sure the contract got to Olivia. We both know that Michael's lawyers could've easily handled that."

Suddenly exhausted, Deacon put his brother on speaker before placing the cell phone on the hotel nightstand and lying back on the king-size bed. Kelly had done a good job of picking out a hotel. The mattress was pillow-top and the bedding plush. It was too bad that his brother had to ruin his relaxing evening in the nice room by pointing out his stupidity.

"Something didn't feel right, Nash. And I couldn't sign until I found out what that something was."

"So don't keep me in suspense."

Deacon ran a hand through his hair and released his

breath. "French Kiss is on the brink of bankruptcy. According to what I could get out of Olivia's assistant and the Parisian designer, the company was struggling even before Michael's stroke."

He was surprised by how disappointed he felt. As much as he might have hated Michael Beaumont, there was a part of Deacon that had also admired him. Unlike Donny John, he had made something of himself. The only Beaumont who had.

"Well, damn," Nash said. "Does that mean that Olivia withdrew her offer?"

"No. The offer still stands."

"So what's the holdup? Sign the contract before Olivia changes her mind."

"She's not going to change her mind. She's got some harebrained idea about saving the company by selling men's lingerie."

"Men's what?"

Deacon snorted. "Exactly. You should've seen the pair of rhinestone thongs. I swear, I don't know who is more crazy—the French designer who designed them or Olivia for putting her trust in the no-talent woman in the first place."

"So I take it that Olivia isn't as business-savvy as Michael was."

"Not from what I can tell. If she were business-savvy, she would jump ship while she could. Instead she's willing to use all her money to buy the shares of a bankrupt company."

"I'm sure she won't go broke," Nash said.

At one time Deacon had been sure of that too. But after seeing the *For Sale* sign at her house, he had to wonder how deep in debt Olivia was willing to go for the company. He massaged his temples. "The crazy woman is gambling on a dream."

"She wouldn't be the first," Nash said. "You sold everything you owned to buy the land by the lake."

"Yeah, but my plan is at least feasible. No man I know is going to buy feathered robes and rhinestone thongs. And Olivia needs to pull her head out of the clouds and realize that. Hell, the woman doesn't even remember to close her garage door. And do you know all the nuts that wander around a big city? When I was leaving her house tonight, I saw some Peeping Tom in a trench coat trying to peek in her windows. The pervert ran off when I jumped out of the car."

There was a long stretch of silence, and Deacon wondered if their connection had been lost. He had just reached for the phone to check when Nash spoke.

"So that's how it is."

Deacon took the phone off speaker and held it to his ear. "What? That's how what is?"

Nash released his breath in one long sigh. "Olivia has become a damsel in distress, and you want to be her knight in shining armor."

"What are you talking about? Have you been drinking some of Dad's moonshine?"

"I'm talking about your Lancelot complex—the one where you feel like you have to come to the rescue of every woman in need."

Deacon laughed. "You have been hitting the moonshine."

"You know I don't drink after what happened, Deke. You have issues with saving women. Don't tell me you've forgotten about getting your butt kicked by those bullies when you defended Katie Day? Or giving Rhonda Lyons money until she found a job? Or fixing that single mom's car for free when it broke down on her way through town? I even think you agreed to be Francesca's cougar cub because you felt sorry for her. And there were at least a dozen more times that you've given money and time you didn't have to help some woman in need. But you can't help Olivia, Deke. Not only because you don't know shit about the lingerie business but also because Olivia doesn't want your help. From what I could tell, she wants us to sign the contract and get the hell out of her life."

Nash paused. "Look, I love you, Bro. You were more of a father to Grayson and me after Mom died than Dad was. And it's not about the money—I don't need much to survive. But this money could help you achieve your dream, Deacon. A dream that you put off because of my screw-up."

"You didn't screw up, Nash," Deacon said. "It was a trumped-up charge."

"Was it?" Nash's reply surprised Deacon—as did the raw emotion attached to the words. He'd thought that Nash had released the past, but it looked like he'd been wrong. "She said no, Deke," he continued. "Did it matter when she said it?"

"Hell, yeah, it mattered. And the jury thought so too." He sat up. "You've got to let this go, Nash."

There was a long pause. "Okay, I'll make you a deal. I'll let it go if you let French Kiss go."

*   *   *

After his conversation with Nash, Deacon didn't sleep well. He woke up still on Central time with a headache and a firm resolve. Nash was right. He needed to sign the contract. It was what his brothers and Olivia wanted. And it should be what Deacon wanted too. If he signed the contract, he could finish his condos, build a new house, find some sweet little Sunday school teacher to marry, and set his brothers up for life. He didn't know anything about the lingerie business. His life was back in Louisiana. Certainly not San Francisco.

Getting up, he showered, shaved, and packed before paying his hotel bill and heading for French Kiss. When he entered the lobby, the pretty receptionist behind the large art deco desk greeted him.

"Good morning. Are you here to see Ms. Harrington again? Because I'm afraid she doesn't get in until around nine o'clock."

"That's okay." He headed for the elevators. "I'm sure her assistant can help me."

Except Kelly wasn't at her desk. But the door to Olivia's office was cracked open. Thinking he would find Kelly inside, he was surprised when he peeked in and saw a thin blond woman in a red power suit bent over Olivia's desk reading the contract he'd left there the day before.

"It's a contract for hundred and fifty million, all right," she said into the cell phone she had pressed to her ear. "What an idiot. Who would pay that much for a company that's going under? So now what? You promised me the position of CEO if I helped you ruin French Kiss. I did everything I could on this end—including overlooking the money that was skimmed."

The woman straightened. Deacon took a step back, but continued to listen.

"Be patient?" she said. "I have been patient. But I'm starting to get the feeling that you're playing me for a fool. And I'm no fool—"

"Good morning."

Deacon turned to see Kelly walking down the hall, carrying a stack of empty boxes. As she peeked around them, the top two went tumbling to the floor. He hurried over to help her, but kept his eyes on Olivia's office. Sure enough, while he was bent over, the skinny blonde slipped out and moved around Kelly's desk.

"I thought I asked you to take those boxes to my office, Kelly?" she said.

Kelly rolled her eyes at Deacon before answering. "I was planning on it, Ms. Bradley, but then I noticed Mr. Beaumont."

Ms. Bradley's eyes narrowed. "Mr. Beaumont?"

After what he'd heard, he couldn't help playing the part. "Michael's nephew... and the new owner of French Kiss."

Her eyes widened before she glanced back at Olivia's office. "But I thought you had..."

"Had what? Ms. Bradley, is it?"

She pulled her gaze away from the door and collected herself. "Yes, Anastasia Bradley. I'm the vice-president of marketing." She held out a hand, and he shook it briefly.

"Then I guess we'll be seeing each other again." He stacked the boxes and picked them up. "Let me help you with these. Where is your office?"

"She's moving into your uncle's office," Kelly said with a gleeful smile.

Deacon lifted an eyebrow at Anastasia. "Really?"

Anastasia quickly took the boxes from him. "Thanks, but I think I can handle it." Then, without an "It's nice to meet you," she turned and headed down the hallway.

She hadn't even disappeared around the corner before

Deacon turned to Kelly. "So what do you know about Ms. Bradley?"

"Besides the fact that she's a class-A bitch?"

He agreed, but he wasn't about to tell Kelly that. The young woman needed to learn a few basic rules of business. He took note of her inappropriate dress with the plunging neckline. Okay, so maybe more than a few.

"There are certain words that should be reserved for happy hours," he said. "Which means that I would like you to answer the question without your personal opinions."

She looked a little taken aback at first, but quickly recovered. "From what I've heard, she came to work here around the same time Ms. Harrington finished college. She graduated cumma sum la-di-da and thinks she should be CEO and not Ms. Harrington."

"And I'm going to assume that she bullies Ms. Harrington."

"That's putting it mildly. The woman not only bullies her she also bullies everyone on the board. And I think she's boinking the old guy with—" Deacon lifted a brow, and she rephrased. "Yes, she's a bully. So are you here to see Ms. Harrington? She usually doesn't get here until around nine. Which doesn't seem right, since I have to be here at eight."

He stared at the door of the office where the contract was waiting. *Don't be stupid, Deacon. Sign the contract and get the hell out of here.* But instead of doing that, he glanced at his watch. "I guess that gives me a good hour."

Kelly seemed thrilled. "I'll be happy to get you a cup of coffee while you wait—black, right?"

He smiled. "You read my mind."

She started to turn when she noticed the opened door

of Olivia's office. Her head cocked. "That's strange. I don't remember unlocking it." She pulled the door closed before heading down the hallway.

Once she was gone, Deacon's mind ticked. If the office had been locked, it meant that Ms. Bradley had done some breaking and entering. He wasn't that surprised. He had met his fair share of women, and men, who were willing to do whatever it took to get ahead in the business world. And it sounded to Deacon like Ms. Bradley wanted to get ahead . . . but not as much as the person she had been speaking to.

"So did you sign it, Mr. Beaumont?"

Deacon was pulled away from his thoughts by the same man who had shown up in Olivia's office the day before. He was a disheveled-looking guy with messy hair, wrinkled pants, and a grease spot on his purple tie. But regardless of his appearance, he seemed to have some guts.

"Jason Melvin." He held out his hand. "I'm the one who drew up the contract."

Deacon shook his hand. "Deacon Beaumont."

"I assumed as much by Ms. Harrington's reaction yesterday." He hesitated for only a second. "So did you sign it? Or would you like to do that now?"

Smart man. He had very politely placed Deacon in a corner. Which made Deacon wonder if he had been the one talking to Ms. Bradley on the phone. It didn't seem likely. A lawyer wouldn't have the power to appoint Ms. Bradley to the position of CEO.

"Call me Deacon," he said. "And may I call you Jason?" Before he could agree, Deacon continued. "Actually, there were a few things in the contract I'd like to discuss. And since you drew it up, I figure you'll be able to answer them better than Olivia can."

"Of course. My office is just—" His face turned a bright red that clashed with his tie as Kelly walked up with the coffee.

"Be careful," she said as she handed Deacon the cup. "It's still a little hot." She looked at Jason and sent him a knowing smile. "Would you like me to get you some coffee, Mr. Melvin, or are you interested in something else?"

Jason's chin lifted. "No, thank you, Miss Wang. There's nothing you can get me that I want."

"Really?" Kelly's smile was more like a baring of teeth, and Deacon wondered if he should step between them or pull out the boxing gloves. "Because it looked like you were...pointing me out the other day."

"If I point you out, Miss Wang, you'll know it." His eyes flashed with anger before he turned to Deacon. "My office is this way."

With a nod of thanks to Kelly, Deacon followed him down the hallway. "So I'm going to make a guess and say that you're interested in Kelly."

Jason glanced at him. "What? That overconfident nympho? Not hardly. She's probably screwed half the guys in San Francisco."

"Doubtful."

Jason stopped and studied him. "What do you mean?"

"I mean that I've met very few women who are true nymphos and addicted to sex. But I've met plenty of women who act sexually aggressive as a way of hiding their insecurities."

"And you think that brassy woman is insecure?"

Deacon shrugged. "It's probable. Kelly is the new kid on the block in a business filled with beautiful lingerie models."

Jason thought for a moment before he cleared his throat. "Well, it doesn't matter. I'm not interested." He turned and led Deacon into a small office that was messier than Grayson's room. The desk was cluttered with stacks of papers and fast-food cups, the trash can filled with empty snack cake boxes, and the windowsill crammed with dying potted plants. The only thing remotely organized was the shelf behind the desk. Sports memorabilia filled each level. It was an impressive collection.

"It looks like you're quite the sports enthusiast." Deacon studied the signatures on a baseball. "Did you play?"

Jason took a seat behind the desk. "No, I just collect. To my father's dismay, I pretty much suck at all sports. But I would imagine that you played and were no doubt the star high school quarterback."

"Actually, I didn't have time to play sports. I was too busy trying to make money." He picked up the framed picture next to the ball. It was a picture of Jason and Olivia with a baseball field behind them. Both were smiling brightly—a little too brightly for Deacon's taste. "Obviously I was wrong. Kelly isn't the woman you're interested in."

"That was at the company charity game," Jason said defensively. "Olivia took pictures with a lot of the employees. She's that kind of a boss—the type that cares about the people who work for her." He cupped his hands on the desk. "And now you don't need to work for money, Mr. Beaumont. Now all you need to do is sign on the dotted line."

Deacon set the picture down and ignored Jason's statement. "If Olivia is such a perfect boss, why is French Kiss going bankrupt?"

Jason looked surprised. "Ms. Harrington told you?"

"We talked about it, and her plan to save the company." He picked up a football. "It's a bad plan."

"How would you know? You don't know anything about the business."

Deacon put the football back in its stand. "You're right. So fill me in." He took the chair in front of the desk. "Starting with Ms. Bradley."

Jason's chair squeaked as he leaned forward. "What's with all the questions? What difference does it make who is in charge if you're planning on selling your shares?" He paused. "Unless you're not planning on selling your shares. Unless you're toying with Ms. Harrington." His eyes narrowed. "Well, I'm not having it, Mr. Beaumont. She's a good person who only wants what's best for this company and the employees who work here. That's why she's using every penny she inherited and selling her home so she can keep French Kiss. And I'll be damned if I'm going to let some Southern, slick-talking con artist ruin that for her."

The loyal speech and protective tone made up Deacon's mind, and he smiled and leaned back in the chair. "Number one rule when dealing with sexual women is don't play their game. Next time Kelly asks you what you want, tell her. No blushing, no sparring, no egos involved. Look her straight in the eyes and tell her."

"Tell her I want to have sex with her?"

"Is that all you want?"

"No. I'd like to take her to dinner."

"So start with that and see where it goes." He leaned in. "And you're right. I've been playing with Olivia, seeing just how much crap she'd be willing to take to get me to sign the contract."

"You asshole," Jason said.

Deacon pictured Olivia kneeling in front of him and had to agree. She hadn't even blinked. To her a little lost pride was no big deal when compared to getting what she wanted. While to Deacon pride came first. Followed closely by honor. And no honorable man could leave Olivia in a pit of scorpions.

"Asshole or not, I own the company," he said. "Or will after it clears probate."

"It already has."

Deacon wasn't surprised by the news as much as the feeling that accompanied it. He suddenly felt overwhelmed by the enormity of owning a huge company and being responsible for it and every employee in it. And he had to wonder if Olivia hadn't felt the same way when Michael had his stroke.

He nodded. "Then I guess that means I'm your boss. And right now, I want to get a look at your accounts."

"Why?"

"Because I think there's another asshole who is skimming money off the top and trying to lower the stock so they can buy out the company." He briefly ran through what he'd overheard Ms. Bradley saying. When he finished, Jason flopped down in his chair in disbelief.

"I knew she was mean, but I didn't think she would do something like that. Who do you think she was talking with?"

"I was hoping you could shed some light on that."

Jason shook his head. "I don't have a clue. She doesn't hang out with anyone that I know of—except Parker Calloway from accounting. They occasionally have lunch together. But he would never do anything to hurt Olivia. They're dating."

So Olivia hadn't been lying when she told Nash she was in a relationship. Deacon didn't know why he felt annoyed by the information, but he did.

"Let's start with the accounts and see what we can find," he said.

Jason studied him for only a moment before he leaned in and grabbed his computer mouse. "I don't have the passcode to get into all the accounts. Only Olivia and Ms. Bradley have those. But I can get you into a few."

"Let's start with the ones you have access to, then once I have the passcode, we'll look at the others."

Jason stopped moving the mouse and looked at Deacon. "So you're on Olivia's team?"

Deacon took his time answering. "It would seem that way. At least until I sign the contract."

CHAPTER NINE

E-e-ek! Are you trying to kill me?" Babette barely made it on board before the trolley started moving. Olivia easily fit between two men in business suits, while Babette had a harder time squeezing in. Once she was situated between a plump woman and the railing, she continued her dramatics.

"I do not understand why zee people in ziss country don't walk to work. In Paris I walked to work every day." She pressed a hand to her chest. "Ohh, how I miss my precious Par-ree. If not for you, I would be enjoying an espresso and cream puff at Popelini right now. Instead of being here in this"—she waved a hand at the traffic that whizzed past—"madness you call home."

"You were the one who applied to French Kiss," Olivia said.

"Because I thought I would get good money. But so far I've been paid less than a street cleaner."

Olivia wanted to point out that she would get her

money when Olivia got her designs. And she wasn't talking about a bunch of flamboyant burlesque costumes. But
she didn't want a repeat of yesterday's dramatics. After
the thong hanging, it had taken the rest of the day to calm
Babette down.

Not that Olivia had been involved in the calming
process. It had been Deacon who carried a sobbing
Babette to the guest room. Deacon who placed her on the
bed and spoke to her in soft French. Deacon who ordered
Olivia to bring Babette some wine to soothe her nerves.
Olivia had opened a bottle of her best merlot and taken
it and a glass to the guest room. Instead of thanking her,
Babette had sobbed even louder.

"You seem to agitate her," Deacon said as he ushered
Olivia out of the bedroom and closed the door. Talk about
agitated. Olivia had been so agitated she wanted to kick
in the door and order him out of her house. The only thing
that kept her from it was the unsigned contract and the
thought of having to deal with Babette by herself. So instead she had gone upstairs and waited. And waited. And
waited. When Babette's loud moans drifted up the stairs,
Olivia couldn't believe her ears. It took a good five minutes of moans before her naïve brain could accept the
truth that Deacon was having sex with a woman right under her nose. Furious, she marched down the stairs with
the intent of kicking them both out of her house. But
when she arrived in the guest room, she found the bottle of wine empty, Babette sleeping like a contented baby,
and Deacon gone.

"So will Deacon be at your office?" Babette's question
pulled her out of her daydream.

Kelly had called to inform her that Deacon had
stopped by the office and was waiting to see her. Olivia

had little doubt that he had signed the contract. He'd made no bones about how ridiculous he thought her idea for a men's lingerie line was. Olivia was relieved. And also terrified. Deacon had some valid points that had her second-guessing the idea. But there was no going back now. Especially when she didn't have another plan.

She glanced over at Babette and tried to give her the brightest smile she could. "I know we've had a little communication problem, Babette. But starting today that's all going to change. I'm going to listen to you, and you're going to listen to me. And together we're going to produce a great line." She pumped her fist in the air. "Viva la Girl Power!"

Babette stared at Olivia as if she were a pair of granny panties. "*Sacrebleu.*"

* * *

By the time they reached the office, Olivia had a plan. Or something of a plan.

"What time is the board meeting tomorrow, Kelly?" she asked as she strode past Kelly's desk with Babette in tow. She wanted to reschedule the meeting for later in the week. Or even next week. But she knew that would only cause panic. Which meant that she and Babette had exactly twenty-four hours to come up with new designs for their men's line. Twenty-four hours to save Olivia from looking like the ditzy adopted stepchild.

"Nine o'clock," Kelly said as she stared at Babette.

"This is Ms. Fontaine," Olivia made the introduction. "She's the Paris designer who is helping me with the new line."

"Should I get you a coffee, Ms. Fontaine?" Kelly asked. "Or would you prefer French fries?"

Babette lifted her nose and strode into the office. "Your American humor escapes me."

Olivia had started to follow her when a thought struck her. "Where is Mr. Beaumont? I thought he was waiting to see me."

"He was. But then Mr. Melvin showed up and they went to his office."

That made things a lot easier. Jason would take care of getting the contract, and Olivia wouldn't have to see Deacon again. The tinge of disappointment that settled in her stomach was easily explained by lack of caffeine.

"Could you get me some coffee, please, Kelly? In fact, bring an entire pot. I think I'm going to need it."

It turned out that not even an entire pot of coffee was enough to help Olivia deal with Babette. The inspired, innovative designer from Paris had turned into a whiny prima donna who couldn't seem to draw anything that didn't look like it belonged in a drag queen's closet. And after seven hours of neon jockstraps, leather briefs, and see-through pajamas, Olivia was ready to admit that Viva la Girl Power couldn't generate enough power to turn on a lightbulb, let alone save an entire company. And when someone tapped on the door, Olivia was relieved to take a break from the madness.

"Hey." Parker peeked his head in. His gaze took in Babette, who was sprawled out on the couch sobbing, then returned to Olivia. "If you're busy, I can come back later."

Babette stopped sobbing and sat up. After giving him the once-over, she sent Parker a weak smile and proceeded to speak to him in French. When he only stared at her in confusion, she flopped back on the couch. "Barbarians."

Olivia wanted to show her "barbarians." She wanted to slap the snot out of her. Instead she walked over to her desk and buzzed Kelly.

"Could you take Ms. Fontaine shopping? I'm sure she would love the break, and you can charge anything she wants to my account."

Babette perked up immediately, but didn't offer one word of gratitude as she got to her feet and walked to the door. "I'm sure I won't find any-zing, but it's better than being held prisoner."

"Be back in two hours," Olivia said as Kelly came in the door and escorted Babette out. When they were gone, Parker spoke.

"Bad day?"

"You could say that." She walked to the coffee table and collected the designs. Parker didn't know about the men's underwear idea, and after Deacon's brutal comments, she didn't want him to. Especially when it looked as if it was a complete failure. She took the designs to her desk and slipped them in the top drawer with the ones she'd been working on before Michael's death. She had just worked on them for fun. She wasn't a designer. She wasn't even a good CEO.

"I tried calling you last night." Parker moved to the desk.

With the Babette drama, she hadn't had time to get a new phone—or go to the grocery store for much-needed coffee.

"Sorry. I'm getting a new phone today." She noticed the wilting plant on the bookcase. Grabbing her empty coffee mug, she went into the en suite bathroom to get it some water. Parker was standing in the doorway when she turned around. For the first time, she noticed that his shirt was heavily starched—almost too heavily starched.

"Olivia. Would you look at me?"

She pulled her attention away from his shirt sleeves and up to his eyes. "I am looking at you."

"No. No, you're not. So what's going on? Do you want to call it quits?"

It? The word seemed as vague as their relationship. And she wondered if it was time to call "it" quits.

But before she could answer, his hands encircled her waist and pulled her close. "I care about you, Olivia. And maybe you're right. Maybe we do need to spend more time away from the office." He dipped his head and kissed her neck. "More time doing a little stress relief." His lips traveled up her neck to her ear, which he gave a very wet lick that caused a shiver to run down Olivia's spine—and not in a good way.

She placed her hands on his shoulders. "Now's not a good time, Parker."

"I think now is a perfect time." He kissed her.

With Deacon's kiss still fresh in her mind, it was hard not to make some comparisons. None of which tipped in Parker's favor. Deacon's kiss was hot and demanding while Parker's was more lukewarm and hesitant. Deacon used the gentle sweep of his tongue to entice. Parker used the quick thrust of his to...annoy. Like, really annoy.

She pulled away from Parker, only to discover the kissing champion standing in the doorway of the bathroom.

Or more like leaning.

Deacon rested his shoulder on the doorjamb, his arms

crossed over the front of his soft-looking chambray shirt. Just the sight of him gave her a jolt of adrenaline that she quickly attributed to the pot of coffee she'd consumed.

"I guess kissing in your office is an everyday occurrence," he said in that silky Southern voice. While Olivia's face flamed, Parker looked between the two of them.

"Who is this, Olivia?"

Before she could reply, Deacon uncrossed his arms and held out a hand. "Deacon Beaumont." He hesitated for only a second. "Your new boss."

The word *boss* hung in the air like an anvil over Olivia's head. She didn't know who was more shocked— her or Parker. They both stared at Deacon while he smiled that annoying smile. Although his eyes didn't look all that happy when they narrowed on Parker.

"And you are Olivia's boyfriend, I take it," he said. "Or just another office fling?"

Olivia had always been a non-aggressive person, but since Deacon had shown up in her life, her mind had been filled with very violent thoughts. Like right now, she wanted to wipe that smile off his face with the jab she'd learned in the one and only kickboxing class she'd taken. Instead she spoke through clenched teeth.

"Parker, could you give Mr. Beaumont and me a moment in private? There are a few things I'd like to clear up."

Looking confused, Parker nodded and turned to leave. Except it was hard to leave when Deacon continued to block the doorway that led back into her office.

"Excuse me," Parker said.

Deacon studied him from beneath his long, dark lashes as if he had no intention of excusing him. But then he pushed away from the doorjamb and stepped back. "Of course."

Once Parker left, Olivia turned all her anger on Deacon. "I'm through playing your little games." She jabbed a finger at him. "For every second that you wait to sign that contract, the amount I'm willing to pay you and your brothers goes down by one hundred thousand dollars. Do you understand?"

Deacon studied her. "So is he your boyfriend?"

"Forty million nine hundred thousand."

"Because if he is, I think you can do better."

She gritted her teeth. "Forty million eight hundred thousand."

"Did you notice that he didn't even hesitate to leave you here with me? I mean, what kind of guy leaves their girlfriend alone with a Beaumont?"

She stood on her tiptoes and leaned in his face. "The kind of guy who trusts me—even with an obvious womanizer." She tapped him in the chest with her finger. "Forty million seven hundred thousand."

"What does *womanizer* mean, anyway? If it means that I go around making women feel like women, than I guess I am a womanizer." He reached out and caressed Olivia's cheek with his finger before running his thumb over her bottom lip. "Are you saying you don't like to feel like a woman, Livy?"

With heat coursing through her veins, it was hard to disagree. But it wasn't hard to step away. "Forty million six hundred thousand and counting. And I don't like the name Livy." She brushed past him.

He followed her to the desk, and for a second she thought there was going to be a fight over who got the chair. Instead he pulled it out and waited for her to take a seat before leaning on the edge of the desk far too close for comfort.

"You haven't even thanked me for saving your crazy designer and putting her to bed." he said.

"Oh, you put her to bed all right. How could you seduce a mentally unstable woman?"

"I did not seduce Babette."

"Then how do you explain all those breathy moans?"

His eyebrows popped up. "Eavesdropping, Olivia?" The sexy smile slipped into place. "Want to try a little of what I gave Babette to make her moan?"

Before she could decline, he stepped behind her and placed his hands on her shoulders. Then, with a technique that would make an experienced masseuse envious, he massaged the tense muscles in her shoulders and neck.

"Good Lord, woman," he said as he used his thumb to roll out a lump, "you're as knotted as pine flooring. You need to relax."

She tried to keep from moaning like Babette, but it was hard when the man had such talented fingers. "I need you to sign the contract."

He released her shoulders and swiveled the chair to face him. "You can't save French Kiss with men's underwear, Olivia. Especially when you have enemies in your camp that don't want you to succeed."

"What do you mean?"

"This morning before you got here, I discovered Anastasia Bradley talking on the phone in this very office. It seems she doesn't mind breaking and entering."

Olivia should've been surprised, but she wasn't. She wouldn't put anything past Anastasia.

"I guess I'll have to fire her," she said.

"You guess?"

"Okay." She lifted her chin. "So I need to fire her."

"You can't." Deacon leaned on the desk, so close that

if Olivia moved an inch, her knee would be brushing his. Didn't the man have any spatial boundaries? "She's working with someone, and you won't be able to find out who it is if you fire her."

Olivia pulled her gaze away from the faded fly of his jeans and looked in his serious eyes. "She's working with someone? What do you mean—?"

There was a tap on the door before Jason peeked his head in. Upon seeing them, he entered the office and closed the door. "I'm glad you're both here." Rather than hand the printouts he carried to Olivia, he handed them to Deacon. "You were right. Someone is skimming money. But I won't know how much or where it's going until I have the passcodes."

"Skimming money?" Olivia felt as if she were in a bad Wall Street movie. Except Deacon and Jason weren't acting. Deacon studied the sheets as Jason leaned over his shoulder and used his pencil as a pointer.

"Here's the discrepancy. Here it is again. And again." He pointed out a few more places on the sheets. "So I talked with her this afternoon at lunch and did what you said. I looked her straight in the eyes and told her that I wanted to take her to dinner."

Olivia sat there stunned, not only because someone was taking money from her company but also because Jason was talking to Deacon as if they were best friends.

"So what did she say?" Deacon asked as he continued to scan the sheets.

"That she wouldn't go to dinner with me, but she'd have sex with me—not at the office, though, because you might fire her."

The phone rang, and Deacon reached down and pressed the speaker button. "Deacon Beaumont speaking."

"Oh...Mr. Beaumont." Kelly's voice came through the speaker. "Um...is Ms. Harrington there?"

Deacon glanced at Olivia and waited for her to respond. She couldn't. Someone was stealing money from her company? No wonder they were going under. After only a moment, Deacon answered Kelly. "Ms. Harrington is a little indisposed right now. What's up?"

"Ms. Fontaine is wanting to purchase a diamond necklace, and I didn't think Ms. Harrington wanted me to charge that kind of money. But when I told Ms. Fontaine that, she threw a major fit. I wouldn't care—I mean, if the woman wants to make a fool of herself, I say let her—but the security guard at the jewelry store is about to call the cops."

"Put Babette on," Deacon said, and only a second later was speaking fluent French in the soothing tone he'd used before. He paused, then went back to English. "I think Babette's shopping spree is over for the day, Kelly. Besides, I need you to help Jason Melvin with some accounting." After he hung up, he handed the accounting sheets back to Jason. "You realize that she's using sex as a smoke screen."

Jason shook his head. "I don't think so." He took the sheets from Deacon. "I'll make some copies of these and keep digging." He looked at Olivia. "You okay?"

She wasn't okay, but she nodded anyway.

When Jason was gone, Deacon walked over to the minibar and pulled out a bottle of bourbon. He splashed some in a glass and brought it to Olivia. "Here, drink this." She downed it in one swallow, the alcohol burning just enough to make her realize that she wasn't in a movie or a dream.

"I'm going to lose French Kiss, aren't I?" she whispered.

"It looks that way." He took the glass from her and re-filled it before handing it back. "And I have to wonder why you care. If you like the lingerie business so much, why didn't you just take the money Uncle Michael left you and start your own company? Why did you want to keep this dinosaur?"

Taking the glass with her, she got up and walked to the window. Fog had rolled in. In the distance thick layers of cotton shrouded the Golden Gate Bridge, giving it the look of some heavenly kingdom rising up from the clouds.

She took a sip of the bourbon and enjoyed the burn, then downed the entire glass. She was halfway through the third glass Deacon had poured her when she finally released some of her pain.

"Michael used to love to walk in the fog. He said on foggy days, he could almost imagine that he was back in Paris, walking along the Seine. For my eleventh birthday, he had the French Kiss designers make me a purple rain slicker with matching boots so I could go with him on those walks. I loved that slicker, but I loved what it repre-sented even more. It meant that I wasn't just a third wheel he'd gotten in the marriage to my mom. Michael actually liked having me around."

"I'm sure he did."

"I'm not." She took another sip. "I'm not sure of any-thing anymore. I thought he was grooming me to take over French Kiss. I thought he wanted me to continue the legacy."

"It's a lingerie company, Livy. Nothing more."

Livy had always been her father's nickname for her. Coming from Deacon it felt wrong...and at the same time so right. She turned. He leaned against the desk, and in the overcast light coming in the window, his eyes looked deep purple.

A French Kiss purple.

"You don't understand," she whispered. "This isn't just a lingerie company. It's my life."

CHAPTER TEN

Deacon was used to working late. In high school he'd worked late cleaning offices. In college he'd stocked shelves at a grocery store. And recently he'd be the last person to leave his land development offices each day. With no one there to interrupt, the hours after everyone had gone home were always the most productive. And this evening had been no exception. He'd spent his time researching French Kiss's financial situation and now knew the extent of Olivia's problems.

They weren't going to be fixed by a new line of men's underwear. The company had been losing money for the last five years. And not from corporate fraud. The skimmed money Jason had found was only a drop in the bucket compared to the money being lost through mismanagement and lost sales. Returns and customer complaints were up. Along with employee dissatisfaction.

The last, Deacon had witnessed firsthand when Kelly

had taken him on a tour of the corporate offices. Everyone seemed jumpy and distracted. No doubt they were worried about Michael's death and what it would mean to their jobs. They were waiting for someone to take charge. And somehow Deacon couldn't see Olivia doing that.

He swiveled the chair and glanced at her diplomas hanging on the wall. For a woman who had a master's degree in business, she wasn't much of a leader. And after hearing the story about the purple raincoat and galoshes, he had to wonder if she'd chosen her major based on her interests or her love for Michael.

Deacon released his breath and scraped the hair off his forehead. What was he doing? What kind of an idiot would hold up a deal for millions because of some story about a kid's raincoat? And maybe it wasn't the story as much as the way Olivia had told it—like a walk in the fog with Michael had been some monumental, life-changing moment.

If that was the case, then her life had sucked much worse than Deacon's. At least Deacon had had his brothers, a loving mother, and a part-time dad. It sounded like Olivia had had only her gold-digging mother until Michael showed up. And if Michael had been as much of a workaholic as the press had claimed he was, he couldn't have been that great a stepfather. From nowhere came another question. One that Deacon had spent the last twenty years of his life trying to avoid.

Would Michael have made a better father to his son?

Deacon's gaze drifted down to the photo on the bookshelf. A photo of Michael and Olivia cutting the ribbon to a new French Kiss store. Both were smiling, but Michael's didn't quite reach his eyes. Had he ever regretted leaving Deacon's mother? Had he ever regretted leaving his son?

His hand shot out and knocked the photo to the floor. The glass didn't break, and Michael's vacant brown eyes continued to stare up at him. Thankfully, Deacon hadn't gotten his father's eyes. He'd gotten his mother's. A mother who had gone to her grave with the secret that her firstborn belonged to her husband's brother.

She had told her sons about her college graduation trip to Paris. Had told them about seeing the Eiffel Tower and the Louvre. She had even made sure Donny John taught them French, and cooked them beef bourguignonne and French pastries on special occasions. But she had never shown them the pictures. Deacon had found them by accident. He'd been looking for a screwdriver to tighten the wheels on his skateboard in the mess of boxes and tools his father kept in the garage when he stumbled on the small photo album. It held pictures of a man standing in front of small shops, looking out at a river, laughing in the rain. At first Deacon had thought it was his father, but then he'd looked closer and discovered that the man had darker hair and harder features.

Deacon had never met his uncle Michael, but he had seen pictures. Of course all he had to do was look in the mirror. Deacon was the spitting image of Michael Beaumont. Something his grandfather had mentioned time and time again before he died. With a sick feeling in his stomach, Deacon had shuffled through the pictures until he found one of Michael and his mother kissing in front of the Eiffel Tower. And one glance at the date on the back of the picture had confirmed Deacon's worst fears.

The date was exactly nine months before Deacon had been born.

The cell phone buzzed in his pocket, startling him. Angry with himself for letting his thoughts wander, he answered without looking at caller ID.

"Beaumont."

"Right back at you, big brother," Nash's voice came through the receiver. "So how goes the contract signing?"

Deacon swiveled in the chair. "I'm taking care of it."

"That's what you said when I talked with you last. You said you were going to take care of it ASAP. Which I thought meant 'as soon as possible,' but now appears to mean 'as soon as you please.' It's been two days, Deacon. Just how long does it take to write your name?"

"I'll be home tomorrow."

There was a pause. "So is that what you're doing in that big office building on this foggy San Fran night? Packing?"

He glanced at the door. "Where are you?"

"Grayson and I are standing outside, waiting for our big brother to finish signing the damned contract so we can go celebrate."

Well, hell. Deacon tossed down the pen and massaged his temples. He could've done without his brothers showing up.

"So are you going to let us in?" Nash asked. "Or did I interrupt something other than contract signing?"

"Hold on," he said. "I'll call down to security and meet you by the elevators."

"You do that," Nash said before he hung up.

On the way to the elevators, he couldn't help noticing the light coming from beneath Jason's door. When he peeked his head in, he was surprised to find Jason and Kelly sitting in front of his computer.

"Sex with me would blow your mind," Kelly said as she used the mouse to scroll through the document.

"More like bore my mind." He pointed at the screen. "Go back. That total isn't right."

She scrolled back and squinted at the screen. "You'll never know until you try. I'll let you be on top."

"I'd rather kiss my grandma. And get a pair of glasses. You're as blind as a bat." He pointed at the line of figures. "Right here."

"I see it," she said, and then clicked on the printer icon. As the copy came out of the printer, she laughed. "This is fun. We're like corperate sleuths." She picked up a doughnut from the box on the desk and took a big bite before offering it to him. "And you want me."

"Not even a little." Jason took a big bite of doughnut.

Before they could spot him, Deacon moved away from the door and continued down the hallway, wondering if he'd created a bad situation that Olivia would have to deal with. Hopefully Jason was professional enough to keep things platonic in the workplace. Kelly certainly wasn't.

When Deacon reached the elevators, he found Parker talking on his cell phone. He didn't like the guy. He didn't like his prissy name. Or his designer suits and the perfect knot of his tie. Or the possessive way he'd been kissing Olivia. And his phone conversation only added to Deacon's dislike.

"No, I'm not imagining things, Olivia," Parker said, completely oblivious to the fact that Deacon stood behind him. "The man is interested in you as more than just a business associate."

Deacon leaned closer and whispered, "But as the boss, isn't it my job to be interested?"

Parker jumped, and the phone slipped out of his hand.

He turned and stared at Deacon with a look that went from surprise to annoyance. "Mr. Beaumont. I didn't realize that you were still here." He picked up the phone. "I'll have to call you back...sweetheart."

Stifling the urge to grab him by the front of his starched shirt and shake him the way his mother used to shake the dust mop, Deacon waited until he hung up before asking, "So what has you working so late, Mr. Calloway?"

"I had some last-minute sales reports to check."

"Hmm? So do you have access to all the accounts?"

"What do you mean?"

"I mean do you have passcodes for all accounts?"

"Why would you ask?"

The elevator pinged as Deacon pinned Parker with his gaze. "As the boss of French Kiss, I don't need to give a reason for anything I ask...or do. Something you need to remember, Mr. Calloway."

The elevator doors opened, and there stood Nash and Grayson. Parker's eyes widened as Deacon's bearded, camo-dressed brothers stepped out. Before they could say anything in front of Parker, Deacon dismissed him.

"Have a good evening, Mr. Calloway."

With his eyes still pinned on Grayson and Nash, Parker sidestepped into the elevator. Once the doors were closed, Nash spoke.

"By the looks of things, I'd say you haven't made any friends, Deke. Who is that guy?"

"I'm starting to think he's the guy that's skimming money from the company." He headed to Parker's office to see if he could confirm his suspicions. Unfortunately, a cleaning lady was there emptying a trash can into her cart. When she saw all three of the Beaumonts, she released a squeal and dropped the can. Documents spilled to the floor as she held up her hands.

"I have no money!"

Deacon tried to calm her. "It's all right. As much as my brothers look like outlaws, we're not here to rob you. We're the new owners of the company."

Her eyes widened before she made the sign of the cross. "Trouble."

Nash laughed. "That's probably putting it mildly."

After Deacon apologized for scaring her, he and his brothers helped her pick up the paper, then headed to Olivia's office. When they stepped through the door, Grayson released a long whistle.

"Damn."

Nash glanced around the opulent room. "I guess I can see why you're not in a hurry to come home. This is pretty much your dream, isn't it, Deke?"

"And this is an original Monet," Grayson said as he studied the impressionist painting behind Olivia's desk. "Do you know how much this is worth?"

Nash ignored him and continued to study Deacon. "But it's not the office you want, is it, Deke? It's the power that goes with it."

It was surprising how quickly Nash had hit the nail on the head. In the last twelve hours, Deacon *had* enjoyed the power that came with being the boss of a billion-dollar corporation. It was a nice change of pace for someone who had spent his life powerless. Powerless to stop his mother from dying. Powerless to stop his father from gambling and womanizing. And powerless to stop life from crapping on the Beaumont brothers. Now, for once, he had the power. He was in control. But only if he was willing to throw away millions on a failing company.

Walking over to the desk, he opened the top drawer and pulled out the contract. He picked up a pen and had started to sign when Grayson noticed the design drawings in the drawer.

"Holy shit. What are those?"

Deacon looked at the drawing of a man in a leather corset and shook his head. "Olivia's idea to save the company."

Grayson walked over and pulled out the stack of designs. "You've got to be kidding. These are ridiculous."

"That's what I told her, but she obviously refused to listen. You should've seen the first set."

Nash sat in the chair across from the desk. "She really thinks men's lingerie is going to sell?"

"I think she's willing to try anything to save the company." Deacon sat down and released his breath. "But after looking at the financial statements, it will take nothing short of a miracle to save French Kiss."

"That's too bad," Grayson said as he flipped through the sketches. "I like Olivia." He stopped flipping. "Now this is more like it. This is what lingerie should look like."

Nash crossed his booted feet on the desk. "Which only supports my theory that you've become a little sissy girl since I've been gone."

"Shut up, Nash." He turned the sketch. "Tell me that you don't think this is hot."

The sketch was of a woman. A woman in a wispy bluish-purple nightgown that left little to the imagination. The drawing wasn't as good as Babette's, but the design was twice as hot.

Deacon sat up. "Where did you get that?"

"It was at the back of the other sketches." He flipped to another page. "And there appears to be more."

Deacon took the sketches from his brother, tossed Babette's crazy creations on the floor, and spread the rest across the desk. Or at least what would fit. There had to be around thirty.

"Damn," Nash said, "how can French Kiss be going under if they sell stuff like this?" He picked up a sketch of a woman in a black studded bra, satin garter belt, and silky thigh-high stockings. "I'd pay a fortune to see a woman in this."

"You've always liked your women dark and edgy, Nash," Grayson said. "I like my ladies in something a little softer." He pointed to the sketch of the sheer pink bra and panties, then tipped his head as he studied it. "But the models need a few more curves to really show off the excellent design of the lingerie."

Deacon stared at a drawing of a purple-and-silver corset. "Whose are these?"

Grayson pointed to the scribble in the corner of the sketch. "I'm not positive, but that looks like an *O.H.* to me."

Olivia had drawn these designs? If so, then why hadn't she chosen these for the new collections? The answer came quickly. Because she didn't think they were good enough. Just as she didn't think she deserved to be the boss of French Kiss—or the daughter of Michael Beaumont.

Deacon sat down in the chair. "She's going to hide these in a desk drawer and walk into the boardroom tomorrow with Babette's pile of crap that will make her the laughingstock of the company."

"And isn't that what you wanted, Deke?" Grayson asked. "I thought you wanted to get back at Olivia for getting you kicked out of Michael's."

It had been what he wanted. Once. Now just the thought of Olivia embarrassing herself in front of a bunch of snobs made him want to hit something. He glanced at the sexy corset. Or come up with a new plan.

He swiveled toward Grayson. "How long would it take you to copy these designs and put them on a curvier model?"

Grayson shrugged. "Five or six hours, probably."

Deacon opened the desk drawers and searched until he found a sketchpad and colored pencils. "Then have at it."

With a grin Grayson took the pad and pencils, grabbed one of Olivia's sketches, and headed for the couch. Deacon turned to Nash, expecting to catch some grief. Instead his brother was putting the sketches into groups.

"These should be put together according to male preference, don't you think?" Nash said.

Deacon started choosing the designs he liked best. "So you aren't going to give me shit about my hero complex?"

Nash glanced up. "This board meeting is pretty crucial tomorrow?"

"It could be the straw that breaks the camel's back. If Olivia doesn't show the board something amazing, most are going to sell their shares for pennies on the dollar to some company that plans on selling substandard lingerie to discount stores. And I have to wonder if that wasn't someone's plan all along."

"The person who's skimming the money?"

"Probably."

A long silence followed before Nash spoke. "As far as I'm concerned, family is family. Now let's help our cousin so we can sign that contract and go home."

CHAPTER ELEVEN

For once in her life, Olivia woke up on time and stayed focused. She showered, dried her hair and pulled it into a French twist, applied her makeup, and then dressed in her most powerful gray suit without once getting distracted by something outside her window, a pimple on her nose, or a random thought. All her thoughts centered around one thing. She was going to lose French Kiss and there was nothing she could do about it.

After a sleepless night, she had finally accepted this truth. And today she intended to walk into the board meeting and lay everything out on the table: Someone was taking money from the company. She had no new line. And she had been totally wrong to think she could fill her stepfather's shoes.

Once that happened, there was little doubt that the board members would vote to sell the company to the highest bidder. With no other plan, she would vote with them. That was if Deacon had signed the contract. Of course, why wouldn't he? He now knew the full extent of French Kiss's trouble and would have to be an idiot not to have signed. Which meant that she now owned controlling shares. It was too bad that owning those shares still left her with little control.

"You look like hell. With your blond hair, gray is zee worst possible color you could wear."

The rude comments greeted Olivia as soon as she stepped into the living room. Babette sat at the breakfast bar eating what looked to be a scone. But since Olivia had yet to go to the store, she didn't know where Babette had gotten it. She only hoped that she had gotten coffee at the same place.

She nodded at her cup. "Coffee?"

Babette shook her head. "All you had was tea. And seeing as how you were trying to starve me, I was forced to whip some-zing up." She held up the scone. "They are not croissants, but they aren't bad."

Olivia didn't feel like eating. She felt like throwing up. "Thank you, but I need to get to the office."

"You Americans. Always in such a hurry." She dunked the tea bag in her cup. "Well, you'll have to wait, because as you can see, I'm not ready."

"That's okay because you're not coming. My plan failed. Therefore, there's no need for you to come to the office with me. In fact, you should be back to your beloved Par-ree by this weekend." If Olivia hadn't felt so crappy, she might've enjoyed Babette's shocked look.

"You are sending me home?"

"Yes, but I'll pay you for your time."

For once Babette had nothing to say. She just sat there at the breakfast bar with her hand frozen in mid-dunk. Since Olivia didn't have anything to say either, she turned to leave, her glance sweeping over the balcony. Jonathan Livingston's beady eyes looked back. But having a pesky bird poop on her balcony no longer mattered. In order to pay off the Beaumonts, she would have to sell her house...and soon. Which meant that Jonathan would become someone else's problem.

As would Mr. and Mrs. Huckabee's dangling parts.

Although when she stepped out of the garage and looked up at their balcony, Mr. Huckabee's parts weren't dangling. Instead they were covered by a rhinestone thong that sparkled like a mirrored disco ball in the morning sun.

"Hel-loo, Britney!" He lifted a hand and waved.

After the tension-filled night, Olivia couldn't help laughing. "Hello, Mr. Huckabee. Are those comfortable?"

"Not at all. But Doris thinks they're hot."

Olivia bit back a grin. "They are that." A movement to the side of her garage caught her attention, and she watched in surprise as the lemon juicer salesman came around from the side of her house.

"Excuse me?" she said. "Can I help you?"

He glanced up, startled, then quickly hurried off with his roller bag clicking on the sidewalk behind him. Confused, she walked through her gate and discovered bright blooms of every color and variety filling the flower bed that ran the length of her small backyard.

It made no sense. Why would some guy she didn't even know plant flowers? And if he'd done it in her backyard, he had probably left the geraniums by her front door. And taken out her trash. She really needed to buy a lemon juicer from him.

Feeling even more depressed, she turned and walked up the street to catch the trolley. When she stepped into

French Kiss's lobby, she struggled to keep the tears from her eyes.

Most people thought she had grown up in a mansion in Pacific Heights. But it was inside these purple-and-silver walls that she had truly grown up. Before school she had sat in the design department and tried to copy the designers' amazing pictures. In the afternoons she had used scraps of satin and lace to make her own creations for her Barbie dolls. In the evenings she'd raced through the deserted halls or sat at Michael's desk and done her homework before they headed home to dinner. On the drive he would ask her about what designs she liked best—what colors—what fabrics.

At the time she'd thought he valued her opinion, but now she realized it had been because he didn't know what else to talk about. French Kiss and business had been his life. And consequently they had become hers. What was she going to do when that life ended?

Kelly wasn't at her desk, which meant there was no one to send for coffee. Olivia thought about going to the break room, but then glanced at her watch and realized that she didn't have the time. Since she wouldn't need her briefcase, she decided to leave it in her office. Surprisingly, the door was unlocked. Or not so surprisingly, since Deacon had been the last one there. Even now she blushed at the memory of sharing the raincoat story with him. He probably thought she was a pathetic nut.

She set her briefcase on the desk and glanced at the contract. Even though she knew what she'd find, she couldn't help walking over and picking it up. As she'd expected, on the last page were three signatures in the left-hand corner. Grayson's was flowing and artistic. Nash's scribbled and illegible. And Deacon's neat and concise.

Deacon Valentino Beaumont was now a millionaire while Olivia Juliana Harrington was penniless. Somewhere the gods of fate were laughing. Deciding that she needed coffee more than she needed to be on time, she headed to the break room.

By the time she got a cup of coffee and arrived at the boardroom, she wasn't surprised to find the majority of the chairs filled. No one would want to miss this. Especially Anastasia, who sat as close to the front as she could get. As she walked past, Olivia had a hard time not punching the woman right in the face. How dare she break into Olivia's office? How dare she consort with someone else to steal money? And how dare she sit there smiling as if she hadn't had a hand in French Kiss's demise?

Pushing down her anger, Olivia sat down in Michael's chair. The reminder of Michael was painful, but not as painful as what she was about to do. She set her coffee cup on the table in front of her, keeping her hands curled around it. The cup appeared to be emitting the only warmth in the room. Everyone's expression was cool and expectant.

She cleared her throat. "Good morning." There was a chorus of "Good mornings" followed by a heavy silence. Taking a deep breath, she continued. "I was hoping to come here today and offer up a bright new future for French Kiss. Unfortunately, I was unable to—"

The door opened, and Deacon came striding in as if he owned the place and everyone in it. He looked like he did. He wore a gray designer suit, pressed button-down shirt, and purple tie. His hair had been combed back from his forehead and only a hint of dark stubble shadowed his square jaw.

"Sorry I'm late." He walked to the front and stopped next to Olivia's chair. And she was embarrassed to realize that in their gray suits, they looked like a matched set.

She glanced at the confused board members before whispering under her breath, "What are you doing here? I thought you left."

"I probably should have, but sometimes you have to go with your gut instead of your head." He nodded at her chair. "I believe this is my seat, Ms. Harrington."

"Excuse me?"

"My chair. Aren't you sitting in my chair?"

Suddenly she didn't care if everyone in the room heard her. "You signed the contract. I saw it."

His smile got a little wider. "Yes, I did sign a contract. But not the one you gave me. I had Jason draw up a new one. And until you agree to and sign that one"—he tipped his head—"you're sitting in my chair."

"But how did your brothers—"

The door opened again, and Nash and Grayson walked in. Unlike Deacon, they looked like they had come straight from a hunting trip—or an episode of *Duck Dynasty*. They wore camouflage pants and worn T-shirts that matched perfectly with their scruffy hair and beards— Grayson's only slightly thicker than before.

Nash took the first seat he came to and reached for one of the pastries in the center of the table. After a big bite, he nodded at Olivia. "Hi, Cuz."

She sent him an annoyed look before turning to Grayson, who gave her an encouraging smile as he sat down next to his brother. Every eye turned to her for some kind of explanation. But before she could speak, Deacon cleared his throat.

"Anytime this week, Ms. Harrington."

Shooting him daggers, she got up and moved to the chair on his right. Once Deacon was seated, he wasted no time with introductions.

"I'm Deacon Beaumont." He held out a hand. "And these are my brothers Nash and Grayson. As you may have heard, our dear uncle Michael willed us controlling shares of this fine company."

A mumble of surprise ran through the board, and Anastasia spoke first. "But I thought Ms. Harrington bought your shares."

Deacon nodded. "She's in the process of buying us out. But for the time being, my brothers and I are...in control." When the mumbles started again, he cut them off. "Now I'm sure you have some concerns, and I'll be happy to address those after Ms. Harrington's presentation."

Olivia felt her stomach drop. What was Deacon doing? Wasn't it enough that her beloved company was failing? Did he have to embarrass her in front of the entire board? Obviously the answer to these questions was yes. But unwilling to give him the satisfaction of humiliating her, she tipped up her chin.

"I'm afraid that I don't have—"

Kelly came hurrying in the door with a laptop. "Sorry it took so long, but I have the PowerPoint presentation all set up, Ms. Harrington." She set the laptop in front of Olivia and handed her a remote before pushing the button on the wall that lowered the projector screen. Deacon got up and motioned to his chair.

"It might be better if you sit here after all." When she just stared at him in confusion, he walked over and pulled out her chair, leaning down to whisper in her ear, "You've got this, Olivia. Let's show these clowns what you're made of."

At the moment she was made of fear, confusion, and anger that Deacon was putting her on the spot. But there was something in his tone—conviction and kinship—that had her tapping the button on her laptop that started the PowerPoint presentation, before getting to her feet.

A title popped up on the screen in scrolled purple letters. She stared at the words for a moment before clearing her throat and reading.

"The Legendary Lovers Line." She clicked the remote. The next frame gave her pause, and she shot a glance at Deacon, who only shrugged. She turned back to the screen and read the words. "The Valentino Collection." She clicked, expecting to see Babette's flamboyant designs. Instead she was shocked to see one of her own designs. The drawing was much better than hers had been. The woman's full breasts and curvy hips were the perfect mannequin for the sheer nightgown and matching peignoir. She glanced at Grayson, and he winked.

Her hand tightened around the remote, and she spoke in a hesitant voice. "I got the inspiration for this collection from the 1940s Hollywood starlets." She clicked to the next drawing. "The colors are dark and dramatic. The material sexy and feminine." It was strange, but by the time she clicked to the next drawing, everything had just sort of fallen into place. She knew the story behind every drawing—what had inspired it. Why she thought it would sell.

She wasn't surprised to find two more collections after Valentino's. Lothario's consisted of her edgier, more erotic designs, while Romeo's were younger, softer, and more romantic. What did surprise Olivia was how perfectly her designs had been organized into collections. And how perfectly the names went with each one.

Deacon might not know the lingerie business, but he knew marketing. With simple organization and titles, he'd changed Olivia's designs into something special— something salable. Halfway through the presentation, she knew it. And by the time she set the remote down on the table and turned to the board members, her heart was beating so loudly in her ears that she was worried she wouldn't be able to hear any questions people might have.

Fortunately, no one seemed to have questions. After only a moment's pause, Deacon started clapping. And everyone in the room soon joined in the applause. Everyone but Anastasia, who looked slightly ill. Although she quickly started clapping when Deacon arched an eyebrow at her.

He stood and reclaimed everyone's attention. To her surprise, Olivia was more than relieved to give it to him.

"Thank you, Ms. Harrington." He nodded at her as she took a seat. "Now I understand why my uncle put so much trust in you." She didn't know why those words made her feel so happy. All she knew was that she couldn't keep the blush from her face or the sincerity from her voice.

"Thank you," she whispered.

He studied her for a long, uncomfortable moment before returning his attention to the board members. "If there are no questions, I think we can adjourn."

Anastasia couldn't wait to jump in. "I just don't see how a few new collections are going to save the company from going under. I think we should take a vote on selling to Avery Industries. They gave us a fair offer."

"Fifty cents on the dollar is not a fair—" Olivia started, but Deacon held up his hand and stopped her.

"You're right, Ms. Bradley. Right now, with the way things are, a couple new collections aren't going to pull the company out of bankruptcy. After looking at the accounts, I think there are—as my grandfather would say—too many holes in the bucket. But instead of throwing away the bucket, we need to find out where all the money is going and plug up some holes. And it's interesting that most of the problems are in your department." He gave her a pointed look before directing his next words to the board. "Now, if you want to take a vote, we certainly can. But I think I can tell you how it's going to turn out. And if you want to jump ship, I'm sure Olivia will be glad to take your resignations. Now, if that's all the concerns, this meeting is adjourned."

After only a few exchanged glances, the boardroom cleared. Although there was little doubt in Olivia's mind that there would be some major discussions on the way out. Once the door was closed, Nash spoke up.

"Impressive, Deacon. I always knew you were meant to be a boss." He grinned. "You certainly practiced enough on Grayson and me."

"I don't think it was Deacon as much as Olivia's presentation that won them over," Grayson said. "Your designs are beautiful."

Olivia couldn't accept the compliment without giving one of her own. "Your sketches didn't hurt. How did you have time to do those?"

Grayson yawned and stretched his hands over his head. "It wasn't that hard, but I could certainly use some sleep now. What hotel are you staying at, Deacon?"

Before Deacon could answer, Olivia found herself speaking up. "After all you did for me, you're not staying at a hotel. You're staying at my house." She grabbed a notepad and pen off the table. "Here's the address and security code—although now that I think about it, the garage door is probably still open." She shook her head. And here she thought she'd been so focused. "Babette is sleeping in the guest room, but you and Nash can take the bedroom next to mine until she leaves."

Nash took the piece of paper. "Thank you, Cousin Olivia." He smirked at Deacon before he followed Grayson out.

When they were gone, Olivia turned to Deacon. "Why'd you do it?"

He started shutting down the laptop. "You shouldn't leave your garage door open. Big cities have high crime."

"I get distracted easily." Right then she was distracted by the way Deacon looked in a suit and by the way his long fingers stroked over the keyboard, all smooth and efficient. She couldn't help wondering if that's how they would feel sliding over her body.

"Nash thinks I have a hero complex," he said.

She was so mesmerized by his fingers and the fantasy they evoked that it took her a moment to catch up with the conversation. "And you see me as needing to be saved?"

He closed the laptop and turned to her, his eyes intent and his expression solemn. "Don't you? You have great ideas, Olivia." He waved a hand at the laptop. "Your designs are amazing. Any man would love to see these on a woman. And any woman would feel sexy as hell wearing them. But for some reason, you decided they weren't good enough and hid them away. Then you came up with some bizarre plan to design men's lingerie with a kook from Paris."

"I still think a line of men's underwear and pajamas will work."

Deacon took a step closer. "Then why don't you design them? Not Babette, but you? I'll tell you why. Because you don't think you're good enough. You don't think you're good enough to design men's underwear. Or women's lingerie. And you don't think you're good enough to be in charge of French Kiss."

Her temper surfaced. "I'm good enough! I spent most of my life around the lingerie business. And regardless of what the board members think, Michael didn't hand me anything. I've worked my ass off for every promotion I've gotten."

"That's not why the board members don't trust you, Olivia. It's not because you're the boss's daughter. And it's certainly not because you're not smart or talented enough. It's because you don't believe in yourself. And if you don't believe in yourself, no one else will."

Olivia tried to pretend that the truth didn't hurt. But it hurt. It hurt so much that she couldn't reply without busting into tears. Even though she didn't speak, one single tear slipped out and trickled down her cheek. She ducked her head and tried to hide it, but it was too late.

"Hey." Deacon stepped closer and tipped up her chin, catching the tear with his thumb. "I didn't mean to make you cry. I just want you to realize that you have everything you need to save this company."

She shook her head. "No, I don't. I could never do what you did today. Not only am I flighty and unorganized I'm non-confrontational."

His eyebrows lifted. "You seem to have no problem confronting me."

"Only because you can be a real jerk sometimes."

He laughed. "Only sometimes? I must be moving up in Olivia's world. Although you've yet to invite me to stay at your house. And technically, while my brothers helped, I was the one who saved your ass."

"And I have little doubt that you're going to make me pay."

His gaze lowered to her mouth. "Oh, you're going to pay, Olivia. Now lift up that skirt and show me your panties."

CHAPTER TWELVE

The words were out of Deacon's mouth before he could stop them. Not that he didn't know where they came from. The moment Olivia had started clicking through Grayson's drawings, Deacon's mind had stripped off Olivia's gray power suit and dressed her in each article of lingerie. From the sheer, sexy nightgowns to the hot leather corsets. And it didn't help that Grayson had put Olivia's features on the model in each drawing. It didn't help at all.

Olivia blinked. "Excuse me?"

He could've teased his way out of it, but he discovered he didn't want to. "Your panties," he repeated. "I want to see them." He watched a blush stain her cheeks, and her breasts lift in a quick inhalation of breath.

"B-but why?"

"Let's just say that your designs intrigued me, and I've been wondering what style you chose as your own."

She released a breath, and the moist heat brushed over his face and relocated beneath the fly of his jeans. She glanced at the door, and then whispered, "Someone could walk in."

The fact that she was even considering it excited him even more. He smoothed back the wisp of hair that had come loose from the clip at the back of her head. "Don't tell me you're too bashful. Not when you've showed me your panties before."

"I was fourteen."

"It was still hot."

Her eyes widened. "You thought I was hot?"

"Yes. So are you going to show them to me or make me guess?" When she only stared back at him with those pretty green eyes, he continued. "Let's see. You have on a gray suit so I'm going to go with the purple satin panties with the little ribbon bows."

She shook her head.

"The white see-through thong with the lace?"

Another shake, and her hair came unclipped, falling around her face in golden waves.

He lifted a strand and held it to his nose. It smelled as he thought sunshine would. Clean, fresh, and hot. "Please don't disappoint me and tell me you've got on a pair of panties that are big enough to dry my two-ton truck after the car wash," he teased.

There was a moment's hesitation before she spoke so softly that he had to tip his head closer just to hear. "What with everything, I haven't had a chance to do laundry." She swallowed and blushed even brighter. "So…"

Her words trailed off, taking all the oxygen in the air with them. He felt light-headed and woozy. Or maybe his condition had more to do with all the blood rushing to his dick. Whatever the cause, he couldn't think past one thing…Olivia wasn't wearing any panties. And hadn't been wearing panties the entire time she'd been doing the PowerPoint presentation.

What had started out as an attempt to get a little peek escalated to an overwhelming desire to touch. In under a second he had her pinned against the wall, one hand cradling her jaw as his lips claimed hers, and the other reaching for the edge of her skirt. And sure enough, above the tops of the sheer, silky, thigh-high stockings was nothing but sweet, warm, welcoming flesh.

"Damn," he mumbled against her mouth as he dipped two fingers into her heat. The hot, wet sheath had him almost ejaculating right then and there like some horny, inexperienced kid. For a man who had always prided himself on being different from his father, on having complete control over his lust, his body's reaction was scary as hell.

He dropped his hands and moved away as if Olivia were a match and he a stick of dynamite. "Look, I apologize. I had no business—"

Before he could finish the thought, Olivia became the aggressor. In two steps she had his hair gripped in her fingers and his mouth scorched by her lips and tongue. Unprepared for her forward assault, he stumbled back and tripped over the leg of a chair, sitting down hard on the boardroom table. And damned if the woman didn't crawl right on top of him.

Between the hot kisses and the sweet center riding the hard ridge of his fly, control seemed like a petty thing to pride himself on. So he let the flame catch and the fuse sizzle toward explosion. Which is exactly what would have happened if the door hadn't opened.

He pulled away to find Nash peeking in.

"Sorry," his brother said with a smirk a mile wide. "I

was just going to see if you were coming." His eyebrows waggled. "But I guess the answer to that would be yes."

"Get the fuck out," Deacon growled.

"Yes, sir, boss," Nash said. "But don't be surprised if someone else comes a-knockin'—someone who isn't as friendly. That metrosexual dude that was hanging out by the elevators last night isn't real happy that you and Olivia are still having a . . . meeting."

"Parker?"

"That would be the one." He flashed another grin before closing the door.

"Oh. My. God," Olivia breathed, grabbing his attention.

She looked sexy as hell with her blond hair all wild around her face and her skirt hiked up to show off the tops of her thigh-highs. It was too bad that her face had gone from flushed passion to pale shock. He had to admit that he felt a little stunned himself. He did not lose it like this. Ever. He was the logical, level-headed Beaumont. And yet from the moment he met Olivia, she'd made him crazy. But he refused to let her know that. Tucking his hands behind his head, he smiled up at her. "Well, I think you've inspired another new line, Olivia. Women might not pay for invisible panties, but I know men would."

Her eyes darkened. "You are such a jerk!" She climbed off him, offering one more view of heaven that stuck with him long after her heels hit the floor. "Would you stop gawking," she hissed, "and get off the table. Parker could walk in at any minute."

Those words made him stay right where he was. "What is up between you and Parker, anyway? I mean, the guy doesn't seem to know where you are half the time. What kind of a boyfriend is that?"

"The type of boyfriend most women want—the non-stalking type." She got on her hands and knees and looked under the table. "What happened to my hair clip? Do you have it?"

"You say that like you think I'm the stalking type. I'm not a stalker. I just like to know where I can find my woman."

Olivia stood and glared at him. "That terminology went out with the cavemen. Women aren't possessions."

"They are if they're mine." He sat up. "And if you're my woman, I don't mind you calling me your man."

Her eyes flickered as if she'd just thought of something. "And are you someone's man?"

"If I were, I wouldn't be looking at other women's underwear—or non-underwear. Just like if you were truly Parker's woman, you wouldn't have let me."

"I-I…"

He lifted an eyebrow and waited for her to continue. Instead she released an exasperated grunt and headed for the door, taking a moment to smooth her hair and her skirt before she opened it. Nash stood guard on the other side, his back to the room and his front to Parker Calloway, who looked about ready to bust like an overfilled balloon. When he saw Olivia, he released some hot air.

"This cretin"—he pointed a finger at Nash, who had stepped out of the way—"refused to let me in the boardroom. He said that you were still having a meeting." He glared at Deacon, but spoke to Olivia. "What is going on, Olivia?"

While Olivia struggled to explain, Deacon hopped up from the table. "This cretin happens to be my brother." He spied Olivia's hair clip under a chair and leaned down to pick it up. "Which means he's your superior. So I'd be careful if I were you."

Parker's gaze ran over a grinning Nash, and his eyes widened. "My superior? You've got to be kidding."

Deacon walked to the door and stood next to Olivia. "One thing you need to learn, Mr. Calloway, is that I never kid. I'm what you would call a no-bullshit kind of guy." He opened up Olivia's hair clip and clipped it to the lapel of her jacket, his hand not-so-accidentally brushing across the top of her breast and turning her face red all over again. But this time he figured it was more from anger than embarrassment. "I enjoyed our meeting, Ms. Harrington." With a wink he shouldered his way past Parker and headed down the hall.

As soon as he rounded the corner to Olivia's office, Kelly jumped up from her desk like an expectant puppy.

"So how did it go? Did they like the new collections?" She came around the desk. "I mean, I thought it was brilliant and the titles are so romantic. Who wouldn't want to own a pair of Romeo panties?"

Deacon headed for the office. "I appreciate you pulling the PowerPoint presentation together so quickly this morning, Kelly." A thought struck him, and he paused and slowly turned. "I'm wondering if you could do something else for me."

"Anything, sir."

"I want you to come up with an emergency that will get Parker Calloway out of the office—like now."

It was a pretty underhanded thing to do. Deacon had no business screwing around in whatever Olivia had going on with Parker. In fact he should be thankful that she was in a relationship and wouldn't put too much time or thought into what had just taken place in the boardroom. But for some damned reason, Deacon wanted her to put some time and thought into it. Probably because he knew he would. Even now he couldn't forget the heat of her kisses or how she'd looked straddling him. And he'd be damned if he let Olivia be alone with Parker when she wasn't wearing any underwear.

"Is Mr. Calloway the one who is skimming money?" Kelly asked with wide eyes. "Are we going to case his office?"

Since it wasn't a bad idea, Deacon pointed a finger at her. "Smart girl. Although until we know for sure, it's best if we keep this under our hats."

"Have you lost your mind?"

Deacon turned to find Nash standing behind him. Not wanting to get into this in front of Kelly, Deacon thanked her and ushered Nash into Olivia's office. The door had barely closed before Nash started in.

"And here I thought you wanted to help Olivia because she was our dear cousin."

"She's not our damned cousin!" Deacon snapped a little too sharply as he walked around the desk and sat down.

Nash stood over the desk. "Which makes it okay for you to screw her?"

"I didn't screw her."

"Only because I interrupted you."

The sleepless night finally caught up with him, and Deacon released his breath and rested his head on the back of the chair. "Fine. I'll admit that things in the boardroom got a little out of hand."

"Who are you trying to bullshit, Deacon? You didn't just let things get out of hand in the boardroom. You let them get out of hand the minute Olivia showed up with the contract. I get it. You were embarrassed when Donny John dragged us here and tried to mooch money from Uncle Michael. And you were really embarrassed that he did it in front of a girl you thought was pretty."

"I wasn't worried about what Olivia thought. And I don't know what you're remembering, but she wasn't what you would call pretty. She was too skinny and had braces. Not to mention the pimple on her chin."

"A pimple? You remember a pimple?"

Deacon grew uncomfortable under his brother's disbelieving gaze, probably because Nash had a point. Why had he remembered a pimple?

"The point I'm trying to make, Deacon," Nash continued, "is that having sex with Uncle Michael's daughter isn't a good idea."

The bathroom door opened, and Grayson walked in. "Deacon had sex with Olivia?"

"So that's where you disappeared to," Nash said. "You've been in there the entire time?"

Grayson flipped a pile of catalogs on the table. "I was doing some research. They need to get a new photographer. The guy they have sucks." He looked at Deacon. "So you had sex with Olivia?"

"I did not have sex with Olivia."

"But he's planning to, once he gets rid of her boyfriend," Nash said. "So what's wrong with the catalogs? I think the models are amazing."

"That's the problem. They're too amazing. I'm not saying that models shouldn't be beautiful, but they should also look real. And beautiful women come in all shapes and sizes."

While Nash rolled his eyes, Grayson flopped down in the chair across from the desk. "So since the board members liked Olivia's lingerie line, when are we going home? I promised Ms. Stanford that I'd paint her kitchen again. Even though I've painted it three times in the last six months." He shook his head. "She seems to like the color on the swatch, but hates it when it gets up on the wall."

Nash laughed. "I bet she does." He looked at Deacon. "So that's a good question, Deacon. When are we going home?"

Deacon looked away from his brother, and his gaze caught on the contract. "Olivia hasn't signed the new contract yet."

"But we all know that she will," Nash said. "Only an idiot wouldn't sign it when we gave her such a deal."

The new contract was set up so Olivia would buy only a portion of the stocks. Then, when the new line of lingerie started making money, she would buy the Beaumonts out for the rest—plus interest.

There was only one small hitch. A hitch that Deacon hadn't exactly made clear to his brothers. If the new line didn't sell and the company went belly-up, the Beaumont brothers would be out millions of dollars. And since he'd convinced his brothers to sign on the dotted line, it was up to him to make sure that the company didn't fail.

"I'm not leaving just yet," he said. "I want to make sure that everything is on the right track before I come home."

"But what do you know about the lingerie business, Deacon?" Grayson asked.

He had a good point. Deacon didn't know shit about lingerie. But he knew about business. He knew that the collections Olivia had come up with were going to sell, but that wouldn't be enough. If French Kiss was going to survive, it would need to be assessed and reorganized from the bottom up. And Deacon had always been damned good at organizing. "You're right, Nash. I don't know anything about the lingerie business. But since I now own stock in the company, I need to learn."

Nash studied him. "Don't you mean *we*, Deacon?"

"Are you saying you want to stay and help, little brother?"

"I'm saying that you're right. As stockholders, we need to keep an eye on our investment." He frowned. "And our big brother."

CHAPTER THIRTEEN

*W*hat the hell is going on, Olivia?" Parker didn't even wait for Olivia to close the door of the boardroom before he started in. And she couldn't blame him. She wanted to ask herself the same question.

What the hell is going on, Olivia? How could you almost have sex with Deacon Beaumont on the boardroom table?

There was no good answer. Save for one. Deacon was very good at giving orders and having people follow them. *Now lift up your skirt and show me your panties.* And she'd done it. Not because he'd liked her designs and given her a way to save French Kiss, but because of the look in his eyes. A hungry, pleading look that wiped out all thoughts of resistance. Then he'd kissed her, and her brain had stopped thinking and desire had taken over. She wanted Deacon. And if Nash hadn't opened the door, she would've had him right there on the boardroom table.

She closed her eyes and cringed.

"Olivia? Are you listening to me?"

Parker's angry voice pulled her out of her thoughts. She opened her eyes to find him glaring at her.

"I'm sorry, Parker." She sat down in the chair and studied her hands like a guilty kid in the principal's office. "I should've explained things to you sooner."

"What things? Don't tell me you're having an affair with your cousin."

Her gaze flashed up. "No! Of course I'm not having an affair with Deacon." Certainly two kisses didn't constitute an affair. "And he's my step-cousin."

"He's a jackass." Parker stood over her. "A jackass you need to get rid of ASAP."

It wasn't what he said as much as how he said it that took Olivia by surprise. He wasn't offering advice. He was issuing an order. Something that he had never done before—not even in the bedroom. Since he had caught her and Deacon in a compromising position and was no doubt allowing jealousy to control his decision-making, she tried to ignore his tone.

"I can't fire him, Parker. Michael left him and his brothers the majority of stock in the company. Which means they own French Kiss."

"So I heard, and I also heard that you were going to buy them out. So do it and get the Beaumonts out of here."

At one time she'd thought the same way. She couldn't wait to have the Beaumont brothers sign the contracts and go home. But things had changed with just one Power-Point presentation. What had made Deacon do it? Why had he taken the time when he could've easily walked out the door with fifty million and left all the problems to her?

"I hope you realize that you won't have a company if you let those hillbillies run it," Parker said.

"I won't have a company if I don't." The words came out before she could even think about them. But she quickly recognized them as the truth. She might not like Deacon, but she needed him. The presentation had been good and Grayson's sketches amazing, but there was little doubt in her mind that Deacon's strong, commanding personality was what had sealed the deal.

Parker knelt in front of her and took her hands. "And maybe that's not a bad thing, Olivia. Maybe it's time to let go of French Kiss and move on. I deal with our accounts daily, and French Kiss isn't going to make it, especially with those cretins running it. So let's forget about French Kiss and start our own lingerie company. I've put a little money aside and, with your money, we could make a real go of it." His eyes got a funny gleam in them. "In fact, why don't we get married?"

Olivia felt like she'd been punched hard in the stomach and had all the wind knocked out of her. And somehow she didn't think that was a normal reaction to a marriage proposal—even a really bad one. The conversation with Deacon came back to haunt her, and she had to wonder if he wasn't right. If she was Parker's woman, why had she let Deacon kiss her? The answer came quickly. Because she didn't see herself as Parker's woman. She saw them as two business associates who occasionally had dinner and sex. And not even very good sex.

"Thank you," she said as humbly as possible. "But I can't marry you, Parker. We don't even know each other. I've never met your parents, and you've never met my mother. I don't even know if you have a pet, and you know nothing about Jonathan." Not that the seagull was a pet. But now that she thought about it, he was the closest she'd come to owning one.

After only a moment's hesitation, Parker released her hands and stood up. "Deacon seduced you, didn't he? Maybe you haven't had sex, but you want to." Olivia couldn't help the heat that filled her face.

"Great!" He threw up his hands and turned away. "That's just great." A few minutes passed before he turned back around. "So you're planning on staying and running the company with that cretin and his brothers?" When she didn't answer, a look of disgust entered his eyes. "I should've known you'd do anything for French Kiss." She couldn't blame him for being angry when she had turned down his marriage proposal and practically told him she wanted to have sex with Deacon. She should've adamantly denied it. Except she couldn't. She did want to have sex with Deacon. Which was wrong. So terribly wrong.

"I'm sorry, Parker," she said.

"Yeah," he said, "me too. This is going to make things much more difficult."

She nodded. "But I hope you don't quit. I'm sure we can still work together—"

A knock sounded on the door before Kelly stuck her head in. "Sorry to interrupt, but I thought Mr. Calloway would like to know that his car is being towed."

"What?" Parker hurried to the door. "Why would it be getting towed? I parked it in the space I always park it in."

Kelly shrugged. "I couldn't tell you. All I know is that the security guy from downstairs called to say it was towed away."

"They already took it?"

Kelly nodded. "I'm afraid so. But the guard did get the name of the company, and I'm sure you can track them down and clear up the matter."

Parker didn't even glance at Olivia before he brushed past Kelly, who seemed to be a little too happy about the situation. Although her smile dropped when she looked at Olivia.

"Do you want to talk about it?"

"Talk about Parker's car getting towed?"

"No. Talk about breaking up with him. Although I can't say as I blame you. That was one sucky proposal. He should've at least taken you to dinner and hidden a huge diamond in a rose. My friend's boyfriend hid the ring in a Ding Dong. The diamond wasn't big, but it was big enough to chip a tooth."

Olivia stared at her. "So you were eavesdropping on our conversation?"

"I had to. You certainly wouldn't want me to interrupt you boinking each other, would you?" She covered her mouth. "Sorry, I promised Mr. Beaumont that I wouldn't talk about sex anymore at the office."

It annoyed her to no end that Deacon had had the discussion with Kelly that Olivia should've had a long time ago—and that Kelly had actually listened. Of course she shouldn't have been surprised. It was obvious that Deacon had a way of getting people to do what he wanted them to.

Kelly moved into the room. "Of course, if we were girlfriends just shooting the shit on our break, he probably couldn't get mad at that." She grabbed a chair and pulled it closer to Olivia. "So what's going on? Did you have sex with Mr. Beaumont? Because if you did, you are my new hero. I mean the man is a god—a walking, talking sex god. And any woman who gets to worship at his altar should consider herself lucky."

"I did not have sex with Mr. Beaumont."

Kelly didn't look fazed. "But you're going to, right? Because anyone can see that the guy would like to bend you over his desk and—"

"Kelly!" she said.

Kelly held up her hands. "Fine. But I think you could use a good boinking to relieve all that stress you carry around with you. Sex is a great stress reliever, and Mr. Beaumont looks like a man who knows his way around the bedroom."

"I'm not worried about getting around a bedroom with Mr. Beaumont," Olivia said. "I'm worried about getting the new designs made in time for the fashion show. Which means that you'll need to set up a meeting with the designers for this afternoon so we can start—"

Kelly cut her off. "I'm sorry, but I can't. Mr. Beaumont has a list a mile long of things I need to do for him."

Olivia bristled. "Mr. Beaumont is not your boss. I am."

Kelly held up her hands again. "Then you need to explain that to him. I'm only trying to do my job."

Olivia's anger boiled as she started down the hall to her office. If the man thought he was going to take her assistant, he had another think coming. He might've saved her butt today, but that didn't mean he could completely take over. Seething, she jerked open the door of her office to find Deacon sitting at her desk, looking like a cover model for *GQ* magazine. His hair was mussed and his gaze intent as he studied the computer screen. He'd removed his jacket and rolled up the sleeves of his shirt, and the muscles of his forearms flexed as he typed.

Just that quickly all her anger melted, replaced with lust so hot and thick that it took her breath away. The whoosh of released air had him glancing over.

"Olivia. Just the person I wanted to see," he said. "I

thought we should meet with the designers this morning. The sooner we start the collections the better, don't you think?" When she didn't say anything, he looked concerned. "Livy? What is it?"

It took a strong will to shake her head while drowning in desire. "Nothing," she squeaked as she took a step back. "Nothing at all. I just stopped by to tell you that I-I'll take care of meeting with the designers." She turned and hurried out the door on wobbly legs. It wasn't until she was on the elevator that her breath came back and her pulse slowed.

Kelly was right. Deacon was a god, and Olivia really wanted to worship at his altar.

* * *

With Michael's stroke, the funeral, and the Beaumont brothers, it had been a while since Olivia had stopped by the design studio. It was a huge, airy room that covered one side of the tenth floor, with full-length windows facing the bay and the Golden Gate Bridge. While you got only a partial view from the large corner offices, here you got the entire view. It was spectacular, but no more spectacular than the sight of worktables cluttered with sewing machines, bolts of fabric, tape measures, scissors, and patterns. Unfortunately, no one was working at the tables. The designers were all huddled in one corner of the room gossiping.

"...I kid you not, bitches." Jose waved his hand dramatically. "I heard the man just walked into that boardroom as sweet as you please and told those uppity snobs what end was up—no please, thank you, or go to hell about it. I swear I just love a man who knows how to take charge."

"I don't care how well he takes charge," Margo said. "I care about keeping my job. Is he going to sell or is he going to keep the company?"

"From what I heard, he's going to keep it. He has three new collections coming out."

"Three?" Effie asked. "That means—"

Samuel Sawyer stepped out of his office. He was the head designer and a man who had always intimidated Olivia. He never had a hair out of place or a wrinkle in his fashionable suits. If he smiled, she had never seen it. He usually wore a solemn look that bordered on a frown.

"If the rumors are true," he said, "then we'd better get busy and quit gossiping like a bunch of overfed hens." He glanced over and saw Olivia standing in the doorway. He acknowledged her with a nod before clapping his hands and getting his designers back to work. When they were busy at their tables, he motioned her into his office. It was as fastidiously neat and somber as Samuel. There were no family pictures on his desk. Not a speck of dust or dirt either. Just a stack of design books and the first laptop ever made.

Once in his office, he gave Olivia an air peck on either cheek. "How are you holding up, doll?"

It was the first time anyone had asked, and Olivia felt like dissolving in a puddle of tears. But knowing that would not go over well with Samuel, she nodded. "I'm fine. I miss him, though."

"Don't we all," he said with no emotion on his face whatsoever. "Now what brings you here today? I'm assuming this has to do with the new owners."

"Have you met them?"

"I think one of them showed up in the studio this morning. It was before any of the other designers had arrived. I was on the phone with a new fabric broker and got a chance to observe him. I'd say he was an artist by the way he studied the design board."

"Grayson," Olivia said. "He's the youngest Beaumont. And he is an artist. An amazing artist. You'll be seeing his work shortly."

"So the rumors are true? These Beaumont brothers from Louisiana are going to take over?"

She walked to the window that looked out on the studio. "For now. They have plans for three collections."

"This Grayson's designs?"

She felt her face flush. "Actually, they're mine."

There was an audible sigh, followed by, "Well, it's about damned time."

Olivia turned to find Samuel smiling. Not a big smile, but a slight lifting at the corners of his mouth. "What do you mean?"

The smile died. "I mean it's about damned time that you figured out where you belong. And it's not behind Michael's desk." He waved a hand. "It's right here in the design studio, creating."

She stared at him. "But why didn't you say anything? All the time I spent here as a kid and you never once acted like I had any talent."

He sat down behind the desk. "I told you all the time, Olivia. You just didn't listen. You couldn't. You were too busy concentrating on every word out of Michael's mouth. And Michael wanted you to follow in his footsteps and run the company."

"Then why didn't he leave it to me?"

"Maybe he actually listened the last time I talked with him."

Olivia moved closer. "You talked to Michael about me?"

Samuel nodded. "It was after his first stroke. I stopped by the hospital to see him." He shook his head. "It was sad to see the commanding owner of French Kiss reduced to someone who had no control of his speech or the right side of his body. But his brain still worked. I started to talk about my ideas for new designs, but he stopped me. After a few grunts and a jabbed finger at your picture, I figured out that he wanted to hear about you and how you were taking care of the business."

Michael had wanted the same information every time she'd visited him. But she'd refrained from talking about the company—mostly because she didn't want him knowing how bad things had gotten. "So I guess you told him."

Samuel leaned back and smoothed out the creases in his pants. "He needed to know—not only about the company going bankrupt but about his mistake in trying to force you to be something you aren't." He looked up. "You know why you're so easily distracted, Olivia? It's because you're a creative person, and creative people struggle to think with the left side of their brain. Their mind isn't on everyday life. It's on their last creation— their last brushstroke, pencil sketch, piano note, or typed word. And Michael couldn't see that because he thinks with his left brain. So he just thought you were forgetful. He didn't know you were a genius."

"I'm not—" she started, but he held up a hand.

"You are. You just needed to have someone give you the confidence." The faint smile reappeared. "And if the new boss is responsible, then I love the man." He winked at her. "And you should too."

CHAPTER FOURTEEN

$\mathcal{D}$eacon didn't know what he expected when he walked into Michael's office for the first time. Maybe he expected to feel some kind of visceral connection. Instead all he felt was anger. Anger over the paintings of Paris that covered the walls, and anger that Michael had died before Deacon could prove that he cared nothing about his biological father.

So it felt good to release some of that anger on the presumptuous woman who sat behind the desk. His plan had been to wait Anastasia Bradley out and see if she led him to the person who was trying to sabotage the company. But the sight of her reclining in the leather chair with one purple high heel on the desk while she leafed through a magazine didn't sit well with him. And he discovered that he'd lost his patience with Ms. Bradley.

He cleared his throat, and she glanced up from *Harper's Bazaar* magazine. The distaste that crossed her face mirrored his own feelings. "Did you need something, Mr. Beaumont?"

"Actually"—he strolled into the room—"there are a few things I need, Ms. Bradley." He held up a finger. "One, I need your resignation." He held up another finger. "Two, I need you out of this office." Another finger went up. "And three, I need the name of the asshole who is trying to rear-end French Kiss." While she stared at him like a largemouth bass, he stepped closer. "The first you have two hours to deliver. The second you'll need to do within the hour. And the last you'll need to give me now. Unless you'd rather I called the FBI."

He didn't want to bring in the federal government. Government and big business didn't mix. But it wasn't an idle threat. If push came to shove, he would have no problem calling the feds. He just wasn't about to call them until he had a handle on what was going on in French Kiss. It didn't look like Anastasia was going to help him out with that.

Shock was quickly followed by anger, and her true colors came out with a vengeance. "You have nothing on me," she hissed as she rose to her feet. "So go ahead and call the FBI."

"Nothing?" He lifted an eyebrow. "What about breaking and entering? I saw you in Ms. Harrington's office. Now who were you talking to?"

A slight flush colored her cheeks, but other than that, she was one tough cookie. "If you're referring to the other morning, that was strictly business. I stopped by to leave Olivia the new catalog mock-ups. When she wasn't there, I left them on her desk."

"In a locked office."

She smiled slyly and shrugged. "I guess her airheaded assistant forgot to lock up."

Deacon crossed his arms to keep from reaching out

and shaking the truth from her. "And the phone call I overheard?"

"What phone call? I don't remember a phone call. And unless you have a recording, it's your word against mine, Mr. Beaumont."

He studied her for a long moment. "On second thought, I think I want you gone from French Kiss now." He picked up the phone and dialed. "Kelly, could you have security send someone up to escort Ms. Bradley off the premises? Thank you." He hung up the phone. "You're right, Ms. Bradley, I don't have proof. But unfortunately for you, in order to ruin a person's reputation, you don't need proof. You just need a rumor. And I intend to start that rumor."

Her eyes narrowed. "As if anyone would believe an ignorant hillbilly."

"An ignorant hillbilly with the power to fire your ass."

She sent him another scalding look before she jerked open the top desk drawer and started pulling things out. He grabbed one of the empty boxes by the door.

"Here, let me help you with that."

"I don't need any help!" she snapped as she grabbed the box from him. He watched her remove everything from the drawers, but stopped her when she reached for the laptop on the desk.

"Unless you have proof that it's your personal laptop, it stays."

She pressed her lips in a thin line. "You won't save French Kiss, you know. You can come up with all the collections you want, and it's still going to end up sold to the highest bidder."

"Why, Ms. Bradley, you sound almost gleeful about that." He cocked his head. "It makes a person wonder if you're not in cahoots with one of the companies that have made an offer. Avery Industries, perhaps?"

The flicker in her eyes was all the answer he needed. Not that he could prove it, but it was nice to know. The guard showed up, then stepped back as Anastasia strode out the door with her box.

"I don't need an escort," she growled. "I know my way out."

When the witch was gone, Deacon was left with the ghost. A ghost that had haunted him for years and refused to let up. Unlike Olivia's office, Michael's had a masculine feel. The shelving and desk were dark wood, the furniture brown leather and overstuffed. The only splashes of color were the paintings—paintings almost identical to his mother's pictures that he'd found in the garage. There was the same bridge over the Seine. The same angle of the Eiffel Tower. The same quaint café. And the same small lingerie shop.

Deacon had always thought Michael had left his mother after finding out she was pregnant. But looking at the paintings, he started to have his doubts. Why would a man want to be reminded of a woman he didn't love? It made no sense. But if it had been his mother who broke it off, why would Michael surround himself with painful memories?

"So you fired her?" Kelly peeked her head in, and when Deacon nodded, she walked in and closed the door behind her. "I could kiss you for getting rid of that bitch." Before he could open his mouth, she held up a hand. "Not sexually. Just as an appreciative employee." She sent him a heavy-lidded look and toyed with her necklace. "Unless you want more than appreciation."

"Kelly," he warned.

Her shoulders slumped. "Fine. You can't blame a girl for trying." She looked around. "Isn't this a great office? Don't you just love Paris?"

"Not really," he said dryly.

She pulled a phone from between her breasts and typed with her thumbs. "Get rid of Paris pictures from Mr. Beaumont's office."

"This isn't my office."

"Why not? You are the boss. Besides, I think Ms. Harrington is ready for you to get out of hers." She walked over and took the painting of the café down and leaned it against the wall. It was funny, but Deacon seemed to breathe easier.

"Where is Olivia?" he asked.

"She called and said she'd be in the design studio for the rest of the day."

"Is Parker with her?"

"Nope," Kelly said. "He's getting his Corvette after I had it towed. Did you get a chance to case his office?"

"Not yet," he said absently. "Are there men who work in the design department?"

"Sorta." She winked. "If you know what I mean. Although I'm not too sure about Samuel. If he's not gay, he's asexual. There are no pheromones coming from that guy at all."

"Good Lord." Jason walked into the office. "Is sex all you think about?"

Kelly's smile drooped as her chin hiked. "As a matter of fact, I think about plenty of other things."

"Name one." While Kelly pondered the question, Jason looked at Deacon. "You want to go to a Giants game tonight? I've got two tickets for right behind home plate."

If Deacon hadn't been up all night, he might've accepted. But he was dead on his feet and envied the fact that his brothers were now tucked into Olivia's guest room sleeping peacefully. Damn them.

"Thanks," he said, "but now that Anastasia is gone, I wanted to get a look at her computer and see what I could find."

"You fired her?" Jason asked. When Deacon nodded, he turned and high-fived Kelly. After the celebration was over, they dropped their hands and looked stunned by the show of solidarity.

Jason cleared his throat. "So how did she take it?"

"How do you think she took it?" Kelly said. "When I saw her being escorted to the elevators, she looked pissed."

"That's putting it mildly," Deacon said. "Although not pissed enough to rat out her accomplice. And I don't think they'll be as blatant as Anastasia was." Even though this wasn't his office, and would never be his office, he sat down behind the desk and turned on Anastasia's laptop. "So did you find any more discrepancies in the accounts?"

Before Jason could answer, Kelly spoke. "I'll go to the game with you." For the first time since Deacon had known her, she blushed. "I mean, if you need someone to go with you, I'm not doing anything else tonight."

Jason's expression wasn't exactly thrilled. "Thanks, but since there's no sex involved, you'd probably be bored to tears. And unenthusiastic fans can really jinx a team."

Kelly snorted. "As if the Giants have to worry about being jinxed. Their record this year has sucked worse than my last boyfriend. Their batting is dismal and their pitching even worse."

Jason's eyes widened. "You follow the Giants?"

"Follow them? I've had sex with half the team." She flipped her hair over her shoulder. "Now, if you gentlemen will excuse me. I have work to do."

Jason watched her go before he looked at Deacon. "What do you think?"

"I think it's doubtful. There have to be at least forty guys on the roster."

"No, I mean do you think I should take her to the game?" Jason continued to stare at the doorway. "Just so the ticket won't go to waste, of course."

"Of course." Deacon bit back a smile.

After Jason left, Deacon checked out Anastasia's computer. He didn't find much. The files were all work-related, and if she'd corresponded with anyone from Avery, the e-mails had been deleted. Maybe he had misread her facial expressions. He was pretty beat, so it was possible. Figuring he wouldn't get anything productive done until he got some sleep, he closed the laptop and decided to call it a day.

When he stepped out of the office, he was surprised to find that Kelly had set up residence at the assistant's desk. All her girlie knickknacks cluttered the top, and she was happily tapping away on the computer with some kind of cartoon cat headphones clipped to her head. He was about to wave a hand in front of her face when she noticed him.

"Oh!" she yelled before slipping the headphones to her neck. "So did you need something, Mr. Beaumont?"

"Okay"—he held up a hand—"I get that you want me to move into this office. But even if I decide to, you're not my assistant. You're Ms. Harrington's."

"Look, I'm not putting down Ms. Harrington. I think she's a real nice lady. But except for a few phone calls and setting up meetings, she really didn't know what to do with an assistant. And if you're worried about her being mad, don't be. I checked in with her just a few minutes ago, and she seems pretty happy right where she is. In fact I've never seen her so happy."

"Where is—?"

"Design studio. Tenth floor." She popped the head-phones on and went back to her computer, yelling her next words. "But beware of Samuel. He doesn't like non-designers in his domain."

But it wasn't some asexual designer who had Deacon pausing just outside the studio door. It was the sight of Olivia standing at a table with all the other designers gathered around her. They were talking about one of her designs, asking questions and throwing out ideas for fabrics. And while she had seemed hesitant in the board-room, here she seemed right at home. She answered each question competently, didn't cut off anyone making a suggestion, and yet stood her ground when she needed to. But it wasn't her confidence that surprised him as much as the happiness that radiated from her like the rays of sunlight that spilled in through the windows.

She had always been attractive, but now she was ut-terly and completely captivating. And there was a part of him that was jealous as hell that he wasn't responsible for her look of joy. Which was crazy. Once he made sure French Kiss was solvent, he was out of there. He had no right to be jealous of a group of designers...or her boyfriend.

He was turning to leave when she glanced up. If he'd thought he was captivated before, it was nothing to how he felt when their eyes met. Suddenly he was drowning in twin pools of lush green and a rush of emotions so intense he had trouble catching his breath. Not just from desire, but also from something much more potent. But before he could examine the feelings more closely, his cell phone rang. With a simple nod, he broke eye contact and headed toward the elevators. Shaken, he answered without checking to see who the caller was. Which he regretted as soon as he heard the throaty voice.

"Did you forget something?"

Deacon waited until he was alone in the elevators before he answered. "Hello, Francesca."

"Hello?" Francesca said. "You stand me up for the Fletchers' benefit dinner and all you can say is hello? You do realize that those tickets were six hundred dollars a plate."

Damn, he'd forgotten all about the dinner.

"I'm sorry," he said as he scrubbed a hand over his face. "But you've heard about my uncle's death. There were things I needed to take care of in San Francisco."

"So I've heard. I talked with your father and he mentioned that you and your brothers have come into some money."

Deacon rolled his eyes. He should've known that his father couldn't keep his mouth shut—especially around a beautiful woman. And even at close to Donny John's age, Francesca was beautiful.

"Not yet we haven't."

"Difficulties with the will?"

"You could say that."

There was a pause before she spoke. "You don't need to wait for money, Deacon. I've already transferred money into an account for you. All you have to do is say the word and work will start on your dream."

This was exactly what he'd hoped for—the reason he'd

spent the past few months escorting Francesca around. And once he got the money from Olivia, he could pay off Francesca and the condo project would be his free and clear. So why wasn't he more excited? He stared at the scrolled *F* and *K* on the elevator doors. Maybe because he'd gotten a taste of something bigger.

The elevator silently slid to the bottom floor and opened with a ping. Before him the lobby beckoned like Emerald City. Suddenly Deacon realized that he belonged in this world as much as Dorothy belonged in Oz. His life was back in Louisiana without this glitter and glitz. And without the confusing emotions a certain blonde evoked.

He stepped out of the elevator. "Let's go for it, Francesca. I'll contact the contractors and we'll start breaking ground as soon as possible."

CHAPTER FIFTEEN

"I was only nine when my father disappeared," Olivia said as she hand-stitched the binding to the mock-up corset. "And yet I still think about him almost every day. Which is silly since he probably hasn't given me a second thought."

Grayson's gaze lifted from his sketchpad. They were the same color as Deacon's and Nash's, but Grayson's eyes held an innocent compassion that would make anyone want to share their deepest hurts. Which made Olivia continue to babble.

"I wanted to blame my mother. I thought if she hadn't been so wrapped up in money, my father wouldn't have left after his company went bankrupt." She re-threaded her needle and went back to work on the deep-purple corset fitted to the dress form. It was one from the Valentino Collection. A sexy confection of velvet and ribbon lacing.

"Then, when I became a self-conscious adolescent,"

she said, "I blamed myself. I thought if I'd been cuter, smarter, more lovable, it would've been enough to make him stay. It was Michael who finally made me realize how wrong I was." She pushed up her glasses. "Not because of anything he said, but because of his actions. He had faith in me." She paused. "Then I went and almost bankrupted his company."

Grayson skillfully wielded the charcoal pencil. "From what Deacon says, French Kiss was on its way to bankruptcy long before Uncle Michael died. And he was right to have faith in you." He stopped sketching and looked around the large design studio. "All these works of art are yours."

Olivia followed his gaze. Sunlight streamed in through the tall windows, gilding the dress forms draped in their colorful satins and silks as if they were princesses in a fairy-tale ballroom. Each designer danced around their princess, their attention completely focused on the design. She understood how they felt. While she struggled to remain on task with everything else in her life, she had no problem remaining focused here.

In the past week she'd completed her own pieces for the new collections, including the dark-purple corset with its silver binding and lavender ribbon laces. And she was starting to believe Samuel and Grayson. She was an artist.

For a long while she and Grayson worked on their own creations without saying a word. The silence would've been uncomfortable with any other man, but with Grayson it just seemed right. There was something so soothing about the glide and pull of the needle and thread accompanied by the wisps of Grayson's pencil as it softly stroked the paper.

"What are you drawing?" she finally asked.

"Just a few ideas I have for the next catalog."

"Can I see them?"

He turned the sketchpad. It was a drawing of Olivia, her expression intent as she worked on the corset. There was nothing sexual about what she was doing—it was just a woman in skinny jeans and a button-up blouse sewing—and yet the entire undertone of the drawing was sexual. She should've felt embarrassed that Grayson had pictured her like that. She didn't. Probably because there was nothing sexual about their relationship. He treated her like a sister, and surprisingly, she felt that way.

"It's beautiful, Grayson," she said, "but we can't use that in the catalog. We need models."

He shook his head. "No, we don't. We need ordinary women in love."

"Are you saying that I'm ordinary?" she teased.

He blushed. "Not at all. I'm saying that even beautiful women are more beautiful when they're doing something they love. You're in love with design, and it shows in every movement, in every emotion that plays across your face."

Before she could even begin to marvel at his perception, a voice broke the silence.

"Here you two are!"

She pulled her attention from the sketch to watch as Nash wove his way through the tables. At least she thought it was Nash. The camouflage pants and T-shirt had been replaced with dove-gray pants and a light-lavender dress shirt. But his new clothes weren't as startling as his clean-shaven face. A face that was so handsome that she understood why the women—and men—of the design staff had stopped work and were now staring in openmouthed lust.

While the attention would've had most men puffing up with pride, Nash behaved as he always did. He stopped to admire each designer's work, said something that had them laughing, and then slapped them on the back before he continued on his way. This easygoing friendliness had endeared him to Olivia. And after only a week, she felt as if she'd known him all her life.

He flashed her a blinding smile before his gaze rested on the corset. "Nice. Is that part of my collection?"

Nash did have a corset in his collection, but with its black leather and studs, it was much edgier than this one. Although Olivia had yet to see the edgy side of Nash. He just seemed like a good ol' country boy to her.

"No," she said. "I have my designers working on yours and Grayson's."

His eyes sharpened, and then twinkled. "So Deacon is all yours?"

She blushed. Until now she hadn't given it much thought. But Nash made her realize that she had taken all the designs Deacon liked. Something she didn't want to acknowledge.

"So what happened to the grizzly bear that made me breakfast this morning?" she asked in an attempt to change the subject. Nash was an excellent cook and had made the most amazing brioche French toast that morning. It had sent Babette into fits of French praise.

Babette was still living with her. Olivia had bought her a plane ticket, but Babette kept postponing the departure date. And Olivia didn't know if it had to do with the fact that she didn't miss her beloved Paris as much as she claimed, or with Nash and Grayson's shirtless morning runs. Even now Babette ogled Nash from the table where she worked. Once Samuel had taken charge of the whiny woman and given her direction, she had turned out to be quite a talented seamstress.

"A grizzly bear?" Nash stroked his chin as if his beard were still there. "I'm crushed."

"Right," Olivia said. "I don't think you'd be crushed over anything a woman said to you. So why did you shave?"

His smile dropped. "I had an idea last night, and I made the mistake of telling my big brother."

"An idea? For the new line?"

"Sorta. It has more to do with the image of French Kiss." He glanced at Grayson, who had gone back to sketching, but now with a smirk on his face. "I wouldn't look so smug about me being beardless, Grayson. Your beard is next on the shaving block. Although with three hairs, tweezers will probably work better."

Grayson lowered the sketchpad. "I'm not shaving my beard. It just got going."

"It doesn't look like it's going anywhere to me. But you'll need to take that up with Deacon. He scheduled some photo shoot for us this afternoon."

"Us? Your big idea was taking pictures of us without beards?"

"No. My big idea had to do with releasing the news that French Kiss has new owners." Nash glanced at Olivia. "At least for a short time. I got to thinking about how much women love men to buy them sexy lingerie. But there are a lot of women who don't have a husband or boyfriend to do that for them. So that's where the Beaumont brothers come in. Since we picked the ones we liked the most from your designs, Olivia, it's like we're choosing lingerie for all the women of the world. I thought we could open up social networking accounts where we can actually tweet and post with the customers."

"That's genius," Olivia said.

Nash looked uncomfortable with the praise. "Look, I'm not a businessman like Deacon, but I figured it was worth a shot."

"It's an amazing idea, Nash," she said. "With the new collections coming out, it makes perfect sense to present the Beaumont brothers as the new faces of French Kiss."

"Well, I think it sucks," Grayson said. "You and Deacon can go barefaced if you want, but I'm keeping my beard."

As popular as beards had become with young men, Olivia knew that they weren't quite as popular with young women. And if the marketing strategy was going to work, Grayson would have to shave.

"Okay," she said, "but I have heard that if you shave off a beard, it grows in thicker."

Grayson's eyes narrowed. "Thicker?"

"So I've heard. And if you want to test the theory, I just happen to have some disposable razors in my bathroom."

It took only a second for Grayson to make his decision. "Fine," he said as he got to his feet, "but only for you, Olivia. And I'm growing it back right after the shoot."

Nash rolled his eyes as he followed his brother. "I'm sure that will only take a few hours."

Once they were gone, Olivia went back to work. But her heart was no longer in it. She kept thinking about the photo shoot. Of course she shouldn't go. If she'd learned anything from the boardroom kiss, it was that she and Deacon couldn't be in the same room without sparks flying. Which was why she'd been hiding out in the design studio. Obviously Deacon had felt the same way. He hadn't once sought her out. Instead he'd kicked Anastasia out of Michael's office and pretty much taken complete control of the company. She should've felt angry. After all, she was the one who was supposed to be in charge. But instead she felt as if a huge weight had been lifted off her shoulders.

Since Michael's first stroke, she'd been responsible for everything. Every concern and complaint from the board, her staff, retailers, customers, and what felt like the world, had been her responsibility to deal with. Until Deacon had stepped into the boardroom.

According to Kelly—who had become more his assistant than Olivia's—in the last week, Deacon had set up meetings with every department in the company and asked for their ideas, opinions, and concerns. Once he had Kelly compile the information, he'd made decisions that Olivia had never been able to bring herself to make. Some people had been fired, some issued warnings, and others promoted. Every judgment he'd made, Olivia completely agreed with. With Deacon in charge, she felt it was possible to save the company. And not just possible but probable.

There was only one fly in the ointment of her contentment. Parker had become a bit of a stalker. Under the guise of remaining friends, he'd started showing up to take her to lunch, and because she felt guilty about breaking up with him, she went. But it was starting to get old. Especially when he talked nonstop about how Deacon was out to get him and was having Kelly send him on wild goose chases just to keep him away from the office and Olivia.

"So are you trying to avoid me?"

The words, spoken in a silky Southern voice, had Olivia pricking her finger with the needle. Before it could spill a drop of blood on the velvet, she stuck it in her mouth and turned around.

Deacon no longer wore jeans and an un-tucked-in shirt to the office. He wore a gray suit similar to the one he'd worn at the board meeting. But this one looked more fitted. The jacket clung to his broad shoulders and tapered at his waist, and the pants hugged his hips and outlined his long legs. His designer shirt was French Kiss lavender, bringing out the deep violet-blue of his eyes. He didn't wear a tie, and it was hard to look away from the open collar of his shirt, where solid chest met 100 percent silk. Since she wore jeans and a loose-fitting blouse, it was as if they had traded places completely. He was the well-dressed boss, and she the casually dressed relative.

She turned back to the corset. "I don't remember being called into a meeting. Not that I've had the time."

There was a long pause, followed by a tired sigh. "Time does seem to slip away from you here. Damn, I can't even remember what day it is." He paused. "Obviously casual Friday." She could almost feel his gaze running over her. He moved closer, so close that the soft wool of his pants brushed against the denim of her jeans. She tried to stay focused on the corset, but her hand shook so badly that her stitches would have to be taken out and redone.

"Mine." He reached out and his fingers entwined in the ribbon she'd yet to tie, sliding down the satin in a slow caress that took all the oxygen from the room. For some weird reason, suddenly Olivia didn't feel as if the sexy underwear was on the lifeless mannequin. She felt as if it were on her—the rigid frame hugging her waist and the low bodice offering up her breasts. Taking the ribbon ends in each hand, Deacon pulled until the crossed lacing gathered and the eyelets almost touched. The air in her lungs rushed out, and her heart jarred almost painfully against her rib cage as he tied a perfect bow.

While she struggled for breath, his fingers slid to one end of the ribbon, his thumb rubbing the smooth satin against the pad of his forefinger. The slow circular motion caused heat to settle between her legs.

"I like it," he said in a voice barely above a whisper. "I like it a lot."

She glanced up from his hypnotic fingers and found him watching her with hot eyes that took the rest of her breath. Then she was leaning toward him, grabbing the front of his shirt, and pulling his lips toward her.

The kiss was hot. Wet. Deep. And over much too quickly. He pulled back, and she opened her eyes to find him studying her with a mixture of surprise and desire.

"Olivia?" Her name came off his kiss-dampened lips sounding so sexy that she leaned in for another kiss. He stopped her. "Unless you want me to take you in front of every designer here, I think we need to stop."

She blinked, and her gaze moved around the room. Sure enough, everyone had stopped working and was watching their boss almost rape the new owner of French Kiss. Samuel looked amused, while Babette shot eye-daggers. Before Olivia could die from embarrassment, Deacon did what he was good at—he took charge. Giving her arms a reassuring squeeze, he spoke loudly enough for the entire room to hear.

"My apologies, Ms. Harrington. Obviously you and your design team are on the right track. That corset had the desired effect."

There was a long pause before people broke out in laughter. Everyone but Babette. Deacon flashed them a slight smile before looking back at Olivia, whose face still burned.

"Two things," he said in a voice for her ears only. "First, I want you to be at the photo shoot in fifteen minutes. I need your creative input. And second, I want you to break it off with Parker."

Before her mouth could finish dropping open, he headed for the door. He stopped halfway there and turned around. "Make that three things: The corset. I'd like to see it modeled...soon."

CHAPTER SIXTEEN

It didn't take long for Deacon to figure out that he hated being photographed. Or maybe what he hated was being photographed by a photographer who had singled Deacon out for his outrageous flirting.

"No, gorgeous." The photographer squatted in front of Deacon with his camera poised. "When I said I wanted a seductive smile, I didn't mean a badass glare that would start a barroom brawl. Why don't you try going to your happy place, sweetheart? Somewhere calming and seductive. Like a candlelit bedroom with a bottle of chilled champagne and a sexy naked woman stretched out on the bed." He winked. "Or a naked, very appreciative man."

His brothers, who were standing beside him, burst out laughing. Which made Deacon wonder if he wasn't going to start a barroom fight after all. He was certainly pissed enough. Not just at the photographer's flirting and his brothers' laughing, but because Olivia had completely ignored him. He had asked her to be here in fifteen minutes and it was going on an hour since he'd tracked her down in the studio. And maybe that was what really pissed him off. He'd had no business tracking Olivia down.

The kiss in the boardroom had made that perfectly clear. He wanted her. Not a couple of stolen kisses, but lots of stolen kisses, followed by lots of steamy sex. And having sex with Olivia was stupid. Money and sex worked only with hookers and porn stars. In real life having sex with business associates could complicate things in a hurry, and things were already complicated enough.

Deacon was enjoying being the boss a little too much. Or maybe what he was enjoying was the challenge of bringing French Kiss back from bankruptcy. It was a pipe dream. In the last few days, he'd discovered the depths of the company's problems, and it would take much more than a hillbilly from Louisiana, even one with a degree in business, to save the company. It would take a miracle. And he had never much believed in miracles.

"I'm done." Tossing the photographer one final annoyed look, he stepped off the set and ducked around a white umbrella that was being used for lighting. He stopped short when he saw Olivia sitting in the director's chair in one dimly lit corner.

"He's right, you know." She sounded slightly breathless. She got up, and for the second time that day he noticed how hot she looked. Her hair was down and hung in soft golden waves around her face. The white shirt was loose and sheer. The jeans tight and butt-hugging. And the purple high heels sexy as hell. They clicked against the tile floor as she moved closer. "Women won't be tempted to buy from a surly man."

"You're here."

She took a soft breath. "I thought it was an order." She

hooked an arm through his and led him back to his brothers, who were grinning from ear to ear.

"Hey, Cuz," Nash greeted her. "Long time no see."

She smiled, and Deacon tried to remember if she'd ever smiled at him like that. It annoyed him that the answer was no. Of course the smile didn't annoy him as much as Olivia's reaching out to straighten Nash's shirt collar. "Kelly mentioned that you and Grayson don't have a car. Feel free to use my Porsche."

Deacon would've laughed at the thought of his tall brother being stuffed into Olivia's tiny Porsche, if he hadn't been so pissed at him for flirting.

"How about if we drive home together," Nash said with a wink. "I'll make you dinner. Unless you've got a date with your boyfriend."

Suddenly Deacon's anger shifted from Nash to Olivia. No doubt she'd been having dinner every night with Parker while Deacon had been staying late and working his ass off. But her next words took all the starch right out of his anger.

"Parker is no longer my boyfriend." As if she'd just commented on the weather, she moved over to Grayson. "I liked your beard, but I like you better without it." She unbuttoned the top button of his shirt. "There, that's perfect." She went to stand behind the photographer. "We're ready when you are, Miles."

Miles studied Deacon. "Do you think you can get Mr. Sexy Pants to stop scowling?"

Deacon ignored him and directed his questions to Olivia. "Why? Why did you break it off with Parker?"

She glanced at the photographer. "Miles, would you excuse me and Mr. Beaumont for a second? We'll be right back." She headed to a dressing room in the far corner, and when he followed, he found her holding the door and breathing rather shallowly.

"Are you okay?" he asked.

"Just a little out of breath," she said before she closed the door and rested her back against it. "I broke up with Parker because I wanted to. Not because you ordered me to."

"I didn't order you."

She laughed, or more like released her breath in a sexy chuckle. "You really need to learn the difference between asking and ordering, Mr. Beaumont. Asking means a person has the right to decline without penalty. Ordering means that they have a right to decline with one."

"And exactly what penalty would I implement if you didn't follow my supposed orders?"

She hesitated for only a second before answering. "You'd sell the company."

The words and her somber expression broadsided him, and it took more than a second for him to reply. "You really think I'd do that? Especially after all the hours I've put in?"

She studied him with her clear, direct eyes. "Why, Deacon? Why have you worked so hard to save a company that you don't even care about? And don't tell me it has to do with the money. You could've had the money without the work if you had just signed the contract."

She was right. After a couple of sleepless nights, he'd figured out that it wasn't about the money. Nor was it about the power and big office that came with the job. But he'd be damned before he admitted the truth to her. The truth that it all had to do with his ego and the desire to prove to her and a ghost that he was more than just a stupid hillbilly from Louisiana. And if that wasn't stupid, he didn't know what was.

"So you broke up with Parker because you wanted to?" he asked.

"I'm not good at taking orders—even with the fear of losing the company. I did all three things because I wanted to."

Deacon's eyes widened. "Three?"

A smile tipped her mouth. "Yep." Before he could get his head around that, she opened the door and walked out of the dressing room, leaving Deacon too stunned to move. It took Miles hustling in to break through his daze.

"Come on, lover boy," he said as he pulled Deacon back to the set. "Time is money." He smoothed Deacon's hair before tapping his nose. "Remember. Sexy thoughts."

Deacon didn't need the reminder. As soon as Miles moved out of the way, his gaze sought out Olivia. She stood to the side, just to the right of one of the umbrellas. The area she stood in was too shadowed for him to tell if she wore something beneath the white shirt. But Miles had no more than crouched down and aimed his camera than she pulled something from the opened neck of her blouse. And it didn't take more than an eye-narrowing to see that it was a ribbon. A purple ribbon.

"Perfect!" Miles yelled before his camera rapidly clicked. "Just keep those naughty thoughts coming, my sweet. Women are going to eat you up with a spoon."

Deacon didn't want women. He wanted one.

*   *   *

Deacon allowed the photo shoot to last much longer than he wanted, but only because it seemed to mean so much to Olivia. She stood right behind Miles, offering up suggestions and a multitude of praises when they hit a pose she liked. Occasionally she would stop the shoot and hurry over to fix a shirt collar or straighten a piece of wayward hair. The ribbon had disappeared, but in the bright lights he had no trouble seeing the outline of the corset through the white of her shirt. And when she smoothed his hair off his forehead, he couldn't help leaning down and whispering in her ear.

"With or without panties?"

She froze with her fingertips resting ever so softly against his temple and her breath falling in warm puffs against the skin of his neck. Her gaze lifted to his. "Without."

He squeezed his eyes shut and tried to control the wave of desire that threatened to overtake him. It was a losing battle. It had been brewing since the moment she'd flaunted the ribbon. Or possibly from the moment he'd first kissed her sweet, plump lips. Deacon opened his eyes to discover Olivia licking those lips with a heat in her eyes that scorched his very soul.

"Enough fawning, Olivia," Miles said. "I only need a few more shots."

Without taking his eyes off her, Deacon spoke. "No more shots. Olivia and I have a meeting to attend." Then without one thought for how it would look to the photographer or his brothers, he took her hand and pulled her around the extension cords and lighting umbrellas and out the door.

"What are you doing?" she whispered as he led her to the elevator. She struggled to catch her breath, and he now knew why. "People are going to talk."

"Let them." He pulled her into the elevator, where

he would've kissed her and taken a quick peek at the corset if two women hadn't joined them. He probably should have let go of Olivia's hand. Instead he continued to hold it as Olivia greeted the women in a strained voice.

"Hi, Elaine... Tiffany."

They nodded a greeting, and then studied their purple high heels until the elevator doors opened on the executive floor. Hoping to avoid Kelly, Deacon headed for Olivia's office. Unfortunately, his assistant seemed to be everywhere these days.

"Oh, there you are," she said as she hustled up. "I was just going to interrupt the photo shoot to tell you that Parker—I mean Mr. Calloway—wants a meeting with you, and he seemed pretty pissed off. Like so pissed off that he might explode. I think it might have to do with the rotten egg I placed in his desk drawer—"

"Later," Deacon said as his hand tightened on Olivia's. "Right now I want you to hold all calls and interruptions." Without waiting for a reply, he pulled Olivia into the office, closed the door, and locked it. His grip loosened, but he refused to let her go. "I think you know where this is headed."

Her breath caught. "Yes."

"And you know that mixing business with pleasure isn't smart."

A smile tipped up the corners of her mouth before she bit her lip as if to contain it. "I guess that depends on your definition of *smart*. A very smart man just recently told me that sometimes it's better to go with your gut than with your head."

He didn't even try to bite back his smile. "And what is your gut telling you?"

She linked her fingers with his. "That it would be really stupid to pass up this opportunity."

Something inside his gut said the same thing. Although he wasn't as concerned with the feeling in his gut as he was with the feeling in his chest. His heart thumped much too rapidly. As if it was scared of an impending doom. He ignored it and tugged Olivia closer.

As much as he wanted to devour her, he took his time. Linking their hands, he lowered his head and sipped at her soft lips. One kiss. Two. Three—followed by twenty more. She tasted like sweet tea. Smooth, amber-colored sweet tea that had been brewed and steeped to perfection. And as with the Southern drink, sipping Olivia was addictive. Something he could've gone on doing forever if she hadn't released his hands, slid her fingers through his hair, and pulled him closer for a deep, wet, tongue-mating kiss that had his cock lengthening and his hands curling around her waist. A waist that had been cinched into a rigid cage of material and ribbon. A waist he could easily span.

She pulled back from the kiss, her eyelids lowered, pupils dilated, and breath coming out in soft pants. "So I guess you want to see the new design, boss."

Before he could do more than nod, she reached for the fly of her jeans. It took more than a few hip wiggles to get the jeans down her hips. She stepped out of the heels before peeling them off.

"Keep the shoes," Deacon said.

Her eyes grew even hotter as she kicked the jeans out of the way and slipped her feet back into the heels. Starting at the top, she slowly unbuttoned her shirt, her nimble fingers twisting and sliding to reveal a peek of soft cleavage, followed by dark purple crisscrossed with ribbon resting against a patch of golden blond. Deacon's breath mimicked Olivia's, and he had to fist his hands to keep from reaching out for her and stopping the seductive show.

And she was seductive. Not only now but in a business suit. Or a wet T-shirt and shorts. Or a sundress and panties. Since meeting him she'd seduced him with whatever she wore. Once the shirt was unbuttoned, she merely shrugged her shoulders and it dropped to the floor.

He had seen numerous women in sexy lingerie, but none had made his heart feel as if it would jump from his chest. Or his breath rush out. Or his knees almost buckle. And maybe it wasn't the lingerie as much as the body inside. Her breasts were small but perfect, offered up like two scoops of vanilla ice cream in a bowl of purple velvet. Her torso, encased in velvet and crisscrossed ribbon, curved down to a small waist before flaring out over shapely hips. Silver binding lined the scalloped edges like a curtain framing the thin strip of hair a shade darker than the golden waves that fell around Olivia's face. He allowed his eyes a long moment of worship before he lifted his gaze.

"So what do you think?" she said in that breathless voice that made him want to devour her.

He pushed away from the door, hoping his knees would hold. "I think we need to up our order." He reached out and lifted an end of the ribbon, rubbing it between his fingers. "What's the population of men in the world?"

"A couple billion, but women are our buyers."

"Believe me, men are going to buy this." He took the end of the ribbon and brushed it over the top of one breast, then dipped into the cleavage before stroking the other breast. He went back and forth until her eyes closed and she swayed on her heels. Then he dropped the ribbon and scooped out her breasts. He gently squeezed and watched with heavy lids as her deep rose-colored nipples puckered up like twin sets of lips. Unable to resist the invitation, he lowered his head and kissed first one and then the other.

Olivia's head lolled back, and her hands grasped his shoulders as if she were falling. He knew how she felt. He felt as if he were falling—free-falling. And while the thrill was like nothing he'd ever experienced, he couldn't help but be concerned about the landing. But not enough to release what he held in his hands. Or what he wanted to hold.

While he deepened his nipple-kisses, his hand slipped down her cinched waist, over the crossed ribbon, to the strip of her hair. He traced the plump seam with one finger before dipping into the heat beneath. Lifting his mouth from her breast, he kissed his way up her arched neck as his finger traveled her hot, moist folds. Then, unable to resist the temptation a moment longer, he slid his finger inside, where she was wet and slick and more velvety than the material of the corset.

Her breath caught and held as he worked his thumb over her clitoris and slowly thrust his finger inside. When she was whimpering, he added another finger. Then one more. Her hands tightened into fists on his shirt, and she tugged as if demanding release. He flicked his thumb faster until her body tightened, including the muscles around his fingers. The only sound she made when she hit orgasm was a startled puff of air. He waited for her to sag against him before he picked her up in his arms and carried her to the desk. He set her on the edge. Then, with one swipe, cleared it off.

He expected her to comment; instead she remained silent—the only sound her labored breathing. She watched with hooded eyes as he slipped off his shoes and unbuttoned his shirt. When he dropped the shirt to the floor and reached for his belt buckle, he realized that he'd never stripped for a woman before. They usually stripped him. It was exciting and a little disconcerting. He'd never cared how a woman viewed his body. But damned if he didn't care now. And when he was completely naked, with the condom he'd taken from his wallet in hand, he was surprised how much he cared.

Deacon stood before her like a green kid with a fragile ego, waiting for one word of praise.

He didn't get it.

CHAPTER SEVENTEEN

Olivia was struck speechless. She had seen Deacon's naked body before, but both times had been too brief for her to truly appreciate the splendor. His shoulders were broad. His biceps bunched. And his chest defined and sprinkled with dark hair. Hair that bisected a hard, flat stomach and ended in a display of virile manhood that left Olivia more breathless than her tightly laced corset. If she had thought his penis was big the first time she'd seen it, that was nothing compared to how it looked now. This time it was fully erect and boldly jutted from his body. Just looking at it caused wet heat to flood the spot between her legs.

"So have you changed your mind?"

At Deacon's words she glanced up and met his gaze. The uncertainty she saw there surprised her. She'd expected him to be as controlling in bed as he was in life. Instead he seemed hesitant and vulnerable. Which gave her confidence.

She shook her head, then leaned back on the desk and slowly spread her legs. "Have you changed yours?"

A growl came from deep in his chest, and in less than a second he'd stepped between her legs and was kissing her hungrily. He tasted like the richest of coffee—dark, strong, and flavorful—and he affected her the same way. Adrenaline surged as her brain focused on every place he touched.

The heat of his fingers in her hair. The slide of his tongue in her mouth. The strength of his thighs against the inside of hers. But mostly she focused on the brush of his erect penis against her hot center. The nudge of smooth, moist tip had her hips lifting and her legs wrapping around his waist. There was a brief, heavenly breach of her womanhood before he groaned and pulled back.

"Wait, baby," he breathed as he opened the condom. But before he could slip it on, she sat up and took it from him, fisting him in her hand as she slid it over the tip. She stroked his length until he moaned, then guided him home.

With his eyes closed and sweat beading on his forehead, he took his time, easing in inch by stiff inch. But she didn't want restraint. She wanted Deacon unleashed. She wanted him hard. And she wanted him deep. Hooking her heels around his waist, she thrust her hips up and took him whole. Deeply embedded, he flung his head back and gave her exactly what she wanted. His next thrust was hard and deep. As was the one after. And the one after that.

He gripped her hips and took control, and she let him, giving herself more freely than she had ever given herself before. When the orgasm hit, she felt like a bolt of satin being unfurled. She soared. Billowed. Then drifted down in shimmery waves. Above her, Deacon blurred, and the last thing she remembered before she lost consciousness was his passion-filled eyes.

She blinked awake to find the passion replaced with concern as he tapped her cheek with his hand.

"Breathe, Livy, breathe."

She tried to obey, but couldn't. There was no oxygen left in the air. Just Deacon. Sexy, disheveled Deacon. She smiled and closed her eyes, but then opened them again when he jerked her to a sitting position.

"Damn it, Olivia! How the hell do you get this thing off?" He fumbled with the ribbon on the corset. Finally he gave up, jerked open the top drawer of the desk, pulled out a pair of scissors, and carefully, but efficiently, snipped it off her. The rush of air that filled her lungs was a relief. She sucked in a good three gulps before she noticed the ruined corset.

Thinking about all the work she'd put into it, her heart sank. "I guess it's too late to tell you that the actual laces are in the back?"

"Jesus," he whispered before he pulled her into his arms. "You scared the shit out of me." Okay, so maybe a ruined corset wasn't that big a deal. She smiled against his hard chest as he rubbed her back in soothing circles. "Are you okay? Do I need to call an ambulance?"

"Now that would set the office to gossiping. Not to mention the tabloids." She couldn't help but run her tongue over the nipple that topped his defined pectoral muscle. He tasted a little sweaty and a whole lot sexy. And when his nipple beaded, she took a little nibble.

His hand stopped rubbing. "You should know by now that I don't care what people think."

She did know that. It was just another thing she liked

about him. Once he'd made a decision, he went with it. To hell with what anyone thought. Which pretty much explained what she was doing on his desk wearing nothing but purple high heels. For some reason Deacon had decided that he wanted her. And she had easily fallen in with his plans.

She waited for the guilt and self-condemnation to set in, but all she felt was happy. Happy. Content. And extremely satisfied. A thought struck her, and she stopped brushing her lips over his nipple and pulled back. "Did you come?"

His eyes looked desire-drugged and confused. "What?"

"Before I passed out, did you reach orgasm?"

He blinked. "The way your mind works is truly confusing. Yes, I came. But it would've been even better if the woman who gave me the amazing orgasm hadn't stopped breathing."

The *amazing* made her feel light-headed all over again. "Amazing?"

He grinned. "Damn amazing."

Her gaze lowered. For a man who had just had an orgasm, he looked raring to go again. And just the sight of his hard, smooth length had her not far behind. "Well," she said as she took him in hand, "I guess we could try it again without the corset."

* * *

One of the nice things about having sex with the boss was that you didn't have to worry about getting in trouble for missing work. Although once Olivia was completely sated by three orgasms, she couldn't help bringing work up.

"So have Jason and Kelly discovered anything else odd about the accounts? I would ask Kelly, but she seems to have switched loyalties."

Deacon adjusted a throw pillow under his head and then caught Olivia before the movement caused her to roll off the edge of the narrow couch. "I hate this damned couch. We should've gone to my office."

She giggled and cuddled closer. "I don't know. It worked out kind of nicely just a few moments ago."

"Because you were on top. If your butt had been pressed against this hard-assed cushion, you would've changed your mind. I think I have bruises." He absently kissed the top of her head before answering her question. "Yes, Kelly and Jason found a lot of inconsistencies. As of now it looks like the total is going to be around a million."

Olivia reared up so quickly that she fell off the couch and landed on the floor. "Dollars? Someone has stolen a million dollars from the company?"

"It looks that way." He sat up and held out a hand, but she was too upset to take it.

"So what are we going to do about it?"

"We"—he sent her a pointed look—"aren't going to do anything. I'm going to turn this over to the feds. We aren't talking about small change anymore, Olivia. People who steal that kind of money can do some pretty desperate things. But I think we've found enough that it won't take long for the FBI to pinpoint the culprit."

"Do you think we can get the money back?"

He pulled her onto his lap. "Probably not, but at least we won't be losing any more." He traced a finger up her arm, over her shoulder, and down to a spot right above her nipple. "I like your mole."

"That is not a mole." She slapped at his hand. "According to my mother, it's a beauty mark I've had since I was born."

"I didn't say it wasn't beautiful." He leaned down and kissed it, causing her nipple to tighten beneath the heat of his breath. Were four orgasms in a row even possible? Unfortunately, she didn't get to find out before Kelly tapped on the door.

"Mr. Beaumont?" It sounded like her mouth was pressed against the crack of the door. "Sorry to bother you, but I'm leaving and I wanted to let you know that your father called three times."

Completely ignoring Kelly, he kissed his way up to Olivia's ear, where he did a gentle flick that had her insides melting. Unfortunately, she couldn't ignore the urgent part of Kelly's message.

"Shouldn't you call him back?" she asked breathlessly.

"He probably just needs some money."

"But if he's called three times, it might be an emergency."

He released a groan and moved her from his lap. "Fine, but remember where I was." He rolled to his feet and went in search of his cell phone, calling to Kelly on his way past the door. "Thanks, Kelly! Have a good night."

There was a pause, followed by a giggle. "You too."

Olivia blushed and covered her face with her hands. Great. She had just gotten over the stigma that came with being the boss's daughter. If word got out about this, everyone in the office would think that she was now trying to sleep her way into the new boss's good graces.

"What did you need, Dad?" Deacon sat down in the chair behind the desk as if he weren't naked...and completely hot. When he noticed her looking at him, he smiled and winked. The smile dropped a second later.

"Yes, I'll send you some money." He glanced at Olivia. "No, not yet." His scowl deepened. "How would Francesca know about that?"

Olivia felt her spine stiffen as Deacon swiveled the chair around and continued in a hushed voice that she couldn't hear—no matter how much she strained to do so. Was this the same Francesca who had repeatedly texted him? Again the image of a beautiful Italian woman dressed in a low-cut peasant blouse that displayed her plentiful breasts popped into Olivia's head. But this time the woman wasn't squishing grapes as much as feeding them to Deacon. Compared to a lush, bodacious Italian, Olivia felt like pale, flat-chested chopped liver. Stupid chopped liver because she'd believed Deacon when he'd said that he didn't have a girlfriend.

Of course he had a girlfriend. How could you not have a girlfriend when you looked like he did? And when your father was the biggest womanizer in Louisiana? He probably didn't have just one girlfriend. He probably had an entire harem. Suddenly Olivia felt like she wanted to throw up. Instead she put on her business face and searched for her clothes. As she drew nearer to the desk, she could hear more of the conversation.

"Look, I need to go. I'll talk to you tomorrow after I get into town."

Deacon was leaving? The news was almost as bad as finding out that he had a girlfriend. She'd known that he wasn't planning on staying in San Francisco forever. But she had thought he would stay until the collections were complete. Instead he was waltzing out as quickly as he'd waltzed in. And had she thought that he was going to stay indefinitely? Yes. That's exactly what she'd started to think. Or at least long enough that desk sex wouldn't make her feel like a sleazy slut.

She located her shirt crushed under a design book and stapler and shook it out with a snap just as Deacon hung up and swiveled back around. His gaze wandered over her, and his eyes turned steamy.

"Come here," he said in a husky voice that made her want to drop the shirt and walk straight into his arms. The feeling fizzled when the image of his grape-stomping girlfriend popped into her head. No doubt Francesca followed every order, but Olivia wasn't going to—at least not anymore. She really hated the feeling of disappointment that welled up inside of her.

"I need to get back to work." Since he'd destroyed her corset, she pulled on her shirt without undergarments.

"At six o'clock in the evening?"

"I like working late. So you're leaving?" She wanted to sound nonchalant, but instead she sounded bitchy and panicked. And she was bitchy and panicked. Bitchy because she felt like a cheap slut, and panicked because the company was about to become her sole responsibility again.

The leather chair creaked as he leaned back, completely unconcerned with his nakedness as he glanced at his watch. "Actually, I was planning on leaving this evening. But since I missed the flight, I'll have to see if I can reschedule for the morning."

Biting back the words she wanted to fling at him, she quickly buttoned her shirt, and in her haste she did it all wrong. There was a good six-inch disparity between one side and the other. Before she could fix things, the leather squeaked and suddenly Deacon stood in front of her.

"You want to tell me what happened in the last few seconds to have you in such a fluster?" Brushing her hands away, he unbuttoned her shirt and buttoned it correctly. The man was like a space heater, his hot fingers branding her bare skin.

"Nothing happened," she said as she tried to keep her gaze off his nakedness. It wasn't easy when his naked chest seemed to fill her entire vision. She would've looked down at her toes, but something else blocked that view. So she turned her head and looked out the window. "I just need to get back to work."

He turned her chin with his finger and tipped it up. There was a sparkle of humor in his eyes that really annoyed her. "I'm going to make a guess and say that you heard the name Francesca and assumed the worst."

"I wasn't thinking any such thing," she lied through her teeth. "It makes no difference to me if you have some Italian girlfriend at home." She pulled away from his heated finger. "But don't expect the same from me. I'm an adult woman with her own mind who understands that what happened here was nothing more than an office fling—"

Her words were cut short by a deep, wet kiss that brought her to her toes and had her arms looping around his neck. When she was thoroughly dazed, he pulled back and pinned her with his laser gaze.

"Let's get something perfectly straight. I don't do flings—office or otherwise. If I want to be with a woman, I want to be with her for more than just one night—or one really amazing hour on a desk. And I want to be with her exclusively." He released his breath, and his eyes softened. "Now I understand that getting naked with someone and sharing what we did can make a person feel a little insecure. After the comment you just made, I'm feeling that way myself. So if you'd like to revise your statement, I'm listening."

It was pathetic how much she wanted to believe him. "So why are you leaving?"

"I have a business." For a second he looked almost embarrassed. "It's just a small development company, but I'm building these condos and I need to get my foreman started on them while I'm working here."

"So you're coming back?"

A smile bloomed on his face. "What happened to the woman who couldn't get rid of me fast enough?"

Relief welled, along with a feeling that was almost giddy. Which was probably why she let her guard down and told the truth. "Maybe she finally figured out that she needs you."

"To save French Kiss?"

That wasn't the only reason, but Olivia wasn't willing to examine the other reason too closely. "Among other things," she said. Standing on her tiptoes, she trailed kisses over his chin that was already dark with stubble, but before she reached his sweet mouth, he pulled away, his eyes serious.

"I don't know if I can save French Kiss, Livy."

This vulnerable side of Deacon made her want to kiss him even more. "I do. And so does everyone else in the company."

"I find that hard to believe. Nobody likes the boss."

She smiled. "I didn't say that they liked you. I said that they believed in you—something they never did with me."

"Maybe you didn't give them a chance."

She shook her head. "Maybe I'm not a good boss." She

paused as she remembered Grayson's sketch of her working on the corset, and a realization hit. "But I am a good designer. And it just took the Beaumont brothers to inspire me."

He effortlessly picked her up in his arms and carried her to the desk. "If that corset is an example, you're not a good designer, you're a great designer. And as far as you're concerned, it's not the Beaumont brothers. It's the Beaumont brother. From now on, I want to be the only one who gives you inspiration, Livy. Got that?"

She did.

CHAPTER EIGHTEEN

The lakeside property was as beautiful as Deacon remembered. Pines and cedars grew thick around the perimeter of the large lake, bordering the deep-blue summer sky with their dark, craggy edges and filling the air with the fresh scent of evergreens.

The area he'd planned for the condos had been surveyed and sectioned off, and the heavy equipment sat in the clearing waiting to start excavation. This had been his dream. Something he obsessed about for years. Now he had another obsession. And it had nothing to do with building condos and making his first million. It had to do with a petite blonde with a wild side that set his hair on fire—something he should've figured out the first time she'd shown him her panties. And maybe deep down he had known. Maybe that was why he hadn't been able to take her offer and run.

They had spent the night together. With his brothers at her house, he had taken her back to his hotel room, where they had explored her wild side…and his. He had missed his flight again. Something that Olivia had found quite amusing. But when he'd grumbled over it, she'd picked up the phone and made a call. Two hours later he'd been on French Kiss's private jet—a slick silver plane with an embarrassing pair of purple lips on the tail.

The plane was now waiting at a small airfield for him to conclude his business. He had planned to come back and get the ball rolling—meet with the foreman, set up a timetable. Instead he stood there like the new kid on the first day of school. He felt disoriented and out of place, like he'd stepped into someone else's life. Which was crazy. Louisiana was his home. He and his brothers had gone duck hunting in these woods and fishing in this very lake with their father.

Perhaps because he had grown up in the bayou, Donny John had never liked to spend much time there. Instead he had brought his sons here to the lake, a good two hours from their home, and taught them how to bait a hook and to wait patiently for the second nibble before they yanked the rod. When they had caught their limit, they'd return to camp, where Deacon's mother would be waiting to fry up their catch. Then they would gather around the campfire and toast marshmallows while his mother told ghost stories that were more funny than scary. The memories were some of the happiest Deacon had.

A shriek of girlish giggles had him turning from the lake and looking at the path that led into the trees. Curious, he followed the sound until he found a clearing and three teenage girls sitting cross-legged in a circle. They appeared to be trying to start a fire with a flint stone and pocketknife. Their efforts were pathetic at best—mostly because they couldn't seem to stop giggling. The giggles died when one looked up and saw Deacon. Her eyes widened, and she swatted each of her friends on the arm. All three looked at him and guiltily jumped to their feet. Each wore shorts and a navy blue T-shirt with the words *Camp Chitimacha* printed on the front. Which pretty much explained what they were doing there.

The real estate broker had informed him that a camp was located on the land, but the previous owner was supposed to have evicted it by now. Which meant it would be up to Deacon. Not that he could evict three young girls.

He nodded at the flint and knife they'd left on the ground next to a pile of sticks. "Trying to start a fire?" When they exchanged fearful glances, he introduced himself. "I'm Deacon Beaumont. I'm building condos down by the lake."

"So you're the jerk who's closing down the camp?" the tall, skinny girl asked.

There was a moment when all three pairs of eyes narrowed on him when Deacon thought about backpedaling and lying through his teeth. Instead he nodded. "I am."

"But it's not fair," the redhead said. "We've been coming to Camp Chitimacha for the last four years and now you're just going to tear down the camp cabins? Where are we going to go next year?"

The short, plump teenager spoke up. "I'm going to fat camp. My mom already said." She glared at Deacon and mumbled something under her breath that sounded a lot like *butthole*.

Realizing that things were about to get ugly, Deacon took a few steps back. "I'll just let you girls get back to building your fire. But you might want to make a tinder nest for the spark to catch."

"Thanks for the tip," the plump girl said belligerently, but the tall, skinny girl had more common sense.

"You know how to start a fire?" she asked.

"Emily!" her plump friend snapped at her.

Emily shrugged. "It's not like we're going to keep him from tearing down the cabins, Izzy. And if he can build us a fire so we beat the Tiger Lilies, then I don't see why we shouldn't let him. They've stomped us every summer for the last four years, and I'm getting tired of hearing Chelsea Watts brag about it." She looked at the redhead. "What do you think, Megan?"

Megan studied Deacon for a long moment. "You sure you can do it? It's not as easy as it looks."

Deacon grinned. "Of course I can do it. I spent every summer camping here with my family. And fire-starting was my specialty." He rubbed his hands together. "In no time at all, you girls are going to be toasting marsh-mallows and enjoying s'mores."

Unfortunately, "no time at all" turned into "much longer than he'd expected." Sweat rolled off his temples and the muscles in his forearm ached from repeatedly flicking the flint against the steel blade of the pocketknife. When a spark finally caught the bark he'd formed into a nest, he was too out of breath to blow on it, so it quickly fizzled. But he refused to give up. Especially since the teenage girls had already lost faith in him. Emily picked at the polish on her big toe, while Megan drew in the dirt. Only Izzy continued to watch with a satisfied, know-it-all smile.

Finally a spark caught, and he leaned down and blew until a flame leaped to life. "Get the kindling!" he yelled. The girls quickly handed him the twigs they'd collected, and soon they had a small fire going.

"We did it!" Izzy did a couple of celebratory dance moves. "We have fire!"

Her friends joined her, and pretty soon all three girls were dancing around Deacon as he smiled with a deep sense of accomplishment. Maybe one day he'd teach his own daughters how to start a fire. The thought surprised him. Since he'd spent most of his life taking care of his family, the idea of kids and more responsibility hadn't been appealing. But suddenly his mind was filled with images of him camping with a couple of cute little girls.

Had Olivia ever gone camping? Somehow he doubted it. She had been too wrapped up in French Kiss and earning Michael's love. The thought saddened him. He hadn't had the best of lives. He had lost his mother at an early age and had worked hard to keep food on the table. But he'd had fun in between the hard work—especially the summers spent here at the lake.

A hand waved in front of his face.

"Hey, are you okay?" Izzy asked. "You look kinda dazed out and sad."

He blinked away the images. "Yeah, I'm good. Now let's get some wood so that fire doesn't go out."

After tending the fire, he had the girls line it with rocks.

"You have to go," Emily said as she placed the last rock in the circle. "Mandy, the camp counselor, will be coming back soon to check our progress. And if she finds you here, we won't win the fire-starter award."

He wasn't exactly thrilled to leave a bunch of girls and a fire unattended, but he figured he'd check on them once he met with his project manager. So after instructing the girls on how to properly put out a fire, he headed to the work site.

On the way down, Deacon enjoyed the view of the

crystal-blue lake and deep-green forest. Or at least he did until his gaze landed on the earthmover and backhoes that sat in the clearing. They seemed as out of place in the beautiful setting as three-story condos would be. The thought came out of nowhere, but he realized it was true. No matter how good a job he did, the buildings would still stand out like a man-made sore thumb in this God-made beautiful setting.

The thought stuck with him as he waited for his project manager, and settled into a hard knot of discontentment. To ease the uncomfortable feeling, he picked up a rock and tried to skip it across the lake. But his rock-skipping was as rusty as his fire-starting. The rock disappeared into the water with a loud *pluck*. It took a few more tries before he got it right.

"Impressive."

He turned to find the project manager getting out of a dually truck. Cory Davis had gone to school with Nash. He was a good guy with a strong work ethic, which was why Deacon had hired him.

"Hey, man." Deacon shook his hand. "Thanks for meeting me out here on such short notice."

"No problem. So as you can see, the equipment is here, and I planned on breaking ground on Monday. Is that okay with you?"

A few hours ago that would've been more than okay. But now Deacon wasn't so sure. Instead of answering, he picked up another rock and tossed it. "So have you ever been to the camp out here?"

"Yeah. My brother's kids have gone to it the last couple years. And I came out once for family day." He picked up a rock and threw it. It skipped twice as far as Deacon's. Which had Deacon grabbing another rock.

"Is it a good camp?" he asked.

"It appears to be, but whoever built the cabins could've taken a course in carpentry. They can't be more than ten years old, and they already need new roofs. But since we're going to be tearing them down anyway, I guess it doesn't matter."

Deacon chucked the rock as far as he could, but it still didn't go as far as Cory's had. Then he remembered what his mother had taught him: rock-skipping had nothing to do with strength and everything to do with technique. He picked up another rock and tossed it—this time letting the rock easily sail from his fingers rather than forcing it. It skipped past Cory's spot and then disappeared into the darkness of the water. Just as so many memories of his mother had disappeared from Deacon's life. And suddenly he couldn't stand the thought of one more disappearing.

"So do you want me to start Monday?" Cory asked.

He turned to Cory. "I don't want you to start at all."

Cory looked confused. "Look, Deke, if you're worried about moving the camp, you don't have to be. The camp could stay right where it is."

"Yeah, but what good is a camp if there's a bunch of condos blocking your view?"

Cory laughed. "You're sounding a little like Nash. He's the one who's always looking out for the underdog. I thought you were more about making money."

It was true. Or at least it had been. Now he couldn't stop thinking about the young girls missing out on their camping summers. Or the thought of his own daughters coming here to swim and fish and...dance around fires.

"People change," he said.

Cory studied him for a second. "Yeah, I guess they do. So you want me to have the equipment picked up?"

"Yes, bill me for the cost. And I'd like you to do another job for me as soon as I get my finances settled."

"More condos?"

Deacon grinned. "I was thinking about fixing some cabins."

Cory lifted his eyebrows. "And how is that going to make you money, Deke?"

"Haven't you heard that money isn't everything?"

Cory laughed. "Yeah, I've heard that. But never from Deacon Beaumont."

*   *   *

After Cory left, Deacon hiked up to check on the girls. He was actually disappointed to find them gone. The fire was out, properly doused with water and covered with dirt. He checked for any live embers before he headed to his rental car. He wanted to get back to San Francisco and Olivia, but he'd never believed in putting off until tomorrow what you could do today. Now that he'd decided to scrap the condo project, he needed to talk with Francesca.

Francesca came from old money, and her house reflected that. Built in the early eighteen hundreds by a French ancestor, the plantation-style had towering columns and wide verandas. At one time Deacon had been impressed by the grandeur of the house. Now it just looked old. It even smelled old. Once he was directed into the front sitting room by the maid, he couldn't help noticing the musty scent that seemed to come from the dark rugs and antique furniture.

He had been in the room before on two separate occasions—once to present his proposal for the condos and ask for money and once to escort Francesca to one of her charity events—and both times he'd felt as uncomfortable as he did now. Not wanting to sit, he walked to the fireplace and looked at the pictures on the mantel. Most were of Francesca. Which wasn't surprising. The woman had an ego the size of Louisiana. But a few were of a dark-haired man close to Deacon's age. Obviously Deacon wasn't the first younger man Francesca had been interested in.

Moving over to the bookcase, he browsed the fiction titles until he came to a high school yearbook. Since she had gone to high school with Donny John and Michael, curiosity had Deacon pulling it out. It was surprising how much Donny's senior picture looked like Nash—his smile was bright and his eyes mischievous. Michael's picture, on the other hand, was like looking in the mirror. He didn't smile, but stared at the camera with a solemn intensity.

"I hope you aren't looking at my picture. I never did take good school pictures."

Deacon closed the book and turned to Francesca. She stood in the doorway with a slight smile on her lips. She was an attractive woman, her hair stylish and her makeup not overdone. She had a voluptuous figure, but didn't flaunt it. Her peach blouse and white skirt looked expensive but demure.

"Just looking up my uncle," he said.

Her smile dropped, and she walked over and took the yearbook from him, sliding it back on the shelf. "It never does any good to talk about the past." When she turned, the smile was back. "You shaved." Her finger traced his jawline. "I like it. But I didn't mind the beard either. It was quite a conversation piece among my friends. Speaking of which…I have a dinner tonight at Madeline Crowley's. I'd love for you to come."

He removed the hand that cupped his face. "I'm afraid I can't, Francesca. I need to get back to San Francisco."

She nodded slightly. "I see. And the condos? I won't trust my money to some construction foreman, Deacon. I thought I made that perfectly clear."

"You don't have anything to worry about. Your money won't be entrusted to a construction foreman. In fact, your money won't be used at all."

Her eyes flickered. "So Michael's daughter paid you for the shares?"

Obviously his father had talked too much. Deacon shook his head. "This has nothing to do with Michael's will. I've just decided not to build the condos."

She studied him for a moment as if trying to figure out if he was kidding. When she realized he wasn't, she released a loud, cynical laugh. "So French Kiss lured you away just like it did your uncle? Why am I not surprised? Obviously cheap lingerie is the Beaumonts' weakness."

Deacon smiled. "It would seem that way."

With anger radiating from every pore, she walked to the door and called to her maid. "Sadie, would you show Mr. Beaumont out? Our business is concluded." As he walked past, she added, "I'd be careful putting all my eggs in one basket, Deacon. From what I hear, French Kiss isn't going to be around very long."

"Then you heard wrong," Deacon tossed over his shoulder as he walked out the door.

CHAPTER NINETEEN

hat are you looking at, Cuz?" Nash asked.

Olivia continued to peer out the kitchen window. "Did you sweep my driveway?"

"No, but I'll be happy to do it once I finish the omelets."

She turned and looked at Nash, who stood at the stove flipping the fluffy yellow eggs with a spatula. In the last two days, he'd become Olivia's shadow. Almost like he was under strict orders not to let her out of his sight. And she didn't doubt for a second that he was. But if Deacon was so worried about her, then why hadn't he called?

"Some guy in a trench coat did it."

Olivia glanced at Grayson, who sat at the breakfast bar, spooning Cap'n Crunch cereal into his mouth. In the last week, he'd gotten more comfortable around Olivia and wasn't quite as soft-spoken or shy.

"You saw him?" she asked.

"Yeah, I caught him after I'd beaten Nash like a drum."

"You did not beat me like a drum." Nash turned from the stove and pointed the spatula at Grayson. "The only reason you got back to the house first was because I slowed down to talk with that cute jogger."

Grayson shrugged and spoke around a mouthful of cereal. "Doesn't matter how, it only matters that I got back here first. So who is the guy, Olivia? The trench coat is more than a little creepy, but he has one righteous beard."

Still stunned by Grayson's revelation, it took her a moment to answer. "He sells lemon juicers to the tourists, but I don't know his name. Nor why he would put out my trash, plant flowers in my garden, and sweep my driveway."

Nash set a plate holding an omelet in front of her. "And you've never met the guy?"

"Not that I know of. In fact when he sees me, he never says a word."

The hardness that entered Nash's eyes took Olivia by surprise. Obviously the easygoing Beaumont had another side.

"The next time you see him, I want you to call me," he said.

"I really think he's harmless, Nash."

"Maybe, but I don't want you taking the chance." His cell phone pinged, and he took it out of his pocket and read the text before quickly texting a reply.

Trying to act nonchalant, she took a bite of her omelet. "So I guess that was Deacon."

Nash put the phone back in his pocket. "Yes, it's hard to get away from Controlling Deacon."

Unless you've had sex with him. Then it isn't hard at all. Two days, almost forty-eight hours, and she hadn't heard a word from him. Talk about feeling insecure. And annoyed. Very, very annoyed.

"So I guess his business took him longer than he thought," she said.

Nash went back to cooking. "There were a few loose ends that needed tying up."

"With his company? Or Francesca?" She had no business bringing Francesca up, especially when Deacon had assured her that the woman wasn't his girlfriend. But she couldn't seem to help herself, and the reactions from both men only added to her jealousy. Nash's eyes widened, while Grayson laughed.

"I'm sure Francesca would love to be tied up with Deke," he said. "She might act like her loaning him money is only business, but we all know that she expects more than interest in return."

Nash reached out and cuffed his brother in the back of the head. "Shut up, Gray."

"Hey!" Grayson glared at Nash. "What's your problem?"

"My problem is that you don't know when to keep your mouth shut. First you can't talk to women, and then you say too much."

"What difference does it make if Olivia knows about Francesca?" Grayson paused. "Unless..." He glanced at Olivia, and she couldn't help blushing. His eyes widened before he released a puff of air. "Well, shit." He ran a hand over his smooth jaw. "I didn't realize it was serious."

"It's not," she said in a rush. "We're just...we just work together." She didn't have a clue why tears filled her eyes.

Seeing them, Nash nodded at Grayson. "Why don't you go outside and see if you can find the trench coat guy? I'd like to have a few words with him."

Grayson's concerned eyes remained on Olivia as he got up. "Sure."

Once he was gone, Nash took his vacated chair. "So it's worse than I thought."

She hadn't thought it was that bad until Grayson placed the image of Deacon tying up Francesca in her head. Now she felt like she might be sick. She pushed away the omelet.

Nash swiveled her barstool toward him. Up close he was just as good-looking as any top male model. Maybe even more so. But Olivia discovered that while she could appreciate his good looks, she wasn't attracted to them. She liked her men a little more bossy and intense.

"You need to know something, Olivia," he said. "We Beaumonts have a weakness for women. And as much as we might want to ignore the gene our daddy gave us, we can't help giving in to our need to paint...seduce...or save any female within a mile radius. And more times than not, this weakness leads to a broken heart."

"Are you worried that I'm going to break your brother's heart, Nash?"

His eyes turned soft. "No, Olivia. I'm worried he's going to break yours."

Since she couldn't talk around the lump in her throat, she just sat there staring at her clasped hands in her lap. Nash had brought everything into perspective. She hadn't had sex with some random guy from the office. She'd had sex with a Beaumont. And after being around them, she knew they were different from most men. They *were* heartbreakers. Men whom women should steer clear of if they had any brains. Obviously Olivia had none. And now it was too late. Her heart might not be broken, but after two days without hearing from Deacon, it definitely felt bruised.

"I'm not saying that Deacon would intentionally hurt you, Olivia," Nash continued. "He's a good man. I'm just saying that you should take things slow."

She had to wonder if having sex on a desk was taking things slow.

"That bird's back," Nash said. "If you have a gun, I could take care of him for you. I'm not as good of a shot as Deacon, but from this distance, I'm pretty confident."

"I'm not. You couldn't hit the broadside of a barn at ten paces."

The smooth Southern drawl had Olivia's heart doing a somersault in her chest. She glanced at the doorway to find Deacon standing there, looking extremely sexy in faded jeans and a white button-up shirt. He gave her a lazy smile, the kind that started slow and unfurled into something hot and primal. It made her feel primal—as if she wanted to pounce and devour him. Instead she took an uneven breath and stated the obvious. "You're back."

The smile grew, displaying a dimple in one cheek. Deacon had a dimple? It figured. "I'm back," he said. His gaze sizzled over her pink suit to the toes of her crossed purple heels before moving back to her face. "You're headed to work?"

After wiping her mouth with a napkin, she got up and smoothed down her skirt. "I was going to catch the trolley."

Without taking his eyes off her, Deacon took the keys out of his pocket and tossed them at Nash. "You and Gray can take the rental car."

"I'd rather take the Porsche," Nash said.

"I'm sure you would." Deacon continued to stare into her eyes. "But it's not happening. Now get Gray's butt in gear and get to French Kiss and keep an eye on things."

"It's Saturday."

"Which is a perfect time to catch someone doing something they're not supposed to be doing."

"And talking about doing something you're not supposed to," Nash said dryly, "where will you be, big brother?"

"Olivia and I are going out of town to do some research."

Nash stepped closer, and the hard look returned. "I'm not liking this, Deacon. She's in over her head."

"What is all zee commotion?" Babette stood at the top of the stairs in a pair of ugly poodle pajamas. "Can't a woman sleep in on a Saturday morning?"

Without a word to his brother or Babette, Deacon took Olivia's hand and led her down the stairs to her bedroom on the second level. She had made up her mind to take Nash's advice. Unfortunately, Deacon had other plans. Within two seconds flat, he had the door closed and Olivia in his arms. The kiss was hot and deep, and almost made up for the lack of communication.

Almost.

Olivia pulled back. "Why didn't you call?"

He looked surprised by the question. "I thought you didn't want a stalker for a boyfriend. So I figured I'd give you some time to consider the question."

"The question?"

His brow knotted. "Okay, what happened while I was gone? Because when I left, I felt like you and I were on the same page. But if something's changed..."

"What question?"

He studied her for a moment before speaking. "Do you want to be my woman, Olivia Harrington?"

Nash's warning dissolved beneath the hard *ka-whack* of her heart. Trying to control her budding happiness, she adjusted the collar of his shirt. "Oh. That question." She smiled. "I guess so."

He tipped up her chin. "You guess so?"

A smile spread over her face. "Okay, yes. I'll be your woman."

The growl he gave was caveman possessive. He picked her up and spun her around until she giggled. Then he gave her another melting kiss before setting her on her feet. "You'll need to pack an overnight bag."

"An overnight bag? Where are we going?"

"That's for me to know, and you to find out." He swatted her on the bottom. "Now hurry up, woman. We're on a schedule. Because in business and pleasure, timing is everything."

This wasn't taking things slow. This was taking things fast and furious. But as Olivia packed, she discovered she didn't care. She wanted to be with Deacon, and if that meant she'd have to deal with a broken heart later, then so be it.

Deacon drove the way he did everything—fast, capably, and with a focus that Olivia envied. Not that she had trouble focusing. When Deacon was near, he became the center of her universe. She spent the ride completely captivated by the man in the aviators next to her. He'd put the top down, and the wind ruffled his thick, dark hair. There were crinkled lines at the corners of his eyes, and since he wasn't much of a laugher, she figured they had come from all that eye-narrowing. It looked like he had forgotten to shave that morning because dark stubble covered his angular jaw and looked extremely sexy.

"What's going through that head of yours?" he asked, as he took a corner like a Formula One racer.

She studied his hand on the gearshift, his forearm muscles flexing as he shifted to a higher gear. "I'm wondering why you're being so secretive," she said. "Especially if we're just scoping out some settings for catalog photo shoots."

He glanced over. "You aren't very patient, are you? I bet you were one of those kids who tried to find their Christmas presents before their parents even got them wrapped."

"My parents didn't wrap presents. They had them wrapped." She grinned wickedly. "Although I did unwrap a few one year. I thought I'd rewrapped them perfectly, but my dad figured it out."

"Michael?"

She shook her head. "My biological father." She glanced out the window, searching for another topic of conversation. Before she could find one, Deacon reached out and took her hand, interlocking his fingers with hers.

"So tell me about your dad."

She shrugged. "There's nothing much to tell. He and my mom got a divorce when I was nine, and he disappeared from my life."

"Disappeared? You mean you haven't seen him since you were nine?"

She shook her head. "He had some kind of a mental breakdown and took off for parts unknown. If you know my mother, it's understandable. If it hadn't been for Michael, I would've run for the hills after I graduated from high school."

Deacon let go of her hand to downshift. Once he had, he took her again and stared out the windshield as if in deep thought. No doubt worried about the genes she'd inherited.

"I was kidding," she said. "I'm not much of a runner."

He glanced over at her. "It's not understandable, Olivia. I don't care what your mother did. That doesn't excuse your father from leaving his only daughter and never once trying to get in touch with her. Donny John wasn't the best dad, but at least he stuck around. And if he hadn't, I would've been pissed."

"What good would that do? Getting mad wouldn't have brought him back."

"No, but sometimes it just feels good to let off some steam. To confront the injustices of the world and yell out your anger about them. Or is keeping your emotions in check something else my uncle taught you?"

"We all can't be like you, Deacon, someone who has no trouble letting people know exactly how you feel."

"And why not? If you let someone know how you feel, then there are no surprises—everything's out on the table." He pulled into a parking lot, and she realized they were at the private airport where they kept French Kiss's jet. He drove straight onto the tarmac, where a man was waiting to open Olivia's door. He helped her out with a smile and then rounded the car to accept the keys from Deacon.

"When can we expect you back, sir?" he asked as Deacon discreetly handed him a tip.

"Not until Tuesday night."

"Tuesday?" Olivia said. "I can't be gone that long! I have too much to do to get the collections ready for the fashion show."

"I spoke with Samuel." Deacon handed their bags to another man, this one wearing a polo shirt. "He assured me that he has everything under control." He took her arm and led her up the stairs of the plane.

Olivia started to argue the point, but was stopped by a

smiling flight attendant in a purple skirt, starched white blouse, and neck scarf in a purple kiss print.

"Welcome aboard." She handed them each a flute of champagne before leading them into the luxurious cabin.

Olivia had been in the plane numerous times since Michael had purchased it. So she barely noticed the fine leather seats, plush carpet, or wood-grain paneling. She was too distracted by being gone so long from work. But she waited until they were seated in facing seats and the attendant had left before voicing her concerns.

"Deacon, I really have a lot that I need to get done before—"

The captain's voice came over the speaker. "Mr. Beaumont and Ms. Harrington, I'm Captain Franks. If you'll fasten your seat belts, we'll be on our way. The flight to New York will take approximately seven hours. We'll refuel, and given any unforeseen weather, we should be in Paris by morning."

Olivia stared at Deacon. "Paris? We're going to Paris?"

He smiled. "Where else would I take French Kiss's new designer?"

CHAPTER TWENTY

*P*aris.

It was like a dream come true, and Olivia couldn't keep the tears from rolling down her cheeks.

Deacon leaned in and took her hands. "I'm going to make a guess here and say that you're crying because you're happy. If that's not the case, tell me now—before the captain gets this bird in the air."

She sniffed. "It's just that I've wanted to go to Paris ever since Michael told me the story of walking along the Seine."

"Then why didn't you, Livy? You had the money and a private jet at your disposal."

She shrugged. "I don't know. I guess because I was always so busy with French Kiss."

"I think *consumed* is a better word. With French Kiss and Michael." He gently squeezed her hands. "I know you idolized him, Olivia. To a young girl, he must've seemed like a god. But, like all men, he had his faults. And one of them was wanting you to be as consumed with French Kiss as he was—so consumed that you forgot that there is an entire world out there that has nothing to do with sales reports and bottom lines."

Uncomfortable beneath his intense gaze, Olivia turned to the window. The plane taxied down the runway, gaining speed until the scenery became a blur, then lifted and fought against gravity and wind currents until it reached the right elevation and was able to level out. Olivia felt the same way. She felt like she had spent her entire life fighting against unknown forces just to find that space where she could finally enjoy the ride. She was brought out of her thoughts by the caress of Deacon's thumb on her knuckles. She turned from the deep blue of the skies to the deep purplish blue of Deacon's eyes. And suddenly everything inside her leveled out.

"So tell me, Ms. Harrington," he said with a slight tipping of his lips. "What else do you want besides a trip to Paris?"

It was a good question. At one time she could've easily answered it: Her father's return. Michael's love. French Kiss's success. But now her mind seemed empty of want...save for one thing.

Unable to help herself, she leaned across and kissed him. His lips were as hot as the rest of him, and she moistened them with her tongue before hungrily taking advantage of their softness. He made to release the clasp on his seat belt, no doubt so he could take control of the situation, but Olivia pulled back and shook her head.

He sent her a quizzical look, but allowed her to take his hand from the clasp and rest it on the arm of the seat. After unbuckling her belt, she did the same with his other hand, curling his fingers around the soft leather of the arm.

The flight attendant appeared, carrying a bottle of champagne. "Can I get you anything to eat, Mr. Beaumont... Ms. Harrington?"

"Maybe later," Olivia said with a smile. "Right now, Mr. Beaumont and I have some business to discuss."

"Of course." The attendant placed the bottle of champagne in the holder on the minibar. "Just buzz if you need me." She pulled the pocket door closed behind her.

Olivia turned to find Deacon watching her. "Please don't tell me we're going to spend the entire trip talking about business," he said.

"What else would we do?" Slipping off her high heels, she got out of her seat and knelt in front of him. "Now the key to any good business meeting is knowing when to take charge and when to keep your mouth shut." She smiled at him as she spread his legs and moved between them. "This time I'm in charge, Mr. Beaumont. Got it?"

One eyebrow arched, but he kept his mouth shut.

Slowly she slid her hands up his forearms. The muscles beneath flexed, and everything inside her melted like polyester beneath a hot iron. This was a man. She slipped her hands to his knotted biceps. A real, honest-to-goodness man. And for this moment, he was all hers.

She caressed his body beneath the silk of his shirt, her hands gliding over his shoulders and along his collarbone until she reached the open collar. Button by button, she opened the shirt to reveal his hard pectoral muscles and the sprinkle of dark hair between. She kept unbuttoning until she reached his waistband. With a tug she freed his shirt from his jeans.

Deacon watched through half-mast eyelids. He had the longest lashes, a thick fringe that would make any woman green with envy. But once his shirt was open, Olivia didn't spend a lot of time admiring his lashes.

Spreading his shirt wide, she let her gaze wander over his masculine perfection before she leaned in to place a kiss in the hollow of his throat. Beneath her lips she felt the vibration of his groan and smiled. She liked being in charge with Deacon. She kissed her way along his collarbone, then down to one pectoral muscle. He didn't make another sound, but he shifted in the seat, his knees pressing into her sides as if to prod her on. But she took her time, gently kissing all around the tiny nipple before she took it into her mouth. She sucked, and his hips lifted. She rolled his nipple against the roof of her mouth, and his hands white-knuckled the arms of the chair.

"Livy," he groaned.

She ignored his plea and moved lower, along each abdominal muscle to the waistband of his jeans. The fabric was worn enough that she could easily unbutton it with just a twist of her fingers. The zipper was a lot harder. Metal tooth by metal tooth, she inched it down to reveal the hard length of him beneath the stretched cotton of his boxer briefs. She spread the denim and, using only a finger, traced his erection from base to tip.

His hips lifted as far as they could beneath the seat belt. "Livy," he hissed through clenched teeth, "you're killin' me, babe."

A giddy feeling joined the desire that gripped her body, and wanting to make him lose it even more, she slid her hand into the opening of his boxers and freed him. She caressed the smooth skin along the shaft before rubbing a thumb over the moisture on the tip. The sound he released was a mixture of a groan and a moan. She lowered her head and took him into her mouth. But after only three strokes, his hands came off the armrests and tangled in her hair, gently tugging her away. Within seconds he had his seat belt off and Olivia on her feet with her skirt pulled up. When he saw that she didn't have on any underwear, his expression was priceless.

"Thank God," he breathed as he pulled her down to straddle him. After only a minor adjustment, he entered her with a hard thrust that had her moaning much louder than he had. "Shhh." He placed his lips against hers. "We don't want to distract the crew."

The funny part about it was that Olivia didn't care whom they distracted. She wanted Deacon, and she wanted him now. But having sex in a leather airplane seat wasn't as easy as she'd thought it would be. Her knees were pinned between the arms of the seat and Deacon's hips, and she couldn't get the leverage she needed to move. Fortunately, Deacon was through being a follower. With a firm grasp on her thighs, he got to his feet and carried her toward the bedroom at the back of the plane. Unfortunately, just then the plane hit a patch of turbulence that had Deacon stumbling and bumping her into the paneled wall.

"Are you okay?" he asked with concern.

"No, I'm not okay." She grabbed his open shirt and tugged. "Fuck me, Deacon."

His eyes widened for a split second before he did just that. Tightening his hands on the back of her thighs, he pressed her against the wall and thrust hard and deep. The sensations that ricocheted through her body had her breath whooshing out. She sucked it back in when he thrust again. Olivia had never had sex standing up and was surprised by how naughty and excited it made her feel. Hooking her feet at his back, she used the leverage to meet each thrust. When the plane dipped again, it set off the most amazing climax she had ever had. Deacon's followed soon after, his body tightening and then slumping against hers. They rested like that for a moment, his head buried in her hair and hers buried in his shoulder.

When he lifted his head, his eyes sparkled and his dimple winked. "I think I'm going to like having business meetings with you, Livy."

* * *

The fourteen-hour trip gave them plenty of time for numerous business meetings and plenty of sleep in between. Which explained the lack of jet lag when they finally landed in Paris. In fact Olivia just felt buoyant as they passed the Arc de Triomphe in the limo that had picked them up from the airport.

Deacon laughed as she rolled down the glass and stuck her head out into the cool night air. "Hello, Paris!"

It seemed even more of a fairy tale when they arrived at the hotel and were shown to their suite. It was decorated in French provincial blues and gold with chandeliers and a huge balcony off the sitting room. She didn't even wait for Deacon to finish tipping the bellman before she hurried over to the French doors. The sight that greeted her had her covering her mouth with her hand and fighting back tears.

The lights of the Eiffel Tower sparkled right outside the thick glass. And the painting in Michael's office didn't even come close to depicting the breathtaking beauty of the monument. So caught up was she in the sight, Olivia barely noticed when Deacon slipped his arms around her waist.

"Breathtaking," he whispered against her ear.

"It is, isn't it?"

"I wasn't talking about the tower as much as the woman looking at it." He nuzzled her neck and then rested his chin on her head. "But you're right. Pictures don't do it justice, do they?" They stood there for a long, silent moment before Deacon released her and opened up the doors. "Shall we get a better look?"

A table had been set up on the stone balcony. The flickering light of the tapers gleamed off the crystal flutes and fine china settings. While Olivia gaped at the beautifully set table and the backdrop of the lit Eiffel Tower behind it, Deacon walked over and pulled out a chair.

"Mademoiselle."

It was just too much, and Olivia released a squeal and flung herself at Deacon. Surprised, he stumbled back a few steps until he reached the balcony railing.

"I guess you like it."

"Oh, Deacon, I don't like it, I love it!" She kissed his ear, his cheek, and the tip of his nose. "And I love you."

The words just sort of slipped out and hung there, causing both Deacon and Olivia to freeze. She felt her face heat as he pulled back and looked at her. She couldn't help but fidget beneath his intense gaze.

"W-what I meant was…" She searched for an explanation, but before she could find one, Deacon pressed a finger to her lips.

"It's okay, Livy. You don't need to explain anything." He released her and pulled out the chair. "Let's eat."

Since it was so late, the dinner was light. Beneath the domed warming lids were a delicious French onion soup and a platter of crusty bread and cheeses. After her faux pas, Olivia thought the conversation would be stilted. But

Deacon seemed to put the subject behind them as he poured her a glass of Chardonnay.

"So tell me about your childhood, Livy," he said as he handed her the glass.

She didn't know if it was the wine or the breathtaking backdrop, but she did tell him about her childhood. About how wonderful her father had been and how confused she'd felt when he left without a word. She told him about attending private school and how she had always felt like the odd man out because she had to struggle to stay focused. And she told him about French Kiss and how much she loved designing. And when she realized that she was monopolizing the conversation, she started asking Deacon questions about his childhood. He wasn't quite as forthcoming, and she was forced to piece a picture together.

It was of a high-energy little boy and a brokenhearted teen.

"I'm sorry," she said as she reached across the table to take his hand. "It sounds like you adored your mother."

Deacon turned her hand over and stroked the palm with his thumb. "She was easy to adore, even though she wasn't as outgoing as Donny John and Nash. She was more quiet like Grayson." He paused. "I guess a little like me too. But she had this laugh that could just make you smile even if you didn't know what she was laughing at." He shook his head. "My dad said it reminded him of a sick goose. It just reminded me of happiness."

Guilt assailed her, and she pulled her hand away and studied the napkin on her lap. "I'm sorry, Deacon. If I had known about your mother, I never would've let Michael think that you'd…" She let the sentence trail off.

"That I had molested you?" The humor in Deacon's voice had her glancing up. He was grinning wickedly.

Olivia didn't see the humor. "It's not funny, Deacon. If I had spoken up, Michael wouldn't have kicked you out. He would've mended whatever had gone on between him and your father."

His smile died. "No. He wouldn't have done anything of the sort. He was pissed from the first that your mother had invited us to stay, and I have little doubt that he was coming to kick us out when he discovered us in the garden."

"No." She shook her head. "Michael wouldn't have done that. Not after he found out that your mother had passed away."

Deacon studied her for a moment as if he were making some type of decision. Then he tossed his napkin on the table and got to his feet. "Okay, you're right. He would've welcomed us like long-lost relatives." He pulled her into his arms and kissed her so deeply that she felt it all the way down to the marrow of her bones. When he pulled back, he was smiling. "Now what are you going to do to make it up to me?"

They stayed awake until close to two in the morning so she could make it up to him—although it wasn't much of a chore. Deacon could be as tender at lovemaking as he was tough at business. In the morning they had breakfast in bed before heading out to see the sights.

They spent most of their time at the Louvre. Olivia couldn't seem to get her fill of the priceless paintings and sculptures. Her mind worked overtime as she imagined how she could use the different colors and textures of the art in her designs. That evening they had dinner at a little café. The same café that had been in the painting in Michael's office.

"How did you know where to find it?" she asked.

"The name was in the painting," he said absently.

Olivia looked at him, noticing for the first time how intently he was studying the shop across the street. It was a touristy shop that sold souvenirs, but there was something so familiar about the bay window and the purple door—

"Oh my gosh. Do you think that could be the shop that inspired French Kiss?" she asked.

"There's only one way to find out."

The woman working behind the counter of the shop confirmed that it had indeed sold lingerie at one time. She pulled out a picture that was almost identical to Michael's painting. Olivia was thrilled and took numerous pictures of the shop.

"It's just like fate wanted us to find it," she said as she stood in front clicking her phone camera.

Deacon waited for her to finish before he took her hand and led her away from the quaint shop. "Yes," he said. "It must be fate."

CHAPTER TWENTY-ONE

Deacon stared out the French doors of the hotel suite at the Eiffel Tower spearing the predawn sky, and he had to wonder if fate didn't play a much bigger role in life than people thought. Too many twists and turns had taken place for Deacon's life to all be accidental. Michael and his mother meeting here. Michael getting her pregnant. And finally, Deacon becoming partial owner and ending up right back where it had all started.

Olivia thought he'd brought her here to make her happy. And part of him had, but the other part was purely selfish. For him, coming here had been a way to cleanse away the past and move on. But after only a day, he realized that the past was as much a part of you as the present. Everywhere they went he couldn't help thinking about his mom. Had she been as excited as Olivia to be in the city? Had her eyes lit up when she saw the Eiffel Tower for the first time? Had she gasped with amazement when she walked into the Louvre? Had she giggled with sheer happiness as she sat at the café and grown excited when she noticed the quaint little lingerie shop across the street?

The lingerie shop had been in more than one of his mother's photographs. And Deacon had to wonder if she had been the one to bring Michael's attention to the shop that had inspired his multi-billion-dollar company. It seemed likely. His mother had loved pretty things and would've enjoyed browsing through the frilly undergarments.

Thinking of pretty things, Deacon glanced down at Olivia, who slept next to him with one arm and leg sprawled over him possessively. The sight sent a wave of contentment washing over him. No, it was more than contentment. It was something deeper. He felt like he had finally come home. Not to a run-down shack on the Louisiana bayou. Or a trendy condo by a crystal-clear lake. Or a multimillion-dollar mansion on the California coast. His home had become a petite, easily distracted blonde with a pair of green eyes that melted his heart.

He hadn't felt this happy since before his mother died, and he was in no hurry to get back to French Kiss. Or his brothers. Or his country. If Olivia wanted to stay in Paris for the rest of their lives, he would gladly do it for just one of her smiles.

That night on the balcony, he hadn't been ready to echo her words of love. He was now. But he could wait until she was wide awake. Brushing a kiss on the top of her head, he smiled and closed his eyes. He had almost drifted off to sleep when his cell phone rang. He would've ignored it if he hadn't been worried about waking Olivia. She was clearly exhausted and needed the sleep. Carefully removing her arm and leg, he rolled toward the nightstand and answered in a whisper.

"Hello."

"Let me guess," Nash said, "you decided to do the photo shoot of your collection at the library."

"Real funny. Actually I'm in Paris."

There was a slight pause. "Then you'd better get your ass on the plane ASAP 'cause we've got problems."

The tone of his brother's voice had him quickly sitting up on the side of the bed. Olivia moaned and rolled over, her hand brushing his back.

"Mmm, Deacon," she said in a sleepy voice.

He got up and tucked the blanket around her. "I'm right here, my love. Go back to sleep." She sighed contentedly before snuggling down into the pillow. He waited until he was in the sitting room before continuing the conversation.

"What kind of problems?"

"You're starting to piss me off, Deacon," Nash said. "'My love'? You're calling Olivia your love?"

"And what's that to you, Nash?"

"A few weeks ago, I would've said nothing. But I've gotten to know our cousin, and I like her, Deacon. I like her a lot. She's like this wide-eyed kid who needs a keeper." The accurate description made Deacon smile as Nash continued. "And I don't want to see her get hurt."

"I don't want to see that either."

"Then you need to end your relationship now." Nash paused. "Look, I get that you and Olivia are sexually attracted to each other. But don't make it more than that, Deke. Don't make her fall in love with you. Because if you break her heart, I'm going to have to break your face."

Deacon walked to the windows and looked out. Fog had settled, shrouding the lattice iron of the Eiffel Tower like fresh-spun cotton candy. "What if she breaks my heart?"

There was a long pause before Nash spoke. "Are you saying you're falling in love with her? Because if you are, then you need a reality check. Whether it's conscious or subconscious, your infatuation with Olivia has to do with your preoccupation with her stepfather. That's all, Deacon. And if you don't cut it off now, things are not going to end well."

At one time he would've agreed with Nash. But not now. For the first time in his life, he was thinking clearly. He wasn't falling in love with Olivia. He loved her. He loved that she was the worst boss ever, and the best designer. He loved the way she looked in a suit and heels and the way she looked in nothing at all. He loved to make her smile and to watch her eyes light up. He loved how she zoned out, but could focus when it counted. He loved everything about her.

"You're wrong, Nash, but I'm not going to get into it right now. Right now I want to know why you called me. Did you find out who was skimming money?"

"As a matter of fact, we did. I put a trace on Parker's computer and discovered the account where the money is going."

"Parker's personal account, no doubt."

"Actually, no. It was going into a Elsa Sanchez's account in Mexico."

"Who the hell is that?"

"French Kiss's office cleaning lady."

Deacon adjusted the phone to his ear. "The one we scared the other night?"

"The same. It seems she didn't empty the trash as much as go through it for passcodes."

Deacon shook his head. "Well, that's surprising. Did she mention anything about Anastasia?"

"No, but we turned it over to the feds and they plan on questioning her about it."

"Good job, Nash. And now, since it's five o'clock in the morning here, I'd like to go back to sleep." But before Deacon could hang up, Nash stopped him.

"Sorry, big brother, but that's not the only news I have for you. There seems to be a problem with Michael's will."

Deacon released his breath. "Look, we've talked about this before, Nash. You're going to get your money. It just won't be in one lump sum."

"I'm fine with not getting a lump sum. But now it looks like we won't even be getting a small trickle."

"What do you mean?"

"I mean that Uncle Michael's will has been contested."

"Contested? Who would contest it?" He glanced back at the bedroom. "Olivia?"

"No. His illegitimate child."

The words were like a one-two punch in the face. It took Deacon a moment to find his voice. "What illegitimate child?"

"We don't know. The only way we found out about it was through a friend of Jason's. I guess the guy works for some big-time lawyer here in San Francisco. He wouldn't go into detail because I think he knew he was pushing the ethics thing, but he wanted Jason to have the heads-up that Michael's illegitimate kid is going to try to get a piece of the pie."

"A piece or all of it?"

"I don't know. But either way, it can't be good."

"Deacon?"

He turned to see Olivia standing in the doorway. She had tossed on one of his shirts, but left it unbuttoned. And as she walked toward him, the edges played peek-aboo with soft breasts, a flat stomach, and a strip of golden hair.

"Is something wrong?" she asked.

Just the sight of her calmed him, and he smiled as he spoke to Nash. "We'll head back as soon as possible. Until then, try to get as much information as you can." He hung up the phone and placed it on a nearby table. Before he had even turned around, Olivia was in his arms. She held him like she never wanted to let go, her arms wrapped tightly around his waist and her head pressed against his heart.

"I woke, and you were gone."

"I'm sorry." He kissed the top of her head. "Nash called, and I didn't want to wake you."

She peeked up at him. "So it sounds like the vacation is over."

He should've told her then about Nash's phone call and what it could mean to the company, but he couldn't stand the thought of ruining her dream vacation. There would be plenty of time to tell her on the return trip.

Sweeping her up in his arms, he carried her back to the bedroom. "Not yet, it isn't."

* * *

Deacon planned to tell Olivia about the will contest on the flight home, but one thing led to another and they spent the majority of the flight in the bedroom—not just making love, but going over the pictures of their trip and looking at Olivia's new ideas for designs. She seemed so happy that he couldn't burst her bubble. Besides, there was a good chance that Jason's friend had gotten misinformation. And until Deacon had all the details, he decided it was best he keep Olivia in the dark so she wouldn't worry.

Due to the time difference, it was only late afternoon when they landed in San Francisco. They were both jet-lagged, but Deacon knew he couldn't sleep until he'd talked with his brothers. So he dropped Olivia off at her house before heading to French Kiss.

As soon as he arrived at his office, Kelly greeted him at the elevator with a cup of coffee. He sent her a curious look.

"Thank you, but how did you know I was here?"

"I told Denny the security guard to keep a watch out and let me know when you arrived. I figured you'd be jet-lagged and need a little pick-me-up. But don't get used to it. I'm not a waitress." She led the way down the hallway. "Your brothers are waiting in your office with Jason." She glanced at him and blushed. "I mean Mr. Melvin."

He took a sip of coffee and sighed. "So I'm going to assume that you and Jason are getting along better."

Her blush got even brighter. "I guess you could assume that. Is that okay?"

Deacon bit back a smile. "I don't mind interoffice relationships as long as it doesn't interfere with work. In other words, I don't want you two acting like a couple of horny teenagers."

"Why, Mr. Beaumont," she said, "I thought we weren't supposed to use words like *horny* at work." She stopped at the door of his office. "But if it puts your mind at ease, we won't be boinking each other on the desk. Jason isn't into sex as much as sports. He says he won't have sex with me until he sees how I do during football season." She pushed open the door.

His brothers and Jason all looked as tired as he felt. Obviously they had been up all night. Nash slumped in the chair behind the desk with his eyes closed. Grayson sat on the couch, his hair mussed and his eyes red-rimmed as he drew on his sketchpad. And Jason paced in front of the large windows, his tie pulled loose and his top button undone. He was talking on the phone and merely glanced up when Deacon entered, before moving into one corner and going back to his conversation.

As soon as Kelly closed the door, Deacon started firing off questions. "So did you get a name?"

Nash dropped his feet off the desk and slowly got up. "I'm afraid not. Jason's friend got a bad case of ethics and clammed up. But the lawyers at his office just called Jason, so we should have news soon."

They both looked at Jason, who didn't appear to be too happy with his conversation. He kept running a hand through his hair and shaking his head. For once he didn't have a stain on his shirt or his tie. Deacon couldn't help but wonder if Kelly was somehow responsible.

Jason hung up his cell phone. "It's confirmed. Thomas, Bentley, and Thomas have been hired to contest Michael Beaumont's will. They filed the contest this morning and would like to meet with you, your brothers, and your lawyers tomorrow morning to discuss settling out of court."

"And their client."

"All Matthew Thomas would say was that the mother is the one who hired them and she has clout, but all it will take is me calling the courthouse to find out. Once the contest is filed, the information is public."

Deacon nodded. "So what does this mean for the company?"

Jason moved over to the chair in front of the desk and sat down. "That will depend on how legitimate their client's claim is and what the client wants. If Thomas, Bentley, and Thomas are willing to take it on, there must be some pretty good proof. And if that's the case, and it turns out that Michael has a child, the kid could ask for controlling shares of the company. After all, you're only nephews, while he's directly related."

Deacon exchanged looks with his brothers while Jason lifted his phone and dialed. "Let me see what I can get from the courthouse clerk."

While Jason was trying to get information, Deacon walked to the windows. It surprised him how comforting the view of the Golden Gate Bridge and the bay was. His brothers soon joined him, Grayson on one side and Nash on the other.

"What are we going to do if it is Michael's kid?" Grayson asked. "I mean, if it is, doesn't he deserve to own the company?"

Deacon turned on him. "And what about Olivia? She's worked her ass off for this company. She doesn't deserve to lose it to someone who doesn't even know a bustier from a corset."

There was a slight pause before Nash burst out laughing. Deacon scowled at him. "What's so damned funny?"

Nash sobered, but a grin still creased his face. "I guess I was wrong, big brother. I guess you can fall in love. Because only love would have you thinking of someone else when it came to billions of dollars."

Grayson grinned. "He does have a point, Deke."

Before Deacon could reply, Jason spoke. "I've got it." He handed Deacon a piece of paper with a name written on it.

A name that was very familiar.

CHAPTER TWENTY-TWO

Something had happened at French Kiss. Something that had Deacon worried. After the phone call in Paris, Olivia immediately sensed a subtle change in him. But surprisingly, she wasn't concerned. She trusted Deacon to handle the situation, whatever it might be. So rather than question him, she decided to take his mind off it. She had never been much of a seductress, but suddenly she found herself seducing...and loving every minute of it. She enjoyed tempting Deacon. Enjoyed watching his eyes darken and his body tremble with need. Enjoyed feeding that need until it consumed them both.

And she didn't just enjoy the sex. She enjoyed being with him. Sightseeing. Talking. Or lying together in bed. Which was why she couldn't help feeling disappointed when she woke and he wasn't next to her. Sitting up, she blinked the sleep from her eyes and tried to get oriented. She wasn't in a hotel in Paris. Or on French Kiss's private plane. She was in her bedroom. An image of Deacon lifting her out of the Porsche and carrying her through the garage came back to her, and she smiled.

He was probably in the bathroom. Or better yet, in the kitchen making coffee. But when she crawled out of bed and shuffled to the bathroom, he wasn't there. Nor was he in the kitchen or in any other room of the house. And neither was anyone else. No Nash. No Grayson. And no Babette.

Seeing that it wasn't yet eight o'clock on a weekday morning, it didn't seem right. The brothers never went to work before a run and breakfast—usually no earlier than nine o'clock. The thought of their morning run had her stepping out on the balcony and looking up and down the street.

"Good morning, Britney!"

She turned to find Mr. Huckabee sitting on his balcony reading the newspaper. She lifted a hand in greeting. "Good morning."

He got up, and she was relieved to find his dangling parts covered by a hot pink thong. "What do you think?" He held out his hands and turned to display his flabby butt. "Your houseguest gave them to me. And I must admit that they're more comfortable than the rhinestone ones. Doris loved the flash, but those stones irritated the hell out of my hemorrhoids—"

She cut him off before things could get grosser. "Well, they look great, and I've heard that neon is making a comeback."

He turned around and grinned. "Babette said the same thing. Once she came down from her LSD trip, she turned out to be a nice girl. I was sorry to hear she's moving out. Is she going back to Paris?"

Babette wasn't going back to Paris. It seemed she liked

America more than she'd let on, and despite her disastrous line of men's lingerie, she had done very well on Olivia's designs. Even Samuel thought so and had hired her as a full-time seamstress.

"No," she yelled over to Mr. Huckabee, "she's not going back to Paris. She's getting an apartment here in San Francisco."

"Well, I'll miss her."

Olivia would too. At times Babette had been annoying, but like a hyperactive poodle, she had something lovable about her.

"You haven't seen her or my male houseguests this morning, have you?" she asked.

"Babette headed for the trolley this morning. But I haven't seen the boys since yesterday." He moved to the railing. "Now that Babette's leaving, I hope you're not thinking about having a little ménage. Because Doris and I tried that a few times and it never worked out—one person always feels like they got the short end of the stick. Now orgies are a different story. In an orgy there's always plenty of sticks to go around."

She tried to keep the orgy visual out of her brain, but there it was in a tangle of wrinkled limbs and limp body parts. She was relieved when her cell phone rang.

"I'd better get that, Mr. Huckabee," she said before hurrying inside to answer the phone. Deacon had bought her a new phone in Paris, along with a cute little cover with the Eiffel Tower on the back. He said it was to remind her of their trip. But she didn't need a reminder. She would never forget Paris as long as she lived.

"Olivia?" Her mother's voice startled Olivia out of her daydream. "Are you there?"

"Sorry, Mom. I guess I forgot to say hello."

There was an exasperated sigh. "You also forgot to come help me go through Michael's things. That annoying real estate broker wants to show Michael's study, and to be honest, I don't trust him as far as I can throw him."

Olivia realized she had put off the job for as long as she could. "Okay, Mom, I'll head over now."

"Fine, but we have to be done by one. I have a tennis match at the club."

After Olivia got off the phone with her mom, she tried calling Deacon. When he didn't answer his cell phone, she made herself a cup of coffee and headed for the shower. Since Deacon had her car, she called a car service. On the way she tried Deacon again, and when he still didn't answer, she called the office.

"Mr. Beaumont's office."

Olivia rolled her eyes. "Hi, Kelly, it's your other boss, Ms. Harrington."

"Oh, hi! Did you have fun in Paris? Nash told me that Mr. Beaumont took you to look for photo sites. Did you find one?"

"As a matter of fact, we did. I think we're going to shoot the catalog in Paris."

"No shit! Oops, sorry about that—but, I mean, Paris. That is way cool."

Olivia couldn't contain her excitement. "It was amazing. Just amazing. I took pictures and will tell you all about it when I get to the office. And Deacon—I mean Mr. Beaumont and I talked about it and think that you should come to Paris with us when we do the photo shoot."

"OMG! Are you kidding? That would be amaze-balls."

Olivia laughed. "But first we need to focus on the fashion show. There's about a zillion things I need to get done. And I'm thinking that since you and Mr. Beaumont get along so well, I might hire another assistant for me. How do you feel about that?"

"Great! Then we can just be friends and you can tell me all about your trip to Paris and the sex you had with Mr. Beaumont."

Olivia laughed. "Speaking of Mr. Beaumont, I've been trying to call him. Is he in his office?"

"Yes, but he's in an important meeting and doesn't want to be disturbed."

"What meeting?"

Kelly's voice became hushed. "I didn't catch all of it, but it has to do with Mr. Beaumont having a mistress."

Olivia felt her stomach clench. "Deacon has a mistress?"

"No, not that Mr. Beaumont. The dead Mr. Beaumont."

"You must be mistaken, Kelly," Olivia said. "Michael didn't have time for a mistress. He was too busy with French Kiss."

"He might've been busy, but he wasn't too busy to knock a woman up and get an illegitimate kid. An illegitimate kid who is contesting the will."

* * *

No more than ten minutes later, Olivia stood in front of Michael's mansion trying to steady her suddenly topsy-turvy world. Michael had an illegitimate child? It didn't make sense. Michael would've told her if he had a child. Of course he hadn't told her about the will and giving the company to his nephews either. So what made her think that he would have shared this? A part of her wanted to head to French Kiss and bust into the meeting. But the other part knew that would do more damage than good. She felt too raw. So raw that she couldn't get a word out when her mother opened the door.

Since Deirdre had a tennis match that afternoon, she wore a formfitting lime-green sports top and matching skirt, and her blond hair had been pulled back into a chic ponytail. While she had never been an attentive mother, she'd always been a perceptive one. She took one look at Olivia and took charge.

"Come inside. You look like you're about ready to throw up or pass out." She led Olivia into Michael's study and sat her down in a chair in front of the fireplace before heading to the minibar.

Unlike his office at work, Michael's study didn't have one painting of quaint Parisian cafés. In fact there were no paintings at all. On one wall were large windows that looked out over the garden, and the other walls were lined with walnut bookcases filled with business awards and books. Not that Michael had been an avid reader. When he took the time to read, he had preferred *Forbes* magazine.

"Here, drink this." Deirdre handed her a glass of brandy. While Olivia took a sip, her mother picked up a box from the cluster by the door. "I know it's sad to have to pack up Michael's things, but we'll get through it. In case you haven't figured it out, the Harringtons are survivors."

Olivia didn't feel like a survivor. She felt like a drowning victim. She cradled the glass in her hands and took deep sips as she watched her mother pack up some of the books. After the glass was empty, she felt less shaky, but not less deceived. She wanted to ask her mother about Michael. But of course she couldn't do that. Not when it could involve a mistress that her mom knew nothing about. Although if Kelly had overheard correctly, the information would be out soon enough.

"So did Michael ever talk about his past, Mom?" she asked.

Deirdre closed the box of books. "Michael talked about three things. Paris. French Kiss. And you." She looked up. "He loved you, Olivia. I don't know why he left the company to his nephews, but I do know that he loved you." She grabbed another box and moved to the fireplace, where she picked up one of the brass statues from the mantel.

Olivia set down her glass. "I thought he loved me, but maybe he just kept me at French Kiss because we were so alike."

Deirdre turned to her. "Don't be ridiculous, Olivia. You're nothing like Michael. Michael got focused on one thing and you couldn't get him off it. You, on the other hand, are just like your father. Distracted by anything and everything." When Olivia stared at her with surprise, she laughed. "Don't tell me that you don't know you drive people nuts with your inability to stay focused. Your poor teachers begged me to medicate you. Of course your father wouldn't hear of it. And Michael felt the same way. He said you just needed something to focus on—so he solved the problem by throwing money at your private schools and taking you to work with him. And you idolized him for including you when everyone else had tried to exclude you."

It was true. She had idolized Michael for including her. And she wondered how he could've included her in his life and excluded his own child. It didn't make any sense.

"I wonder if these are worth anything?" Deirdre examined the bottom of a bronze statue of two little boys fishing. "Michael had them specially commissioned by a famous sculptor."

Olivia got up and walked over to the fireplace to look at the sculptures. Since they had been too high up for her to notice as a child, and too familiar when she was an adult, she had paid little attention to them. Each depicted a different scene. Two barefoot boys fishing on a riverbank. An old man hunting with a rifle poised for the shot. An old woman in a rocker on the porch of a ramshackle house. A laughing woman sitting at a café. A little girl splashing in puddles in a rain slicker and boots.

"Michael commissioned these?" she asked as she reached out to reverently touch the little girl in the rain slicker. "This is me."

Deirdre leaned closer. "Hmm, I don't remember you being so cute."

Olivia rolled her eyes. "Well, it's me in the exact raincoat and boots he gave me for my eleventh birthday." She pointed to the two boys fishing. "And I bet that's Michael fishing with his brother Donny John. And these two old people must be his parents." She leaned closer to the woman at the café. It looked exactly like the café in the painting—the one she and Deacon had gone to. "Is this you, Mom? I didn't know you went to Paris with Michael."

"I didn't. You know I hate traveling out of the country. It's hard to find a clean public bathroom."

"So who—?" Olivia stopped, realizing too late what she was asking. But Deirdre didn't seem to be upset.

"I don't have a clue. Although she must've rated with Michael if he had her bronzed. It would appear that only the people he loved got the distinction. And don't look so forlorn, Olivia. I knew that Michael never loved me. But he was good to both of us and I'll always love him for that." Her eyes narrowed on the laughing woman. "I wonder if this is the woman who had his child."

Olivia turned to her. "So Michael told you about his child? Why didn't you tell me?"

"Because I found the letter she sent him by accident, and since Michael never mentioned it, I figured it was a secret he wanted to keep. How did you find out?"

"Michael's child is contesting the will."

Deirdre's eyes widened. "The company? The house? Or everything?"

"I won't know the details until I talk with Deacon, but it doesn't sound good." She looked at the bronze. "So who is she, Mom?"

"I don't know, but maybe we can figure it out." She walked to the bookcase behind the desk and slid a stack of books to the side to reveal a wall safe.

Olivia followed and stood behind her. "I didn't have a clue this was here."

Deirdre started dialing the combination. "I'm sure Michael told you in the instructions that were left with the house. But knowing you, you got distracted before you got to that part."

Between French Kiss and Deacon, Olivia hadn't even gotten a chance to read the sheets of information the lawyers had sent her. But as soon as she got home tonight she planned on doing so.

"How do you know the combination?" she asked.

"I used to keep my jewelry in here." The lock clicked, and Deirdre pulled open the safe door. She reached in and took out a stack of papers and handed them to Olivia. "Somewhere in here is the letter. I need a drink."

While her mother walked to the liquor cabinet, Olivia took the papers to the desk and sat down. There were the usual documents that one would find in a safe: Deeds. Stocks. Michael's birth certificate. But beneath the legal papers were two letters and a sketchpad filled with designs. Olivia leafed through the pages and recognized the drawings immediately as Michael's original designs. There was even a design for the French Kiss logo. But what she hadn't noticed in the designs she'd seen before was the scrolled *A* at the bottom. Why would Michael sign his designs with an *A*?

Hoping to find the answer, she picked up the first letter. It was addressed to Michael and held one thin sheet of stationery with tiny purple flowers running along the top and bottom. The writing was artistic and beautiful.

Dearest Michael,

There are no words to express how sorry I am for the way things turned out. But I want you to know that it wasn't a lie. I'll always cherish the time we spent in Paris. I also want you to know that I gave birth to a son tonight. I'm hoping that he will be the one to mend your heart, the one who will make you understand the importance of family.

Love,

A

Olivia stared at the letter. "So Michael does have a child."

"Maybe." Deirdre came over and took the chair across

from the desk. "And maybe she was just some weirdo trying to get money from a wealthy man. You remember that song that Michael Jackson made popular. Although I always thought he protested too much about Billie Jean not being his lover and the kid not being his son." She took a drink of her gin and tonic and nodded at the other letter. "What's that?"

"It's another letter." Olivia put down the first and picked it up. It wasn't from the same woman. The handwriting was stronger—more masculine. She opened it and a picture fell out. She barely glanced at it before reading the words written on the piece of lined notebook paper. Five harsh lines with no heading or signature.

How could you do it? How could you love my mother and let her die without ever trying to help her? As far as I'm concerned, you're a piece of shit! And I want nothing from you! Nothing except for you to go straight to hell!

"So what does it say?" Deirdre asked. "Please don't tell me we have another illegitimate child who wants a cut."

Without answering, Olivia reached for the photograph. It was a picture of Michael and a woman standing in front of the Eiffel Tower. The woman was looking at the camera, but Michael was looking at the woman. It wasn't his expression of adoration that Olivia noticed as much as the familiarity of his features. At this young age, Michael looked exactly like Deacon. Except for the eyes. Deacon didn't have Michael's eyes.

He had this woman's.

CHAPTER TWENTY-THREE

The hotel was one of the most expensive in the city, which wasn't surprising considering the woman who was staying there. As Deacon pulled the Porsche up to the front, a young valet hurried over to open his car door.

Deacon got out. "There's an extra twenty in it if you keep it parked out front." He didn't plan on staying long. Just long enough to find out what was going on.

The kid nodded. As Deacon pushed through the revolving door, he heard the grinding of gears. It barely registered. Even after a good night's sleep, he still felt jet-lagged. Or maybe what he felt wasn't jet-lagged as much as broadsided. He hadn't expected someone to contest the will. And he certainly hadn't expected someone he knew to contest it.

At first he'd thought it was a joke. But after speaking to her lawyers that morning, he'd realized it wasn't. Now he wanted answers. And the best place to get them was at the source. Since the person he'd come to see had a penthouse, a bellboy accompanied him up in the elevator. The kid tried to start a conversation, but Deacon didn't feel much like talking. There were too many questions running through his head. He didn't even wait for her to finish opening the door of the suite before he started asking them.

"What the hell is going on, Francesca?"

Francesca smiled like a satisfied cat. "Well, hello to you too, Deacon." She held open the door. "Won't you come in?"

"Since you wouldn't explain things on the phone, do I have a choice?" Deacon stepped into the foyer of the opulent room, but refused to go further. "Since when do you have a kid?"

She laughed, a harsh sound that grated on Deacon's last nerve. "You've always been so impatient, Deacon. Something that doesn't always work in business transactions." She swept past him in a waft of expensive perfume.

"And this is a business transaction?"

She went to the minibar and pulled out a bottle of orange juice. "I learned from my workaholic daddy that everything is business." She poured some orange juice in a glass, followed by a splash of vodka. She held up the glass. "Drink?"

He ignored the offer and moved farther into the room. "So where is this illegitimate kid?"

"He's in New Zealand right now. He lives there with his wife and two kids."

Deacon snorted. "You'll have to forgive me if I have trouble seeing you as a grandmother."

Instead of getting angry, she just shrugged and took a sip of her drink. "You're right. I've never been much of a grandmother. Or a mother for that matter. Which is why he was quite happy to take his inheritance from my father and leave the country."

"So if he has money, why are you contesting the will?"

Her smile dimmed. "It's not about the money, Deacon. It's never been about the money. It's about setting things right." She ran her long nails along the back of the couch on her way to the windows. "Do you realize that this is the first time I've been here? I've always resented the city for taking Michael from his hometown . . . and me."

She stood with her back to him, her voice taking on a hard edge. "He wasn't supposed to go to Paris and fall in love. He was supposed to come back to Louisiana and marry me. I gave him my love, and I gave him my virginity when we were in high school, and how does he repay me? By bringing home his fiancée who he knew for all of two weeks. Two weeks." She laughed. "What kind of idiot wants to marry a woman after only two weeks?"

Francesca turned. "But then fate took charge. Your mother fell in love with Donny John and broke it off with Michael."

So his mother *was* the one who had broken it off. Deacon didn't know why that made him feel better, but it did.

"So if this isn't about money for your son, Francesca," he said, "what is it about? Revenge for Michael not loving you like he did my mother? Because in case you haven't figured this out, Michael's dead. You contesting his will makes no difference to him now."

She downed her drink and refilled it with straight vodka. "As it turned out, Michael didn't love your mother—he didn't even return home when she was dying. No, he loved money and power. He loved French Kiss.

And as long as it continues, memories of Michael's betrayal continue."

At her words, the pieces of the puzzle slipped into place for Deacon. "You were the one Anastasia was talking to on the phone that day. You're the one sabotaging French Kiss. Let me guess, you own stock in Avery Industries."

She smiled. "You are just like Michael. Smart and business-savvy. Which is probably why I'm so attracted to you. Of course you won't be able to prove any of it. Nor will you be able to stop French Kiss from being sold—especially when all Michael's money will be tied up in a lawsuit."

Deacon stepped closer. "That's it, isn't it? This isn't about your son. You just want to tie up Michael's money long enough to buy French Kiss for pennies on the dollar."

Her smile died. "This isn't your fight, Deacon. So why don't you just let it go and take the money Michael's wimpy stepdaughter offered you? We're not enemies. In fact, we could still be friends."

"We were never friends, Francesca." He turned and walked out the door.

Once he left the hotel, he drove around to clear his head. Francesca was right. Unless Anastasia was willing to talk, he couldn't prove that Francesca had had anything to do with trying to lower French Kiss's stock for a buyout. And he couldn't see Anastasia talking, especially when she would become CEO when Francesca took over. As for the will contest, given Francesca's connections and money, she could tie up Michael's assets long enough to cause major problems for French Kiss—especially with the expense of the new collections. Which meant there was a good chance that French Kiss would be sold to the highest bidder.

He needed to tell Olivia—something he should've done sooner. Since it was almost noon, he figured he knew where to find her. He headed straight to French Kiss and the design studio.

He hoped to catch her working on one of the designs in his collection—something sexy that she could model for him later. Instead the studio was empty except for Grayson, who sat at Olivia's table, sketching.

"Is Olivia still at her house?" he asked as he walked in.

Grayson looked up. "No. She was gone when Nash and I got back from our run this morning. She left the garage door open again."

Deacon couldn't help smiling. "She does that often."

"That's why Nash stayed there today. He has some plan to put sensors throughout her house and then connect them to an app on her cell phone so she'll get an alert if something is left open or on." Grayson shook his head. "I guess our brother is smarter than he looks. So did you meet with Francesca?"

Deacon nodded. "And the woman is as crazy as a shit-house mouse. I gather she was in cahoots with Anastasia to sell the company to Avery."

Grayson continued to draw as if Deacon hadn't just dropped a huge bomb. "That doesn't surprise me. The woman has always been crazy, Deke. You were just too money-hungry to see it." Since there was more than a little truth to that, Deacon couldn't argue the point. "So what about her son?" Grayson asked. "Do you believe he's Michael's?"

"He could be, but I think it's more likely that this is all some grand scheme that Francesca cooked up to get back at Michael."

Grayson stopped sketching and looked up. "Isn't that

what you wanted, Deke? Didn't you always want to get back at Uncle Michael? And not just for the way he treated us when Donny took us there to beg for money. But even before that, you seemed resentful of him for making millions when Dad couldn't seem to make a dime."

Grayson was right. Deacon had wanted revenge. Revenge for Michael ignoring him and his mother when she was dying. And revenge on Olivia for making him feel like a beggar. But not anymore. Now he wanted to save French Kiss and Olivia. Or maybe he wanted French Kiss and Olivia to save him. "Okay, so maybe I was consumed with Michael. But he could've helped us, especially when Mom was so sick."

Grayson stared at him. "Michael couldn't have kept Mom from dying, Deke. Her cancer was too advanced for his money to have made a difference." He set the sketchpad down on the table. The top drawing was of a stern businessman in an expensive suit—his eyes intent, his mouth unsmiling. It took a full minute before Deacon realized it was a drawing of him. Was that how Grayson perceived him? Or was that how he really looked?

"Nash thinks that you're using Olivia to get back at Michael," Grayson said. "Using her just like you used Francesca to get money for the condos. Is it true—?" His gaze swept to the doorway, and his eyes registered regret.

Deacon turned to see Olivia standing there. She was dressed casually, her sweatshirt faded, her jeans holey, and her flip-flops inexpensive. With her golden hair falling out of its ponytail and her face completely devoid of makeup, she looked young, fresh, and wholesome. Just seeing her filled him with an uncontainable joy. In two strides he had her in his arms and was breathing in all that wholesome goodness. It took a moment before he realized that she wasn't hugging back. In fact her body was stiff and unresponsive.

Deacon pulled away and noticed what he hadn't noticed before.

Her normally warm green eyes were cold. The kind of cold that froze a man's heart.

$\mathscr{C}$HAPTER TWENTY-FOUR

$\mathscr{O}$livia felt cold, and even the warmth of Deacon's arms couldn't dispel the iciness that seemed to be hardening around her heart. She had come to French Kiss to talk with Deacon. To give him a chance to deny that he had written the letter. To deny that he was Michael's son. But deep down she knew that there would be no denial, and Grayson's words only confirmed this.

Nash thinks that you're using Olivia to get back at Michael.

There was only one reason he'd want to get back at Michael, and that reason made everything that had happened between them nothing but a lie. All the deep kisses. All the passionate lovemaking. All the sweet talk about her being his woman. All of it had been nothing but lies. Nothing but a way to get back at Michael for not acknowledging Deacon as his son.

But even knowing this, her body still wanted to melt into his embrace. To feel his hands on her waist. To hear his heart beat against her ear. And it took everything she had to ignore the confusion in his eyes and keep her voice steady.

"So you're Michael's son."

It wasn't a question. Just a tired statement filled with all the pain she felt.

His eyes flickered with surprise, and then he did what he did best—he took charge. Without a word to Grayson, he led her from the room and guided her to the elevator with his hand on the small of her back. She wanted to slap it away. To yell at him not to touch her. To never touch her again. But the elevator was crowded so she just stood there like a zombie while he greeted the people around them. They greeted him back, completely oblivious to the fact that they were only pawns in the game Deacon played.

Just like Olivia. Except now she knew.

When they got to his office, Kelly and Jason were talking at the desk. For once Kelly wore a conservative suit with the trademark purple high heels. Although her headband was Hello Kitty. She was giggling at something Jason had said, but when she saw them, she quickly got to her feet and brushed at her skirt.

"Good afternoon, Mr. Beaumont...Ms. Harrington. I put your messages on your desk, Mr. Beaumont. And I'll get you some coffee—"

"No thank you, Kelly," Deacon said. "Just hold all calls, please."

She must've read their solemn expressions, because her smile dropped. "Yes, sir." She exchanged looks with Jason as they walked into Michael's office.

Once inside, Deacon removed his hand from her back and closed the door. The paintings of Paris were back

up on the walls, and everywhere she looked she was reminded of the time they'd spent together. She realized he
had taken her to the exact spot in every single painting.
The Eiffel Tower. The Seine. The small café.

And the quaint shop that had started it all.

An uneasy feeling crept up her spine as she tried to
place all the pieces into a coherent picture. But what she'd
thought was the truth was starting to get muddled. Even
the images of her in this room as a child weren't the same.
At one time she'd pictured herself doing her homework
or drawing in her design book at Michael's desk. But now
she realized that he had never allowed her to sit at the
desk with him. She had sat on the couch while he worked.
And the morning-coffee-and-pastry image turned into her
taking hurried notes as he rattled off orders.

Suddenly her legs felt like they were made of the
sheerest of nylons. She slumped down in a chair and tried
to remember how to breathe.

"Are you okay?" Deacon stood over her. He wore another gray suit—this one as tailored as the one he'd worn
for the photo shoot. She looked away and stared out the
windows.

"Answer Grayson's question, Deacon," she said in a
voice that didn't sound like her own. "Are you just using
me to get back at your father?"

Her mind knew the truth already, but her heart still
held out hope for a quick denial. Instead she got silence,
followed by a question. "How did you find out?"

With shaky hands she unzipped her purse and pulled
out the letters and sketchpad. "I found these when I went
to the house to pack up Michael's things."

Deacon took them cautiously, almost as if he was
afraid to touch them. He glanced at the letter on top—

and, hoping that she was somehow mistaken, that it was some kind of prank, she couldn't help asking, "Did you send that to Michael?"

He nodded slowly. "Since he never replied, I thought he hadn't received it."

The acknowledgment had Olivia's breath seeping out of her as if she were a punctured tire, and it took a moment for her to reel it back in. "And the other one, did your mother write that one?"

It took him a while to look at the other one. He seemed to be preoccupied with the first. She watched myriad emotions cross his face before it settled into the stern scowl he had worn when she'd first met him. At the time she had thought his anger was directed at her. Now she realized that it was directed at Michael. She was just the scapegoat.

He moved around the desk and sat down in the chair. She now understood why he looked so comfortable in Michael's office. Like father, like son. She watched as he opened the letter and read through it. Usually his face was hard to read. This time it was easy. Pain. Hurt. Betrayal. Anger. They all played across his features, and when he lifted his gaze, they shimmered in the bluish-purple depths of his eyes. Eyes that matched the French Kiss emblem on the plaque behind the desk. Suddenly, Olivia realized that purple wasn't just a random color that Michael had chosen. The color had reminded him of Althea's eyes...and his son's.

"Why, Deacon?" Olivia said. "Why didn't you tell me?"

"Because until this moment, I didn't know for sure." All emotion seemed to drain from his face. "And what difference does it make? Michael didn't want a son. And I sure as hell didn't want him as a father."

"Then why are you contesting the will?"

"Me?" He stared at her in shock. "You think that I'm the one contesting the will? Why would I do that?"

"Because you're Michael's son!" Regardless of her wobbly legs, she got up and moved to the windows. When she turned, he was studying the designs in the notepad with his steepled fingers pressed to his chin as if in prayer. But Deacon wasn't the type to pray. He was a man of action. A man who created his own destiny. A man who took care of his own revenge.

"So what's your plan, Deacon?" she asked. "Why are you contesting the will when French Kiss is yours? Or do you want it all? The mansion? The cars? The entire lifestyle? All so you can then have revenge on a father who never acknowledged you?" She hated the tears that sprang to her eyes, but couldn't seem to stop them. "And did you just want to make me look like a fool because it pissed you off that I had Michael's love and his money?"

In one fluid movement he got up from the chair and slammed his fist on the desk. "You're damned right I'm pissed off! But not because of Michael's love or his money. I'm pissed off my mother's dead and he didn't once try to save her. Not fuckin' once! And I'm pissed that he couldn't even reply to his own son." He jerked up the letter and ripped it in two with one twist. "But what pisses me off the most is that you still think he's some kind of a god. He wasn't a god, Olivia. He was a selfish bastard who didn't love anything but power and money."

He moved closer and held up the sketchpad. "Do you realize what these are?" She did realize, which was why she'd brought them along. But she didn't say a word as he continued. "They're my mother's dreams." He waved a hand around the office. "This is my mother's dream.

None of it was Michael's. Not one damned bit of it."
He threw the sketchpad across the room, and it hit the
wall and pages scattered all over the floor. She cringed as
Deacon laughed.

"I often wondered how a redneck from Louisiana
could come up with an idea for a lingerie company. And
now I know. He couldn't, so he had to steal them from
a sweet little seamstress who fell in love with a lingerie
shop in Paris and with his baby brother."

With her last question answered, like a sleepwalker,
Olivia moved over to the designs and started to collect
them. Lifting first one and then another, she carefully
placed them in a neat stack as if they were made of
the most fragile glass. As each design went back in the
book, everything became crystal-clear. Almost too clear.
Michael's hatred for his brother and his brother's sons.
His refusal to talk about the past. His almost rabid desire
to see French Kiss succeed. It had nothing to do with
his love of the company. It had to do with revenge on
Deacon's mom.

Emotions welled up, and tears dripped from her eyes,
landing on the drawing of the French Kiss logo and
smudging the purple pencil etchings like raindrops on
sidewalk chalk.

"Don't cry, Livy," Deacon said as he pulled her into
his arms. "I'm sorry I didn't tell you sooner." He hugged
her close. But she was too numb to feel his arms or the
heat of his body. "I'm not contesting the will, Olivia," he
spoke against the top of her head. "Francesca Devereux is
the one contesting it—she claims she had Michael's son.
But I think she just wants to keep Michael's assets tied up
so that her company can buy French Kiss."

Olivia recognized the name, but couldn't bring herself

to care. It was just one more piece of bad news heaped on the pile that had formed around her. She felt weighted down. As if she were drowning under yards upon yards of brocade and there was no way out.

After a moment Deacon pulled back to study her with his intense eyes. "I know you're scared, Olivia," he said. "But you don't need to worry. I'm not going to let French Kiss fail. I'm going to fight for the company. And I'm going to make it bigger and better than Michael ever could—for you and my mother." He smiled and traced a tear track with his finger. "Marry me, Livy."

His words snapped her out of her trance, and she felt as she had when she'd fallen out of the pirogue and into the bayou. A wave of emotion closed around her, and she couldn't find her way to the surface.

Her inability to talk made him smile even wider. "I know it's crazy. Especially since we've only really known each other for a couple of weeks—and when for most of that time, you didn't like me. But I love you, Olivia Harrington."

It was ironic. Olivia had spent her entire life looking for a man's love. Her father's. Michael's. And here Deacon was offering it to her. It was too bad that, like her father's and Michael's, it wasn't real.

"I can never marry you, Deacon," she said in barely a whisper.

His smile faded. "What do you mean? I thought...in Paris..."

It was hard to speak when looking into his eyes, so she turned away and walked back to the windows. "It wouldn't work," she said. "Not when Nash is right. You are using me. Using me to get back at Michael." She paused. "And maybe I was using you too. Maybe I was using you to keep French Kiss." She turned and glanced around the opulent office. "But now I realize that I don't want it. I don't want any of it."

Deacon looked confused for a second before he walked over and took her hands. "You're upset, Olivia," he said. "The jet lag and going through Michael's things were too much for you. You don't know what you're saying."

"No. For once in my life, I know exactly what I'm saying. I don't want this." She waved her hand to encompass the room. "I've never wanted this. This was Michael's dream, and I wanted it because I thought it would make him love me. But now I realize that you can't make people love you. They either do or they don't." She looked at him and lied. "And I don't love you, Deacon."

The hurt in his eyes looked real. But she was learning that sometimes what you thought was reality turned out to be only a dream. The truth of that came when the look of hurt faded to be replaced with nothing.

Nothing at all.

After a moment he laughed. It was a harsh sound that echoed off the high ceiling and tightened the knot in Olivia's stomach.

"I guess what they say about Paris is true. It does make you look at life through rose-colored glasses."

CHAPTER TWENTY-FIVE

Deacon woke to a blast of frigid water. The spray forced his head back against the cold tile of the shower with a thump that resonated through his already throbbing head like a sonic boom. He might've cussed if he hadn't been drowning. He rolled to his side to avoid the frontal spray, choking on the water he'd already sucked into his lungs. The movement made him aware of the queasiness in his stomach, and the choking soon turned to gagging.

The water was turned off, and Nash's voice cut through Deacon's misery. "From what I just found in the toilet, I would say that you don't have anything left, big brother."

After a few minutes of trying to throw up, Deacon had to agree. He leaned back against the shower wall and took a deep breath before slowly opening his eyes. He was in the en suite bathroom of his office. Nash sat on the lid of the toilet with a grin on his face, while Grayson stood by the sink with a more solemn look.

"So it looks like you had a serious go-around with the

minibar," Nash said. His eyebrow lifted. "And the minibar won."

"Very funny." Deacon massaged his temples. "What time is it?"

"A little after nine o'clock in the morning."

Deacon dropped his hands and stared at his brother, trying to figure out how he'd lost almost twenty-four hours. The answer came too quickly. Olivia. Just the name drove a knife through his heart and had his stomach clenching. He leaned up and gagged. A glass of seltzer water appeared, along with three aspirins. He accepted them from Grayson with a slight nod of thanks.

His brother waited for him to down the aspirins before asking, "So what happened, Deke?"

"Nothing. Nothing happened." He got to his feet and leaned against the glass door for support. "I just tied one on, is all. I guess the pressure of running a big business got to be too much for me."

A towel hit him hard in the face. He caught it and glared at Nash, who was no longer smiling.

"Cut the bullshit, Deke. You thrive on pressure." Nash got to his feet, blocking Deacon from getting out of the shower. "So what happened with Olivia? You weren't kidding, were you? You really fell in love with her."

He laughed and tried to ignore the pain in his head. "Now who is full of shit? Move out of the way so I can get ready for the meeting with Francesca's lawyers."

"Not until you tell us what happened."

"It's none of your business. Now move, Nash, or I'm going to pound your ass."

"Not likely."

If Deacon hadn't had the worst hangover on God's green earth and a meeting only minutes away, he might've taken his brother up on the challenge. But as things were, his brother's pounding would have to wait. Rather than fight with Nash, he stripped out of his clothes and tossed them at him before pulling the shower door closed. The hot water soothed his muscles and the ache in his head, and by the time he'd finished showering, he felt a little better. The feeling dissipated when he stepped into his office and found Nash sitting at his desk, Grayson sketching on the couch, and Donny John standing looking at the painting of the Paris lingerie shop, which had been slashed right down the middle.

"Dad?"

Donny John didn't look away from the painting. "It looks like you have something against Paris, Deacon."

Deacon had a lot against Paris and could vaguely remember taking a mail opener to the painting the night before, but right now he wanted to know what his father was doing there.

"How did you get here, Dad?"

Donny John finally turned to him. "You look like shit, Son." He waved a hand around the office. "I would've thought that all this would keep you as happy as a preacher on Sunday. You always loved the finer things in life. Although I must say that I enjoyed my trip in that jet with the kiss-on-the-ass end. With that cute little stewardess waiting on me hand and foot, I felt just like Hugh Hefner on the bunny plane."

Since that didn't explain how he'd gotten there, Deacon looked at Nash.

"Don't look at me," he said. "It was Grayson."

Grayson stopped sketching and turned his direct gaze on Deacon. "After what happened with Olivia, I think we need to have a family meeting."

"I'm not talking about Olivia." Deacon strode past Grayson and leaned over the desk to push the button on the phone. "Kelly?"

There was a click before she replied. "Yes, sir."

"Set the meeting with the lawyers up in the conference room, please," he said. "And could you bring me a cup of coffee?" Not more than three seconds later, the door opened, and she waltzed in with a tray of cups.

"You are getting efficient," he said as he took a cup from the tray.

She laughed. "I was on my way in when you buzzed." She cocked her head. "So I guess you're done tossing your cookies."

Instead of commenting he took a sip of coffee.

"Don't worry," she said. "I've been there and done that. Just be glad you didn't wake up next to some guy with tattoos of Chip and Dale on his pecs. The sight of those little chipmunks nibbling on his—" Deacon lifted an eyebrow and she stopped in mid-sentence. "Fine," she said. "I'll save the story for my girlfriends." She moved over to Nash and handed him a cup of coffee. "And speaking of girlfriends...Olivia didn't come in today. And when Jason stopped by to see her, he said her office was cleaned out. Is she moving into Samuel's office in the design studio?"

What the hell? Did everyone want to talk about Olivia?

"No," he said, "she's not moving into Samuel's office. She's leaving French Kiss."

Kelly froze in the process of handing his father a cup of coffee. "But why?"

"I don't know. You'll have to ask her. Now if you'll excuse us." He waited for her to walk out the door before closing it behind her. When he turned, his brothers and father were studying him with suspicious looks.

"What?" he said. "Don't look at me like I'm responsible for her leaving. Olivia left because she finally figured out what she wanted. And it's not French Kiss or...a bunch of rednecks from Louisiana. And I say good for her." He took a sip of coffee, enjoying the scalding of the hot liquid, which seemed to detract from the searing pain in his chest. "And good for us. With her out of the way, we can concentrate on dealing with Francesca."

"You did something, Deke," Nash said. "When she came back to the house last night, she didn't say more than two words to me before she closeted herself in her room. Later Grayson heard her crying."

Deacon had never liked for women to cry—especially Olivia—but this time he felt more than a little satisfaction. He wanted her upset. As upset as he had felt...as he still felt. "She made her choice. She made it perfectly clear that she doesn't want anything from us."

"From us? Or you?" Nash got up and walked around the desk. "And I've got to tell you that I'm getting a little sick of you calling all the shots, big brother. You wanted to come to San Fran. Okay, we came to San Fran. You wanted to help Olivia—we helped Olivia. Now you want us to forget Olivia and help you take the company away from Michael's only kid. Why? Because you got a little taste of power and can't let it go? Well, I'm not quite as power-hungry as you, Deacon. I say we give Francesca what she wants and sell whatever is left." He glanced at Grayson. "What about you, Gray?"

"Wait a minute." Donny John held up his hands. "What's this about Francesca and Michael's only child?"

"Michael's other child."

Everyone turned to Grayson, who had spoken the words in his usual calm voice. Deacon was surprised for about a second before he remembered that Grayson had been in the design studio when Olivia had shown up and asked him the question.

"What are you talking about, Grayson?" Nash asked.

Grayson went back to sketching. "Deacon thinks he's Michael's son. Which is why I thought we needed to have a family meeting."

While Donny John looked at Deacon with shock, Nash laughed. "Is that your new plan to keep control of French Kiss, Deke? Because I've gotta tell you that it's almost as ridiculous as Michael willing us shares in the first place."

Deacon didn't want to hurt his brothers or his father, but now that the truth was out, there was no way around it. "It's the truth, Nash," he said.

"Where would you get that crazy notion?" Donny John's expression confirmed Deacon's belief that he knew nothing about Althea's being pregnant when they got married.

"I found Mom's pictures in the garage. Pictures of her and Michael in Paris. I guess they knew each other before she met you."

"Of course they did," Donny John said. "Mikey was the one who introduced us. But what I don't understand is why those pictures made you think that you were his son."

"Because you never mentioned Michael and Mom dating and because the date on the back of the pictures was nine months from my birth," Deacon said. "And if that's not enough, just look at me. I look exactly like him, Dad. Hell, I even act like him. I've got a bad disposition and put money before everything else."

The right hook that Donny John delivered had Deacon stumbling against the desk and wondering if he might pass out. It took a couple blinks to clear his vision. And a couple more to find his voice.

"What the hell?" he said as he tested his jaw.

"What the hell is right, Deacon Valentino Beaumont." Donny John pointed a finger at him. "How dare you think that your mother and I would keep such a secret from you. You were conceived on our wedding night. A good two weeks after Michael headed for California. And we couldn't help it if you decided to come early, Deacon."

The pain in his jaw took a backseat to disbelief. "But she wrote him a letter telling him about me."

"She did that in hopes that he could forgive and forget. That a new nephew might heal his heart." He shook his head sadly. "But if she had asked me before she sent it, I would've stopped her. I knew our having a child would only upset him more."

Deacon stared at him, having trouble believing what he was hearing. "But why didn't you tell us about Michael being in love with Mother? Then when I found the pictures I wouldn't have been so surprised."

"That wasn't any of your business. What happened was between me, Michael, and your mother."

Feeling a little woozy, Deacon sat down in the chair behind the desk. Donny John motioned to Nash. "Get your brother a bag of ice and a stiff drink, then you and Grayson leave. I need to talk to your brother alone."

"I think he's already had the stiff drink," Nash said dryly. "And I'd like to hear this story too."

Donny John pointed at the door. "Out."

Nash scowled, but followed Grayson to the door. When they had gone, Donny John went to the minibar and put some ice in a paper towel and brought it to

Deacon. Deacon was still so stunned by Donny John's revelation that it took him a moment to take it.

"I should've known that Mom would never lie to me," he whispered as he placed the ice pack on his jaw.

"No, she wouldn't." Donny John walked to the window and looked out. "She hated hurting people—especially people she loved. It tore her up when we had to tell Michael that we'd fallen in love. Of course it tore me up as well. The first woman my brother ever brought home and I had to go and fall in love with her." He shook his head. "At first Mikey just laughed as if I was playing some kind of joke on him. But when your mother and I didn't join in, he got this look in his eyes that I can't even describe. It was like I'd given him a right hook when he wasn't expecting it." He paused. "And I guess that's exactly what I did."

"That didn't give him the right to steal Mom's dream," Deacon said.

Donny John turned. "And why not? We had stolen his. Your mother thought that it was only fair."

Deacon got to his feet. "But it wasn't fair! Not Michael taking her dream. And not her dying. None of it was fair, Dad."

Donny walked over and pulled Deacon into his arms. It had been a long time since his father had given him a hug. "You're right. Life isn't fair. But we can't spend our lives trying to make things even. That's what Michael did, and he died a lonely man. Your mother never once looked back, and she died with a smile on her face, surrounded by the ones she loved."

Unable to bear the pain, Deacon had pushed that memory from his mind. But his father was right. His mother had died with a smile, surrounded by her family. "So she never regretted it?" he asked around the lump that had formed in his throat. "She never regretted letting her dream go for Louisiana and a bunch of unappreciative boys?"

Donny John pulled back. "I worried about that every time a French Kiss fashion show came on television." He smiled, and his eyes brimmed with tears. "And as if reading my mind, your mother would always pull me close and whisper, 'You and my boys are worth much more to me than a bunch of panties.'"

Moments passed before Deacon could speak. "So you think that's why Michael left the company to us? It was a way of repaying Mom for taking her idea?"

"I think that was some of it. That, and I think he still loved her." He stared at the picture of Michael and Olivia with tears in his eyes. "You once asked me about the purple flowers that showed up on your mother's grave every week. I told you that I didn't know. But there was only one person who would want forget-me-nots placed on her grave."

"Uncle Michael?"

He nodded. "I caught one of the groundkeepers putting them on. He said that someone had paid to have the flowers put there each week. Since Michael's death they haven't been there."

Suddenly too tired to stand, Deacon fell back in the chair and pressed the ice on his chin. His father gave him the time he needed to digest what he'd just learned by walking back over to the windows. But after a few minutes, he spoke. "So what happened to Olivia?"

"She realized that French Kiss wasn't her dream."

There was a long pause. "Is it yours?"

It was a good question. A week ago he would've said

yes. But that was before Paris. Before he'd started to dream about something else…someone else.

"I don't know," he answered truthfully.

His father glanced at the window. "Can you fish in those waters?"

Deacon smiled, then flinched when pain shot through his jaw. "Yes."

Donny John rubbed his hands together. "Well, what say we grab your brothers and some fishing poles and see what we can catch?"

There was nothing Deacon wanted to do more. Fishing had always cleared his head. Unfortunately, he still had some business to take care of. He glanced at his watch.

"We'll have to do that later, Dad. Right now I have a meeting I need to attend." He swiveled in the chair. "Did you know that Francesca loved Michael?"

"I wouldn't say *love*. That woman is like a spider. She doesn't love as much as feed on men. She got it in her head she wanted to snare Michael, and when he wasn't interested, she got spiteful. Why? What does she have to do with the meeting?"

"Francesca claims her son is Michael's."

Donny John tipped back his head and laughed. "Well, she can claim anything she likes—and Michael might've had sex with her. But I know for a fact that she didn't have his child."

"What makes you so sure?"

"Because Michael was sterile."

CHAPTER TWENTY-SIX

*O*livia was miserable. And whenever she was miserable, she became focused and extremely productive. She cleaned out every closet in her house, the flatware drawer, and the refrigerator and freezer, and then she went to Trader Joe's and stocked up on cheese and coffee, and she was now industriously working on the stained rug on the balcony. Jonathan Livingston Seagull watched her from his perch on the back of the rattan couch with what appeared to be a slight smirk on his long beak.

"It's not funny, you know," she said as she brushed in the eco-friendly carpet cleaner. "How would you like it if I used your nest as a toilet? You wouldn't be laughing then, now would you?"

He sidestepped to the arm of the couch and leaned closer to the opened can of sardines she'd placed on the table. She didn't know if seagulls liked sardines. They were the only things she'd been able to think to buy at Trader Joe's. With eight cans now in her well-organized cupboard, she was relieved when Jonathan reached out his beak and snatched one from the can. The others followed in short order.

"I shouldn't be rewarding you for bad behavior." She sprayed more carpet cleaner on the rug. "In fact I should've let Nash get rid of you when I had the chance. Now he's gone." She brushed in the cleaner. "And so is Grayson."

The Beaumont brothers had left that morning. She should've expected it. After all, they were Deacon's brothers—or at least half brothers. But that didn't explain why she got so teary-eyed when they'd said their good-byes. Of course they'd said they would be back to visit. But she didn't believe it. Now that she wasn't part of Deacon's life anymore, she wouldn't be part of theirs. She would miss them. She would miss Nash's flirting and his bright smile. Miss Grayson's calming presence and inspiring talent. Now the house seemed so empty. So lonely. Maybe she should call Babette and invite her back. Even her snooty arrogance would be better than this silence.

She gave up on getting the stains out and sat back on her butt. "At least I have you, Jonathan—"

"Hammond!" Mrs. Huckabee's loud yell scared Jonathan, and in a flap of wings he took flight. His poop landed almost dead center on the spot Olivia had been cleaning.

"I'm busy, Doris!" Mr. Huckabee yelled back. "I'm sitting out here on the balcony listening to Britney talk to her new lover. Now that the two so-called cousins left, she's got some guy over there who goes by the name of Jonathan."

Olivia rolled her eyes and got to her feet. Mr. Huckabee was sitting on his balcony holding a pair of binoculars that were directed straight at her. Not that he needed them when their houses were so close. She waved. "Hello, Mr. Huckabee. See anything interesting?"

He lowered the binoculars, not at all embarrassed that he'd been caught spying. "So you remembered to close the garage today when you left for the store."

She didn't know how Nash had done it, but somehow he'd set up an alarm on her phone that went off when she pulled away from the house without closing the garage door. "Thank you for always keeping an eye on my house," she said.

Mr. Huckabee nodded. "So where's this Jonathan?"

She could've explained, but she was coming to realize that Mr. Huckabee didn't want explanations as much as some excitement. Excitement that he could no longer get for himself.

"Passed out cold," she said as she looked down at the empty couch. "He must've eaten too many of my magic brownies."

Mr. Huckabee grinned. "That will do it." He set the binoculars on the table. "You should try Mrs. Huckabee's some time. She has them down to a science—just enough buzz without the side effects of a gassy stomach."

"She sounds like quite a cook."

He craned his neck and called back into the house, "Doris! I'm going to invite Britney over for dinner."

"Olivia!" Mrs. Huckabee yelled.

Mr. Huckabee didn't miss a beat. "Who is Olivia?"

* * *

Surprisingly, and fortunately, Mr. and Mrs. Huckabee dressed for dinner. Mrs. Huckabee wore a peasant blouse and long skirt, and Mr. Huckabee wore a tie-dyed T-shirt and ripped jeans. Mr. Huckabee was right. His wife was an excellent cook. Olivia had seconds of the vegetable couscous, but declined the brownie for dessert. Instead she had a glass of wine and listened to the couple relive their life together.

They had married right out of college and traveled the world. Africa. South America. India. After living in a commune in Arizona, they'd settled in San Francisco and opened a restaurant for vegans. By the end of the evening, it was plain to see that they had lived a long and adventurous life. One that made Olivia's life look dull by comparison. By the time the dinner was over and she'd walked back to her house, she was feeling more than a little morose. Not only because the Huckabees had experienced so much of life but also because they had done it together.

All Olivia had was her mother and a pooping seagull. She had wasted her adult life on a company...and on a man who hadn't even cared enough to tell her about his son. If Michael had told her, she would've understood his leaving the company to Deacon. And it would've saved her the last few weeks of hell. Of course not all of it had been hell. Most of it had been heaven. She had loved designing. Loved having Grayson and Nash around. Loved...Deacon.

Yes, she loved Deacon. The time away from him had allowed her to finally accept it. But it didn't change the fact that they could never be together. She would always remind him of the man who had stolen his mother's dream.

As she punched in the security code for the garage, she caught a movement out of the corner of her eye. She whirled to find the lemon juicer salesman sneaking away from the side of her house. When he saw her, he dropped the empty flower containers, grabbed his roller suitcase, and made a run for it. She didn't know if it was the wine or her guilt about not thanking him sooner that had her chasing after him. She caught up to him after a block and grabbed the sleeve of his jacket. It was a surprisingly nice trench coat, the material an expensive nylon-and-polyester mix.

"Wait," she said as she pulled him to a stop. "I just wanted to thank you."

He stared down at his shoes. "You don't have to thank me," he said in a gruff whisper.

"Of course I do. You've taken out my trash, swept my driveway, and planted those beautiful flowers in my garden. I really appreciate it, and I'd like to buy a lemon juicer."

He quickly unzipped the roller bag and pulled a juicer out. It looked a little like a gun. There was a round chamber where the lemon went, a handle you squeezed, and a long barrel the juice came out of. He handed it to her.

"This is ingenious," she said. "Did you design it?"

He nodded, continuing to stare at his shoes. "You don't have to pay me. I want you to have it."

"Absolutely not." She dug through her purse for her wallet and then pulled out a twenty. Although twenty didn't seem like enough for all that he had done for her. "Look," she said, "I know this probably isn't any of my business, but do you have a place to sleep? I mean, I know how expensive this neighborhood is and—" She stopped when she realized how arrogant she sounded. "What I'm trying to say is...if you need a place to stay, I have an extra room."

His head came up. "What? Are you crazy, Olivia Harrington?"

It wasn't just her name that had Olivia looking closer. It was the familiar voice that went with it. A voice she'd thought she would never hear again.

"Dad?"

Her father pointed a finger at her. "Don't you Dad me, young lady. What were you thinking asking some stranger to live in your house? Why, I could be some kind of lunatic who kills you in your sleep, for all you know."

Olivia was struck speechless as she stared into her father's green eyes. Then she took Deacon's advice about letting your emotions out and got pissed. "What was I thinking? What were you thinking?" She pointed a finger at his finger. "You haven't contacted me once since I was nine, and then you show up at my house masquerading as a lemon juicer salesman? Urrgh! I hate men! All men!" She turned and strode back toward her house. Then stopped and came striding back. "How could you do that to me? How could you do it to Mom?"

She was yelling, but she didn't care. "For years we thought you were dead and here you are selling lemon juicers." She pointed the juicer at him like a gun.

"Lower your voice, Livy," he said as he glanced nervously around.

"No! I'm not nine years old anymore. And I won't take orders from a father who couldn't even call me to tell me he wasn't injured or sick."

His gaze settled on her. "But I am sick."

Some of her anger drained away. "You're sick?"

He nodded. "That's why I didn't contact you. It was better if you thought I was dead."

She tried to think of a disease that would keep you away from your daughter for twenty years. "Leprosy?"

A smile tipped the corners of his mouth. "I wish it was that simple."

The front door of the house across the street opened, and an older woman in baggy pajamas and UGG slippers stepped out. "Is that man bothering you?" she yelled. "Because if he is, I'll call the cops."

Olivia pulled her gaze away from her father long enough to answer the woman. "No, he's not bothering me, ma'am. But thank you for checking."

"Are you sure? Or is he making you say that?" The woman held up her smartphone as if taking a picture.

Since Olivia didn't want to end up on Facebook or the front page, she took her father's arm and pulled him back toward her house. "Come on. I'll make you some coffee."

She put in the code, and the garage door opened. And she was halfway to the door when she realized her father wasn't following her. Instead he stood in the driveway as if he couldn't bring himself to step over the line that divided the driveway from the garage.

"What's wrong?" she asked.

He paused before taking a hesitant step. "Nothing. Nothing at all."

Once inside her house, he became even more fidgety and nervous. He refused to let her take his coat and sat perched like Jonathan Livingston on her kitchen barstool—as if he were ready to take flight.

"I don't drink coffee," he said. "It reacts badly with my medication."

Since it was late and she probably shouldn't have any either, she put the empty carafe back in the coffee maker and sat down across from him. She studied him and wondered why she hadn't recognized him sooner. Despite the beard and a few extra wrinkles around his eyes, he looked the same. No signs of decaying skin or flesh-eating disease.

"So why?" she asked. "Why did you leave? And why didn't you ever contact me?"

He fidgeted with the buttonholes on his coat. "I wish it was easy to explain." His gaze bounced around the room until it landed on a picture of her and Michael standing in front of a Christmas tree. "I wanted to be there." His gaze returned to her. "But it was better for you that I wasn't."

"Funny, it didn't feel better. I was devastated when you left. I thought it was my fault because I didn't do well in school—because I couldn't stay focused."

"No!" He rose from the stool and shook his head. "It was never you, Livy." He hit himself in the chest. "It was me. I was the one who couldn't live a normal life—who couldn't be the father that you deserved."

He started to pace back and forth in front of the breakfast bar. "I wanted to be the perfect father. I did. But then the pressure at work became too much and your mother and I weren't getting along...and I couldn't keep it together." He stopped and looked at her with sad eyes. "Not even for my most precious daughter."

His shoulders sagged in defeat beneath the trench coat. "My condition isn't physical, Olivia. It's mental. One doctor thought I was schizophrenic, and another diagnosed me as bipolar. But none were exactly sure what caused my mental breakdown. After years of trying to figure it out, I think it boils down to one thing: Your father can't handle pressure of any kind without going nuts."

It wasn't what she had been expecting. Not what she had been expecting at all. And all she could do was sit there while he continued to pace and fiddle with his buttonholes.

"Even now I can't stand being surrounded by walls. They seem like they're closing in on me." He got a desperate look in his eyes. "Like they're squeezing me from all sides."

Since it looked like he was about to have another mental breakdown, Olivia got up and hurried to the balcony door. As soon as she had it open, he pushed past her and stood at the railing, panting like he couldn't breathe. Not knowing what to do, she rubbed his back the way he used to do when she was a little girl and upset.

"It's okay," she said in a soothing voice. "There are no walls. Just open sky and fresh air." She pointed at the sky to distract him from his panic attack. "Look. Cassiopeia."

He looked up, and his breathing slowly returned to normal. "Do you remember the story?"

Olivia knew it and all the stories he'd told her by heart. "Cassiopeia was a vain queen who bragged to the sea spirits that she and her daughter were much more beautiful than they were. They reported back to Poseidon, who sent a sea monster to destroy their city. The king, Cassiopeia's husband, decided that the only way to stop it was to sacrifice his daughter to the monster."

Her father turned to her. "I couldn't sacrifice you or your mother to the monster that lives inside me. So I left. But I love you, Livy. You have to believe that."

Olivia looked away. "I don't know what to believe anymore, Dad. Every man I've ever trusted with my love has abused it. And I don't understand any of it. Because if you love someone, you don't leave them without an explanation. Lie to them. Hurt them. That's not love."

There was a long stretch of silence before her father finally spoke. "I'm sorry, Livy. But you're wrong. I do love you." He fiddled with his buttonholes. "I guess love isn't always perfect."

Not knowing how to reply, she just stood there next to him and tried not to cry. It was a losing battle. Soon tears streamed down her cheeks. Her father shifted toward her and placed a tentative hand on her back. It wasn't a hug, but it felt nice. Maybe he was right. Maybe love wasn't perfect. Or maybe what wasn't perfect was people. Maybe Olivia was like Cassiopeia's daughter, a princess who felt as if she'd been sacrificed to the sea monster of life and was waiting for a savior.

The squeal of tires on asphalt had her eyes opening. She might've looked down to see who was driving so recklessly if a bright beam of light hadn't blinded her.

"They're up here!" Mr. Huckabee yelled. "The bum's trying to make a move on her, but I've got him in my sights."

Heavy footsteps sounded on the stairs. She turned to see who it was, but before she could blink the spots from her eyes, someone stepped out on the balcony and attacked her father.

"If you've hurt her, you sonofabitch, I'll kill you."

Olivia's vision cleared enough to see Deacon holding her father by the throat while Mr. Huckabee held his flashlight on them and yelled.

"Keep a tight grip, son. The police are on their way."

Olivia grabbed Deacon's arm. "Let him go!"

Deacon squinted in the bright light before he called over to Mr. Huckabee, "Could you please turn that off?" The light clicked off, and Deacon turned to Olivia. "What's going on? Mr. Huckabee called me and said that the street bum had broken into your house and was accosting you on your balcony."

"He wasn't accosting me. I invited him here."

Deacon pointed a finger at her father. "So he didn't break in?"

"No."

"And you're not hurt?"

"No."

"Then what are these?" He reached out and touched her wet cheek with the pad of his finger. It amazed her how much heat the simple touch generated. And how much she wanted to fall into his arms and continue to cry.

Instead she took a quivery breath. "I've had an emotional day."

He studied her for a mere second before he spoke. "Haven't we all." Then he tossed the keys to the Porsche on the coffee table and left.

Before she could sort out all the thoughts and emotions that raced through her, Mr. Huckabee turned the flashlight on them. "I guess I'll call the police and tell them it was a false alarm. But, Britney, I sure wish you'd mentioned having an affair with the street bum at dinner. It would've saved everyone a lot of grief."

CHAPTER TWENTY-SEVEN

And here I thought all the Beaumont brothers were straight."

Pulled out of his daydreams, Deacon turned to Samuel, who was dressed as impeccably as usual in a gray designer suit and lavender tie. "Excuse me?"

Instead of answering, Samuel turned to Babette, who was crouched in front of a model and pinning her corset—the exact corset that Olivia had worn. Which was what had prompted Deacon's daydreaming. He still couldn't look at it without all the memories flooding back. Not to mention the pain.

"Make sure the satin binding looks smooth, Babette," Samuel said. "And don't lace her up too tightly for the show. We don't want her passing out onstage."

Babette sniffed. "You act as if I have never stitched a stitch before, but I'll have you know that I could've designed this in my sleep."

"Doubtful." Samuel leaned back with one finger pressed

to his lips and studied the corset before he nodded his satisfaction. "Perfect. Absolutely perfect." He turned his attention to Deacon. "I said that I thought all the Beaumont brothers were straight, but it seems I was wrong."

Deacon's eyes narrowed. "You weren't wrong."

"Then explain why a heterosexual man who is surrounded by half-naked supermodels isn't smiling." He nodded over at Nash, who stood in one corner, grinning like a Cheshire cat high on catnip. Grayson stood next to him. He wasn't smiling as much as sketching furiously. "Your brothers seem to be enjoying themselves." He glanced at Donny John, who was chatting up a model. "And your father."

"Because they don't realize how much is riding on this fashion show."

Samuel studied him for another second before turning to the roomful of designers and models and clapping his hands. "Okay, everyone, let's see if we can finish up with the fittings before nine tonight. I want everyone getting a good night's sleep because tomorrow is going to be a busy day." He glanced back at Deacon. "Would you please step into my office, Mr. Beaumont? There are some last-minute decisions I'd like your input on."

Deacon nodded and followed him to the office. When the door was closed, he took a seat in front of the immaculate desk. "I've told you before that you can call me Deacon. I'm sure Michael had you call him by his first name."

Samuel took the chair behind the desk. "Actually, the only one who got away with that was Olivia."

"It figures. The more I learn about my uncle, the more of a jackass he becomes."

"Michael Beaumont had his flaws just like the rest

of us. One was his arrogance, and the other his love of money." Samuel hesitated. "Is that true of you too, Mr. Beaumont? Is that the only reason you're working as hard as you are? You want to make the fashion show a success so you can sell the company for more money?"

Deacon had thought about it. He had spent the last two weeks thinking about it. And last night he had finally come to a decision. "I'm not selling French Kiss." He got up and walked to the window that looked out on the design studio. "I'm trying to save it for the one person who deserves it."

"I assume that we're not talking about Michael's illegitimate son."

Presenting the doctor's records of Michael's football injury and consequent infertility to Francesca's lawyers had been the highlight of the past few weeks. Thomas, Bentley, and Thomas had immediately backed out of the will contest, and Deacon had yet to hear from Francesca. He hadn't heard from her even when the board voted to decline Avery's offer to buy French Kiss.

"No," Deacon said. "He wasn't Michael's son."

"And are you?"

He turned. "How did you know about that?"

"I've talked with Olivia." Samuel leaned back in his chair. He was the only man Deacon knew who could lean back and still not look relaxed. "She calls me almost every day. She claims it's just to chat, but I think it's to keep track of what's happening here. So I'm going to assume that she's the one you're saving the company for."

Deacon nodded. "She's worked hard all her life for French Kiss. She deserves to have it. And I don't know why my uncle didn't will it to her."

"I think he finally realized that he had imprisoned

Olivia in the walls of French Kiss, and he wanted to set her free to live her own dream...not someone else's."

Deacon shrugged. "It was still a shitty thing to do. Olivia loves French Kiss more than anything."

Samuel pressed a finger to his lips and studied Deacon just as he had the corset. "I don't think that's still true. As for Olivia running the company, it's a bad idea. She's too kindhearted to be a good boss. The company needs a controlling hard-ass...like you."

"Well, they'll have to do without this hard-ass. I'm leaving first thing in the morning."

For the first time, Samuel showed emotion. He sat up, his eyes concerned. "Before the fashion show? You can't do that. People will want to see the new owners—they'll want to know the faces that go with the names on the collections."

"My brothers will be here. And people won't care about us as much as the designer who created the collections. That designer is Olivia. She should be the one who gets the accolades—the one walking down the catwalk at the end of the show to all the applause and camera clicks." He crossed his arms. "Now what last-minute details did you want to go over?"

Samuel rose from the chair and walked around the desk. "There aren't any. I lied to get you alone so I could find out the truth."

Deacon held up his hands. "Look, I don't know what vibes I'm sending out, but I'm not gay. And if you come any closer, I'm going to have to prove it with my fist."

Samuel smiled, the first smile Deacon had ever seen on the man, and before Deacon could stop him, Samuel gave him a stiff hug followed by a peck on each cheek. "Thank you for being the kind of man I hoped you were."

Feeling uncomfortable and more than a little confused, Deacon only nodded before he left the office. Since Samuel seemed to have things under control in the design studio, he headed back to his office. He had a few more details to finish up before he called it a night. Seeing the light beneath Jason's door, he stopped and peeked his head in.

Kelly was on the desk with her legs wrapped around Jason as he kissed her. Deacon might've ducked out before he was spotted if Kelly hadn't chosen that moment to break the kiss and glance over Jason's shoulder. "Oh! Mr. Beaumont."

Jason whirled around, then smiled sheepishly. "Hi, Deacon. We thought you were down in the design studio."

Deacon nodded. "Yeah, well, I'll just let you get back to..."

"We weren't having sex." Kelly got off the desk and smoothed down her skirt. A professional skirt in a nice somber gray. Although her belt was hot pink with a rhinestone cat buckle that made Deacon smile. He was glad Kelly hadn't lost all of her style. "Jason and I have decided to wait until we're married to have sex."

"Married?" Deacon glanced at Jason, who only shrugged.

"She asked me on the Jumbotron at AT&T Park. How does a guy say no to that?"

Deacon laughed and walked in to shake his hand and give Kelly a quick hug. "Congratulations. When's the wedding?"

"Not until next summer." Kelly grinned from ear to ear. "We're thinking about having the ceremony performed at home plate during the seventh-inning stretch. I know you're leaving, but you'll come back, right? If you hadn't declined the Giants tickets, we never would've figured out that we could stomach each other."

"I'd love to attend," he said, even though it was doubtful that he would return for the baseball wedding. Olivia would be there, and Deacon didn't think he could survive seeing her again. The night several weeks before had been bad enough. Everything inside him had ached at the sight of her. He'd wanted to touch her, to hold her, to absorb every inch of her into his body. All she had done was look at him as if he were crazy. And maybe he had been a little crazy at the sight of another man touching her. He still couldn't figure out what she'd been doing with the trench coat guy. But she had made it perfectly clear that it was none of his business.

"Well, I better get back to my office," he said. "I have a few things I need to finish up." He nodded at Jason. "Thanks for being my right-hand man."

Jason walked him out to the hallway. "I wish we could've found something on Anastasia."

"After word gets around, she won't be working as an executive in the industry she loves. That's punishment enough."

Jason's eyes turned sad. "I wish you'd stay, Deacon. French Kiss needs you."

"It doesn't need me. It has you, Kelly, and Samuel." He put a hand on his shoulder. "And I'm counting on you three to advise Olivia and keep her focused."

"Yes, sir."

Not wanting to prolong the goodbye, Deacon thumped him on the back. "You might not be good at sports, Jason, but you're a damned good team player." He smiled at Kelly, who stood in the doorway with tears in her big brown eyes. "And so are you, Ms. Wang."

Once in his office, Deacon didn't feel much like working. So he wandered over to the window and stared out at the view.

The night was as clear as a bell. The lights of the Golden Gate Bridge gleamed in the distance. He would miss this view. Miss the city. And miss French Kiss. But mostly he would miss Olivia.

"We thought we'd find you here."

He glanced over his shoulder to see Nash entering the office, followed by Grayson.

"So I guess the fittings are over," he said as he turned back to the window.

"Actually they're still going on." Nash joined him.

"And you two left?"

"I think Donny John is more than enough Beaumont for those poor models to have to deal with. He claims he's found nirvana." Nash looked out at the view. "And you have to wonder if he doesn't have a point. I've grown kind of attached to this view...the cool weather...the hot women."

Grayson stepped to the other side of Deacon. "It is funny how much it feels like home."

They stood there absorbing the view until Nash finally spoke. "So you're still leaving tomorrow?"

"Ten thirty flight."

"Does Olivia know?"

"No. And she doesn't care. I told you how she reacted to me when I raced over there like an idiot."

"You did drop everything when Mr. Huckabee called," Nash said. "It's the hero complex you've got going. And if anyone needs a hero, it's Olivia."

Deacon stared out at the view. "She doesn't want a savior, Nash. Nor does she need one. She'll do fine without me. Especially if you two stay to guide her."

There was a long stretch of silence before Nash spoke. "We're not staying, Deke."

"What?" He turned to Nash first and then to Grayson, who smiled and lifted one shoulder.

"We might not always get along, big brother. But we're family. If you go, we go."

CHAPTER TWENTY-EIGHT

In the past few days, Olivia had learned that life was full of twists and turns. She had thought she'd one day own French Kiss, but now she was jobless. She had also thought that she'd never have a father, and now she had one. He might live on the street and have a few psychological issues, but he was living proof that when life gave you lemons, you needed to make lemonade. And it was easier if you had a great lemon squeezer to do it with. Her father sold great lemon squeezers. Which explained why he could afford to offer Olivia money to start a lingerie business.

"Two million dollars?" Olivia's voice hit a high note as she helped him set up his sidewalk stand. "You made two million dollars selling juicers on a street corner?"

Her father glanced around. "Over, actually. And I don't just sell them on the street. I sell them on the Internet. People seem to like a good product, and money accumulates quickly when you don't use it." There was a flap of wings, and Jonathan Livingston landed on his shoulder. Her father barely paid attention as he unloaded his lemons from his roller suitcase and placed them in a large Del Monte tomato can.

Olivia shook her head. "I still can't believe that Jonathan is your pet."

"He's not a pet. He's free to come and go as he pleases."

It seemed this was very important to her father. He couldn't have ties that bound him to a house with walls or to a person. He needed to be able to come and go as he pleased. Which meant that he would probably disappear again. As hard as it might be, Olivia needed to accept that.

"So how did you get him to hang out on my balcony?" she asked.

"Maybe he just knows good people when he sees them." His eyes twinkled. "And maybe I tossed up a few pieces of garbage. I wanted someone to keep you company in that lonely house."

"It's not that lonely."

He studied her. "So tell me about the man that came rushing to your rescue the other night. He looks a lot like Michael Beaumont."

"You met Michael?"

"I've been keeping an eye on you for a long time, Livy. And while I never personally met Michael, I did some research on him at the library. Although that didn't tell me whether or not he was a good stepfather. Was he?"

She had been giving that question a lot of thought lately. In fact, with nothing else to do, she'd spent a lot of time thinking. About Michael. Deacon. Her life. And she had come to a conclusion. Love came in all different shapes and sizes. Michael was a good example of this. He hadn't been a verbal kind of guy, but in his own way, he had loved her.

She had finally gone through the documents the lawyers had sent over, and among them was a letter from Michael. A letter explaining why he hadn't willed her the company. It seemed that, on his deathbed, he'd realized what was important. And it wasn't a lingerie company. He wanted Olivia to realize this too. He wanted her to experience the world outside of French Kiss and to enjoy life to the fullest.

She looked at her father and smiled. "Yes, Michael was a good stepfather."

Olivia stayed with her father for a few hours, watching him wow a crowd of tourists as he made lemonade. Then, catching his eye, she blew him a kiss before hopping the trolley for home. When she got there, she realized that she had left her cell phone on the counter. She had twenty messages. One was from her real estate broker, telling her that they had gotten a good offer on her house. And nineteen were from Samuel. Rather than listen to all of them, she called him.

"Where are you?" he asked. For once he didn't sound like the calm, demure man she knew. "I've been trying to get ahold of you since last night."

"I was with my father. You would not believe how much money he makes—"

"Not now." He cut her off. "Right now you've got to get to the airport and save the fashion show from being a complete disaster."

"Calm down, Samuel. The fashion show is going to be amazing. I'm sure Deacon has everything under control."

"He would if he were still here," he said. "But he's not."

She froze. "He left French Kiss?"

"Yes. And his brothers left with him."

"But they can't leave now—not when their faces are scheduled to be plastered all over magazine covers and billboards across the country. Without them the new collections won't mean anything."

He released his breath in a long sigh. "Exactly. Now are you going to the airport to stop them or not?"

* * *

Olivia drove to the airport faster than she had ever driven in her life. Not wanting to waste time on parking, she left the Porsche at the flight departure curb and got out.

"Hey! You can't park there." A young security guy came jogging over.

"I know," she said as she grabbed her purse from the front seat. "But this is an emergency." She handed him all the cash she had in her wallet. "Please. I'll just be a few minutes."

It took her more than a few minutes. When she didn't find them at the curb check-in or the airline counter inside, she was forced to buy a ticket for the flight so she could get through security. Standing in line, she glanced at her watch before she slipped it off and put it in the plastic security bin. The Beaumonts' plane boarded in less than fifteen minutes.

Once the TSA officer had waved her through the scanner, she quickly stepped over to the conveyer belt to get her shoes and purse. Unfortunately, her purse had been confiscated by one of the TSA officers.

"Excuse me, ma'am," the officer said, "but we need to search your bag." He took her out of the line and over to a table where he emptied the contents of her purse. He held up the lemon juicer her father had given her and that she'd forgotten about.

"What's this?" he asked.

"It's a lemon squeezer."

He held it like a gun. "It doesn't look like any lemon squeezer I've ever seen."

"Well, it is. My father designed it."

"Hey"—another officer came over—"I've seen those. Some guy sells them on Pier Thirty-Nine. I got my wife one for her birthday, and at first she wanted to beat me over the head with it for not getting her that charm bracelet she wanted. But then she used it to make her aunt Martha's lemon cake—you know, the one I bring to work every Christmas—and now she thinks it's the best gift ever. She says it gets the juice out of a lemon like no-body's business." He took the squeezer and demonstrated how it worked.

Olivia glanced at her watch as she put it back on. "Look, I really need to get to my plane before it leaves. You can keep the squeezer if you want to."

The officer studied it for a second more before putting it back in her purse. "Fine. But next time you should leave the squeezer at home."

"Thank you." She grabbed her purse and hurried toward the gate. She arrived just as they were making the last call. Which meant that she had to board the plane. She intended to walk down the aisle until she found them, and then by any means possible get them off the plane before it took off. She didn't plan on a large woman with an even larger suitcase stopping her.

It seemed that the woman was planning an extended trip to Louisiana and had something against checking bags. The suitcase she was trying to shove into the overhead compartment didn't fit, but that didn't stop the woman from trying. She shoved, repositioned, and shoved again while the flight attendants were occupied elsewhere and didn't seem to realize the woman was blocking the aisle.

"Maybe you should check it," Olivia said.

The woman glared at her. "And maybe you should mind your own business."

Normally Olivia would've kept her mouth shut and waited patiently. But this was an emergency, and she was getting a little tired of always being the nice one.

"And maybe there's a reason these overhead bins are small." She rose up on her tiptoes so she was at eye level with the woman. "Maybe it's because they're not meant for suitcases the size of a cargo trunk."

"Why you little pip-squeak—"

A flight attendant finally showed up. "Is there a problem?"

The large woman gave her suitcase one last shove and closed the compartment with a slam. "No, there's no problem."

"Good," the attendant said, "because we're getting ready to leave the gate."

"No!" Olivia shook her head. "You can't take off. I need to get some people off the plane."

"Off the plane?" the man sitting to her left said. "Why do you need to get people off the plane? Is something wrong with the plane? And what's that hanging out of your purse? Is that a gun?"

"Gun!" A woman yelled.

"No." Olivia pulled out the squeezer and held it up. "It's just a—"

"Hijack!" someone yelled, and the entire plane erupted in chaos. The flight attendant dove to the floor as people cowered behind the seats in front of them with frantic screams and squeals of terror. There were only four people who didn't duck: An attractive older gentleman Olivia immediately recognized as Donny John Beaumont. And his three extremely good-looking sons. One son was grinning from ear to ear, the other was smiling just enough to show his dimples, and the last was looking as if he'd just drunk an entire glass of her father's lemon juice. Of course it was Deacon who took charge—who unbuckled his seat belt and stood, his large frame filling the aisle.

Suddenly she forgot how to breathe. Because even though he was still scowling, he was the most beautiful, gorgeous, amazing thing she'd seen in days. And she realized that she had driven fast, parked in an illegal zone, and almost gotten in a fight with a large lady all because she didn't want him to leave. Not because of some fashion show. Or her designs. But because she couldn't stand the thought of his leaving. It didn't matter if he was Michael's son. It didn't even matter that he only wanted to use her to get back at his father. All that mattered was that she get a chance to tell him how she felt.

Unfortunately, before she could, the large woman clocked her with her tote bag. The last thing Olivia saw was Deacon's face going from angry to concerned. The last thing she felt was his arms around her. The last thing she heard was the strong, steady beat of his heart.

When Olivia woke up, she wasn't in Deacon's arms. Nor was she on the floor of the plane. Instead she was being rolled through the airport on a stretcher by a male and female EMT who seemed to be deep in conversation.

"It looked like a gun," the woman said. "I understand why that woman knocked her out."

"It did not look like a gun." The man pushed her around a group of travelers. "Which is why they didn't handcuff her."

The woman glanced down at Olivia and finally noticed that her eyes were open. "Welcome back. How are you feeling?"

Olivia took inventory before she answered. "My head hurts a little, but other than that I think I'm okay."

While they were still moving, the woman took a flashlight out of the pack on her waist and flashed it at Olivia's pupils. "I don't think you've got a concussion, but it might be best if we took you to the hospital."

Olivia came fully awake. "The hospital? I can't go to the hospital." She tried to sit up, but she was strapped down to the gurney.

"Calm down," the woman said. "We're just going to take you there for a few tests."

"I don't have time for tests." She struggled with the straps. "Please! I have to get to Deacon."

"I'm right here, Olivia."

She stopped struggling as Deacon moved to the other side of the gurney. He took her hand, and the entire world brightened. "How do you feel?"

It was hard to talk with those beautiful eyes staring back at her. She felt as if she were floating in an indigo sea of warmth.

"It looks like she got her bell rang but good." Nash appeared on the other side of the gurney, right next to the EMT, who blushed profusely when he gave her a smile. "So how are you doing, hijacker?" He winked at Olivia. "You gave us quite a scare."

"Mostly Deke." Grayson moved next to Deacon. "I thought he was going to throttle the woman who hit you."

"Now, your brother would never hurt a woman, Grayson." Donny John joined Nash. "Beaumonts don't hit women—even large manly ones." He took Olivia's hand. "Do you remember me, darlin'? Don Juan Beaumont at your service. After seeing you all grown up, I see why you have Deacon all aflutter."

"That's enough, Dad," Deacon said. "So what were you doing on the plane, Olivia?"

She swallowed hard. Suddenly all the things she'd wanted to say to Deacon got jumbled up like Scrabble tiles. "Well...I..."

Her cell phone rang. And since she was strapped in, Deacon pulled it from her purse, glanced at the screen, and then answered it. It wasn't hard to hear Samuel's loud prayer of thanks.

"Thank God she stopped you in time!"

"What's going on, Samuel?" Deacon continued to hold Olivia's hand and walk next to the gurney as they headed for the elevator that would take them to the exit. This time Olivia couldn't hear Samuel's answer, but Deacon must not have liked what he said because his eyes turned stormy. As soon as they were out of the elevator, he released her hand.

"Fine," he said. "I see your point." He hung up the phone and placed it back in Olivia's purse before his gaze pinned her. His eyes were cold as the gel ice bag beneath her head. "So that's why you came to the airport," he said. "Why you were so frantic to stop the plane. And here I thought you had come for me." A sad smile tipped his mouth. "But it's always been about French Kiss, hasn't it, Olivia?"

Before she could even try to deny it, he looked at his

brothers and father. "Grayson, you and Dad stay with Olivia and make sure she's okay. Nash, you come with me to the fashion show. Two Beaumont brothers should be more than sufficient for the press." He was almost out the front doors when Olivia finally found her voice. It wasn't a timid, unsure voice. It was a strong, commanding voice that had Deacon stopping in his tracks.

"Stop right there, Deacon Beaumont!"

She looked at the EMTs. "Get these straps off me. I'm not going to the hospital." They glanced at each other before they did what she asked.

Deacon came striding back over. "Oh yes, you are going to the hospital. Now lie back down, Olivia."

"No." She hopped off the gurney and met him toe to toe. "I'm not going anywhere until I've said what I came to say."

Deacon released his breath. "I get it, Olivia. If your designs are going to make it, we need to be at the fashion show. And if you hadn't pissed me off so much the other night, I would've realized that and stayed until after the show."

"I pissed you off?" She pointed at his chest. "You punched my father."

He blinked. "Your father? That street bum is your father?"

"He's not a street bum. He's a salesman who just happens to prefer the outdoors to four walls."

Deacon studied her. "So why didn't you tell me that?"

"Because you never gave me the chance. Like always, you just barged in and took over. Just like you did today. You answered my phone—my phone—then assumed you knew why I was here without once waiting for me to tell you."

"She is right, Deke," Nash said.

Deacon shot him a mean-looking glance before he turned to Olivia. "So are you telling me that Samuel didn't call you and ask you to stop me from getting on the plane?"

"No, I'm not telling you that at all. Samuel did call me. And he did want me to stop you from leaving. At first I thought I rushed to the airport because I didn't want my designs to fail." Her voice lost some of its belligerence. "Those are my designs that are going to be on the runway tonight—designs that I have spent most of my life working on. And I'll admit that I want them to be a success." She tipped up her chin and tried not to lose herself in the deep purple-blue of his eyes. "But when I saw you sitting on the plane, I realized that my designs had nothing to do with me not wanting you to leave. I don't want you to leave, Deacon, because I realized that I don't want to live without you. And it doesn't seem to matter that you're Michael's son—"

Donny John cut in. "There seems to be some confusion on fathers here. Deacon is my son, not Michael's."

When she sent Deacon a questioning look, he nodded. "It's true. Michael was infertile. The letter my mother sent Michael was just to tell him about my birth in the hopes that a nephew would mend things between the two brothers." He stepped closer. "Now what were you saying about not being able to live without me regardless of who my father is?"

She might've been annoyed with his arrogance if the hopeful look on his face hadn't been so cute. "I don't care who your father is. To me you'll always just be Deacon. The arrogant, controlling boss who walks into a room and takes charge. The sweet, caring man who took me to Paris. The polite Southern gentleman who pulls out my chair and opens my doors and makes me feel like a woman. Not a weak woman, but a strong woman who can be anything she wants to be. Even if the only thing she truly wants to be is your woman." She tried to continue her speech in a strong voice, but it was hard to appear strong when a tear leaked out of her eye. "I love you, Deacon. That's why I drove like a maniac to get here. Why I bought a ticket to Louisiana. And why I got on the plane and made a fool of myself."

Deacon studied her as if he were studying a sales spreadsheet, his gaze intense, as if he were ferreting out all her secrets. Finally, after what felt like a lifetime, he spoke. "Okay."

"Okay?" Her eyes narrowed. "I spilled out my heart to you and all you can say is 'okay'?"

"No. I have some other things I'd like to say, but they'll need to wait. Right now we need to get you to a fashion show." Without waiting for a reply, he swept her up in his arms and carried her out the door.

*C*HAPTER TWENTY-NINE

When Deacon and Olivia arrived at the hotel where the fashion show was being held, the main ballroom was already filled to capacity. Celebrities and honored guests sat in the rows of chairs that surrounded the catwalk, and television equipment and cameras filled every other available space.

The backstage was even more chaotic. Designers, hair stylists, and makeup artists swarmed around supermodels, adjusting bras and panties, fixing hair, and touching up makeup. Reporters and photographers circled, taking notes and snapping pictures, while a camera crew interviewed the models as they were being primped. In the midst of the mass confusion, Samuel stood, his usually perfect hair mussed and his tie crooked. When he saw Olivia, he hurried over.

"Thank God you're here," he said. "One of the models has the flu. Another went on a doughnut binge this morning and looks pregnant in the Romeo bra and panty set.

And the stage backdrop for the Lotario Collection is all wrong."

Olivia expected Deacon to start issuing orders, and when he didn't, she glanced over to find his eyes wide and his mouth partially open in stunned shock. For the first time, he looked like he didn't have a clue what to do. That alone was enough to put a smug smile on her face. Especially after his lame reply to her heartfelt speech at the airport. And after he hadn't spoken a word on the way to the hotel. Not one word. He'd just driven the Porsche like a movie stunt man in a car chase while Olivia fumed.

"What, Deacon?" she said. "Don't tell me that you don't know what to do." She might've continued to rub it in if the show wasn't starting in mere minutes. Looking around at a scene she had witnessed dozens of times before, she felt an invigorating excitement.

"Which model has the flu?" she asked as she took Samuel's clipboard.

"Leila."

Olivia flipped through the list of models. "It's too late to call one of the alternates, we'll have to divide up the designs Leila planned to wear." She ran her finger down the list. "Charlize and Renee have similar measurements. Get them fitted now. Let's not worry about the backdrop. Once the models are on the runway, no one will be looking at it anyway. And as for the poochy tummy, let's go with it. It might make women around the world feel a little better about their own bodies. Also, you'll need to call Kelly and have her bring me something from my house to wear on the runway—she can choose."

While Samuel raced off to do her bidding, the side door opened, and Donny, Nash, and Grayson walked in and joined Deacon, who still stood by the door. He no longer looked shocked. In fact he was smiling. And surprisingly, Olivia smiled back before she started issuing orders.

"Grayson, you'll need to get dressed. You'll be going out with two of the models at the end of your collection. And the same goes for you, Nash."

Grayson nodded while Nash gave her a salute. "Yes, ma'am."

"Deacon, you'll go out last." She didn't wait for him to reply before she clapped her hands. "Now let's get to it. We've got a fashion show to pull together."

But her excitement left quickly enough as one problem after the other cropped up. The pop singer they'd hired to open the show split a seam in his pants and had to have them quickly stitched, but once he got onstage, he rocked the house. Olivia adjusted the deep-purple bra of the first model before sending her to Samuel, who stood at the top of the stairs wearing a headset and issuing orders into the microphone.

Once the model stepped out onstage, there was nothing for Olivia to do but hold her breath and watch the backstage monitors as the model pranced down the runway like a pony on parade. It wasn't until she made her first turn that the crowd broke out in deafening applause, and Olivia's stomach released a mere fraction. But this was only one design. There were dozens more to come. And with each model and each round of applause, she relaxed a little more.

During a commercial break, Kelly arrived with a dress flung over her arm. It wasn't one of Olivia's business suits. It was a sleeveless purple-polka-dotted dress with a flared skirt that Olivia had bought on impulse and never worn.

"I thought it was time for our top designer to strut her stuff," Kelly said with a smile. "And I think this shows off your creative personality better than those stuffy suits you've been wearing."

Olivia held up the flirty dress and smiled. "I think you're right, Kelly. And call me Olivia."

Kelly laughed. "I get the feeling that we've both done a little evolving since the Beaumonts have arrived." She took Olivia's arm and led her back to one of the makeshift dressing rooms to help her change into the dress.

Because she was still confused and needed some advice, Olivia spilled her guts about what had happened at the airport.

"'Okay'? That's all he said?" Kelly zipped the dress and handed Olivia the purple high heels she'd brought.

"That was it. And since you've dated a lot of guys, I was hoping you'd know what it meant."

Kelly blushed. "Actually, I haven't really dated that many guys—okay, so I've only dated five guys. And one was in third grade. But I know a good guy when I see him, and Mr. Beaumont is a good guy. If he said 'Okay,' then I think everything is going to be okay. Now we better hurry before the show ends without you."

Once the makeup artist gave Olivia the once-over with his brushes, she and Kelly hurried back to watch the rest of the show.

Grayson and Nash turned out to be naturals. Grayson even gave the camera a sexy little smile as he walked down the aisle with a model on each arm. Nash was a little more theatrical. He had coached the girls he walked with, and when they reached the end of the runway, they gave him a kiss on either cheek as he flashed a brilliant smile and winked.

The Valentino Collection was the grand finale, and Olivia couldn't help taking extra time with the models before they climbed the stairs to the stage. The last one out wore the purple lace-up corset. Olivia had just retied the bow in front for the third time when Deacon spoke.

"I liked it better on you."

She glanced behind her. He had changed into a gray suit, purple shirt, and silver tie, and the supermodels couldn't seem to take their eyes off him.

"You look nice," she said.

"So do you," he said, even though his eyes remained locked with hers. "New dress?"

Before she could answer, Samuel hissed at them, "Stop gawking at each other, you two, and get up here. You're on next."

Olivia looked away from Deacon and realized that all the models had moved out onstage and Samuel was frantically motioning to the two of them. Deacon took her arm and helped her up the stairs, where Samuel fussed with her hair before giving her an air kiss on either cheek.

"You did it, love. You've knocked their socks off." He held back the curtain and waited for her to step out onstage.

She turned to follow his directive, but then froze. The runway spilled out in front of her, lined with beautiful models all wearing her designs. Suddenly Olivia was terrified. She didn't belong here amid all the lights and cameras. She took a step back and ran into Deacon.

He placed his hands on her waist and leaned down to whisper in her ear, "It's okay, Livy. I'll be right beside you." He paused. "Forever."

Before she could absorb his words, the announcer spoke. "And now I'd like to introduce to you the new CEO of French Kiss, Deacon Valentino Beaumont, and the designer of tonight's entire collection, Olivia Harrington."

Deacon moved next to her and took her hand, his warmth and strength giving her the courage she needed to take the first step. They walked down the runway together while cameras clicked and the audience rose to its feet in applause. The applause continued long after Olivia and Deacon reached the end.

"They love you," he said as he smiled at the crowd. "Almost as much as I love you."

"You love me?"

Uncaring of the camera on a hoist that moved in for a close-up, he turned and brushed a strand of hair from her cheek. "Completely. Now tell me you'll marry me and be my woman for life."

It was hard to keep from flying into his arms. But since it would be her job to keep this arrogant man in line, she shrugged. "Okay."

His eyebrow quirked before he laughed. "I guess I deserved that. Now, shall we seal the deal?" Then right there in front of the audience and millions of television viewers, he kissed her. Not a quick kiss but a long, deep kiss that had the runway models sighing and the applause getting louder. When he pulled back, all she could do was beam with happiness.

"I love you, Deacon Valentino. Although it would've been nice if you'd asked me at the airport instead of in front of millions of people."

He flashed a smile. "Haven't I always told you that perfect timing is everything?"

There was a staccato of pops, and purple lip-shaped confetti filled the air. As it floated around them like a billion kisses, she had to agree.

Reporter Eden Huckabee's dedication to chasing a story leads to a steamy Q&A with Nash Beaumont, French Kiss's kinkiest VP. But a highly personal confession is the real scoop...

Please see the next page
for a preview of

A Billionaire
After Dark.

CHAPTER ONE

If you want to make it in this business, you must immerse yourself in the story."

That was the advice Eden Huckabee's editor had given her. But what Eden was getting ready to do was more than immersing herself. It was out-and-out insanity. Especially when the man who waited behind the double doors of the penthouse suite could be another Zodiac Killer. Or the real Zodiac Killer, since he'd never been apprehended. All Eden had was the word of a prostitute that he wasn't.

"He's a really respectful guy," Madison had said, "who must be afraid of women. That's the only reason I can think of for the 'no touching' rule."

No touching. That's what had cinched the deal for Eden. She could immerse herself in the story as long as there was no touching. Taking a deep breath, she tapped on one of the doors before she used the room key that had been in the envelope she'd picked up at the concierge's desk. But before she could reach for the door handle, it turned. Eden tensed for flight, but her body relaxed when a young man who looked like Harry Styles from the boy band One Direction peeked out. He had long hair and pretty eyes, and still carried baby fat in his cheeks.

This was the man Madison called the Dark Seducer? No wonder he kept the lights off; he probably didn't want the escorts carding him. She bit the inside of her cheek to keep from laughing. It appeared that all she needed to worry about now was being asked to perform a cheer in a parochial pleated skirt. Pleated skirts made her butt look the size of a front-loader washer, and she had never been what you would call coordinated.

While she was trying not to laugh, the young man was giving her a thorough once-over. His gaze wandered over her damp hair, rain-drenched coat, and wet high heels. It was raining cats and dogs, and since she had forgotten to bring cash to tip the valet, she'd been forced to park a good block and a half away. San Francisco had a lot of things, but parking wasn't one of them.

"So are you a hooker?" The teenager finally spoke. "Because you don't look hot enough to be a hooker."

All the cuteness drained right out of him, and she had the strong urge to pinch his baby-fat cheeks until his eyes watered. "I believe that hot is in the eye of the beholder. And we're called escorts, not hookers."

"What's the difference?"

Eden had wondered the same thing, but after meeting Madison, she'd learned that there was a big difference between being a hooker and being an escort. Hookers had pimps. Escorts had services. Hookers worked nightly. Escorts worked rarely. Hookers barely made enough to keep them in drugs. Escorts made a boatload of cash—not to mention the jewelry, vacations, and homes they received as bonuses. Hookers weren't picky about their clients. Escorts were very picky.

Which didn't explain why Madison had chosen this smart-mouthed yahoo.

"Are you going to let me in?" she asked. "Or am I not hot enough?"

He shrugged and opened the door.

The suite was over-the-top lavish. The marble floors of the entryway gleamed in the light of the overhead chandelier. There was an opulent contemporary dining room table on the right. And in the living area, white couches and chairs surrounded a coffee table with a circular bed of blue quartz in the center that flickered with gas flames. Being wet and cold, Eden wanted to move closer to the fire. Instead she stood there, dripping on the marble floor and staring with awe at the spectacular view of downtown and the Bay Bridge. Obviously the kid made money. No doubt one of the growing number of Internet baby billionaires who struggled to spend their money. It wouldn't be a bad angle for a story. But one story at a time. This story was about Madison. It was Madison's perspective she needed to channel. What ran through her head when she walked into a hotel room? What did she see? Feel? And ultimately, how did she deal with selling her body for—

Eden's mind came to a screeching halt when hands settled on her shoulders. She jumped and then turned to point a finger like a mother with a naughty toddler. "No touching, young man."

Looking duly chastised, he held up his hands. "Okay. Okay. I was just going to take your coat."

"Oh. Sorry." She slipped off the coat and handed it to him. Beneath she wore a black sequined cocktail dress that she'd worn to the Christmas office party. She thought it was sexy, but Baby Cheeks seemed thoroughly disappointed. His eyes lost their gleam of anticipation, and his shoulders slumped in the ill-fitting burgundy jacket. A burgundy jacket with a gold name tag pinned above the breast pocket. *Jeremy Ross*.

Eden's eyes widened. "You work at the hotel?"

"Yeah," he said. "I wanted to work at Starbucks but they won't let you have a tattoo on your neck. Not that I have one, but I want to get one. I'm thinking that one of those Chinese dragons on my chest with its tail wrapping around my throat would be so wicked—"

A cell phone rang, and he pushed aside his jacket and took the phone off his belt clip. When he spoke, he used a lot more respect than he had with Eden. "Yes, sir. Okay, I'm leaving now." He hung up. "I gotta go. The concierge said that if you need anything, just call down." He was almost to the door when she stopped him.

"Wait! Where is my...date?"

He shrugged. "I don't have a clue. I just dropped by the complimentary fruit basket that goes with the suite." He nodded at the basket of fruit on the bar. "Maybe the guy stiffed you." He gave her the once-over. "If so, what could I get for twenty-one dollars?"

Eden lifted an eyebrow. "How about a swift kick in the seat of your pants?"

He rolled his eyes. "I don't see how you make a living as a hooker. You've got way too much attitude." He turned and walked out the door.

When he was gone, Eden stood there for a few minutes not knowing what to do. Part of her was relieved that she wouldn't have a hand in sexually corrupting a minor, and the other part had gone back to being scared. So much so that she thought about helping herself to a couple minis from the bar. But Eden wasn't a drinker. Or a smoker. Or a midnight toker. Something that really annoyed her grandparents. Pops and Mimi believed that a glass of wine or the occasional hit of marijuana kept you from being an uptight asshole.

Which probably explained Eden's personality.

Trying to stay focused on the goal, she glanced around the suite and started her story: *The blue flames of the fire reflected in the floor-to-ceiling windows that offered a spectacular, rain-drenched view of the city. A view that had been bought for a price. But Madison had learned early on that anything could be bought for a price... even your soul.*

Or was that too dramatic? Eden's boss, the editor of the small newspaper she worked for, always got on her for being too dramatic.

"You should write romance novels," Stella would say. "Because with that kind of mushy prose, you'll never make it as a serious writer."

But Eden would make it. She might write a little dramatically, but she had something that other people didn't have. Her father called it true grit. Her mother called it enlightened aura. And her brothers called it pain-in-the-ass stubbornness. Eden called it goal-setting. And she had never left a goal unaccomplished.

Never.

And right now her goal was to become the next Woodward and Bernstein. She wanted to do investigative reporting like her father had done before he had started teaching college journalism. So far she'd been given only human interest stories. Charity walks, doggy costume contests, and a night at the opera. But now she had a story that she could sink her teeth into. A story about the underbelly of prostitution. It was the first real news story Stella had given her, and Eden was determined to knock her editor's socks off with it. Even if it meant Eden had to go above and beyond. And this was certainly going above and beyond.

Taking her phone from her purse, she made a few notes describing the furniture, fireplace, and view. But the living room wasn't what she needed to describe as much as the bedroom. She glanced at the double doors to her left, and after only a moment's hesitation, she walked over and opened one.

Light from the living area sliced through the dark across plush white carpet and the puffy satin duvet on the bed. Was this the room where she would be expected to strip? Not that she was actually going to strip down to her skin. She wasn't about to go that far for a story. All she needed was a taste of what it felt like to be in Madison's shoes. Just a glimpse of the debauchery of the escort world. Once she had that glimpse, she intended to contract a bad stomach virus and get the heck out of there.

But for now she might as well get a feel for her part. Channeling Mimi's favorite actress, Mae West, Eden placed a hand on her hip and strutted seductively into the dark room. "So what do you want, big boy?" She ran a finger along the cool, slick fabric of the duvet. "You want a slow burn or a fast trip around the world?"

There was a rustle before a smooth Southern voice spoke. "Personally, I've always liked things slow and hot. But I am a little curious as to what going around the world consists of."

Eden dropped her phone, and it thumped to the carpet,

but not half as loudly as her heart thumping against her rib cage. "I-I'm sorry," she stammered as she turned toward the voice. "I didn't realize someone was in here."

"Then who were you talking to?"

She tried to collect herself, but it wasn't easy when her knees felt like overcooked spaghetti. "I was just"— unable to think up a lie, she told the truth—"practicing."

There was a long pause before he spoke. "Close the door."

She tried to clear the fear that clogged her throat. "There's no touching, right?"

"I thought I explained the rules to your service." His voice sounded closer. "No talking and follow my instructions to a tee." The door slammed closed, causing Eden to almost jump out of her heels.

Being in the dark with a complete stranger had her reevaluating her goals. And being a good investigative reporter took a backseat to self-preservation and getting the hell out of there.

"Look." She took a step closer to the door. "I'm sorry, but I don't think I can do this."

"Obviously. You seem to have a problem keeping your mouth shut."

Suddenly she wasn't scared as much as annoyed. "And you seem to have control issues."

"I believe I'm paying two thousand dollars for that control."

"Two thousand?" Eden couldn't hide her surprise. She knew that Madison made a lot of money as an escort, but she hadn't thought it was that much. "Are you kidding me?" Realizing that she didn't sound like an escort, she backpedaled. "I mean, Madison told me that I'd make much less."

"She lied." The words were spoken so close to her ear that she released a squeal. She backed away and bumped into the bed, sitting down with a bounce on the down comforter. The mattress dipped as his hands pressed on either side of her hips. "There will be touching."

"B-but that wasn't part of the deal."

"I don't know what kind of deal you made," he said, "but the deal I made was for a woman who will do exactly what I say."

"Exactly?" she squeaked.

He leaned closer, his breath falling against her lips like steam on a bathroom mirror. "Exactly."

Before Eden could make it very clear that she wasn't about to do exactly what he said, he moved away. A few seconds later, a light clicked on. Not a light that lit up the room, but a soft recessed light that shone only on the bed. The Dark Seducer stood by the window, his tall, lean body outlined by the small amount of light that filtered in through the curtains.

"But you're right," he said. "I won't be doing the touching. And you won't be touching me. Now take off your dress."

With his words and the light on, Eden's determination to succeed returned. All she had to do was slip off her dress and endure just a brief sampling of the humiliation that Madison went through. Of course thinking you could do something and actually doing it were two different things. Her hands shook so badly she had to fist them for a few seconds before she reached for the straps of her dress. She tried to calm her nerves with a little mental justification: *This is no different from going to a nudist beach with your grandparents.* Except she hadn't been to a nudist beach with her grandparents since she was three. *The human body is beautiful and should be shared.* Except her body wasn't beautiful and she had never been good at sharing. *This is only a few minutes of your life.* Except as the dress slipped to her waist and revealed her bra, time seemed to stand still.

Then he spoke. "Take it all the way off."

She swallowed, and her heart thumped in her ears as she wiggled out of the dress and dropped it to the floor. She thought about removing her heels, but Madison had said that he liked the heels left on. Just the heels. She tried to assess all the emotions racing through her so she could write them down later. Humiliation. Fear. Excitement. Excitement? Yes, it was there nibbling at the edges of her humiliation and fear.

"Now the bra and panties...slowly."

This was her cue to exit, to grab her dress and phone and get the hell out of there. But her curiosity wouldn't let her. "Why do you do this?"

"Excuse me?"

"Why do you hire women?"

There was a pause, and she thought he wasn't going to answer her. And then his voice came out of the darkness, low, deep, and Southern-soaked. "Why else? Because I'm sexually deviant."

His blatant response should've just reinforced her belief that he was a wealthy man who enjoyed victimizing women, but somehow it did the opposite. It made her see him as a human being with flaws. And Eden had always had a weakness for flaws. Probably because she had so many herself.

"Watching a woman pleasure herself while you sit in the dark really isn't all that deviant." She scooted closer. "I'm sure a lot of men would want to do the same thing if they had the money."

His laughter wasn't filled with humor as much as derision. "Really."

"Okay, so maybe they would want to do more than watch." They also wouldn't worry about being seen. She squinted. Was he ugly? Disfigured? A pitiful Elephant Man shunned by society? The questions swirled around in her head. "Why the dark?" she asked. "Are you afraid that women won't find you attractive? Because that shouldn't be a concern. Unlike men, women aren't hung up on physical looks. And with all the dating sites, you should have no trouble whatsoever finding a companion."

"The problem isn't finding a companion."

She thought for a moment until the truth dawned on her. "Oh. I'm sorry. But look on the bright side. They have medicine for that now. One little pill and things are looking up. And you shouldn't be afraid to tell a doctor. Lots of people suffer from it. Even me."

"What?"

Eden's face filled with heat. She had never shared this information with anyone and didn't know why she did now. But since it was out, she continued in hopes that if she shared her truths, he'd share more of his. "I don't know if it's called impotency with women, but it runs along the same lines. I've never experienced an orgasm." She gestured as she talked, something she did when she was nervous or trying to get a point across. "Weird but true. And I don't think it's a physical problem as much as a mental one. I just have other things besides orgasms to concentrate on right now. Although I have faked a few. Men seem to get very depressed if you don't make them think they're good in bed."

There was a long stretch of silence before the light clicked off. Eden barely had time to tense before her dress was slipped over her head and she was effortlessly lifted her to her feet.

"What are you doing?" she asked.

"It's time for you to leave." With a hand on the small of her back, he pushed her toward the door.

"But—" Before Eden could finish, she was standing outside the closed bedroom door, listening to the click of the lock. Obviously faked orgasms had been the wrong subject for an escort to bring up.

Cassie McPherson falls for the sexy escort she hires for her company's holiday party. But James isn't an escort—he's her fiercest business rival...and all he wants for Christmas is *her*.

Please see the next page
for an excerpt from

Hunk for
the Holidays.

CHAPTER TWO

A few hours later, Cassie wasn't sure if she looked festive or like a desperate hooker. The dress was a *shirt* with a hem and neckline that ran at opposite angles, showing off her right shoulder and a whole lot of left thigh. The "few little Christmas gifts" Amy had left included a strapless bra that shoved her boobs together and a satiny pair of panties that covered very little of the front and none of the back. Then there were the shoes, which weren't shoes at all, but some kind of torture chambers that imprisoned her feet in skinny, crisscrossed red straps that ran from ankle to toes and kept her feet from sliding off the skyscraper spiked heels. Mike would have drooled over these puppies, she thought. Not that his size thirteens would've fit in them.

The entire ensemble made Cassie feel like a tall, flashing red light that said something like SEX FOR SALE; COME AND GET IT or DESPERATE, SEX-STARVED WOMAN NEEDS BREAK FROM SHOWER NOZZLE.

But Cassie didn't have much of a choice. Her burgundy dress and shoes had mysteriously disappeared from the executive bathroom. Or not so mysteriously, considering how devious Amy was. Cassie could've gone home and changed, but her escort for the evening was bought and paid for and hopefully on his way to the office to meet her. There was no way she was going to dole out five hundred bucks so some college kid could go home and play video games for the evening.

So Cassie did what she always did in a no-win situation—she went with it, applying more makeup than she normally wore and leaving her hair to fall down her back in long dark waves. The only thing she didn't apply was lipstick. Her lips were full enough without drawing attention to them. She gave her reflection in the mirror one last annoyed look. If this wouldn't degrade and undermine her authority in front of all the employees, nothing would.

On the way back to her office, the phone rang, and since everyone else had left for the night except for Juanita the cleaning lady, Cassie wobbled over to the receptionist's desk and picked up the receiver.

She adjusted it around her dangling diamond earring, the only thing she had planned on wearing, and answered, "M and M Construction."

"Hi, Mama's angel. I'm glad I caught you."

"Hi, Mom. What's up?"

"I wanted to let you know that I'm making your father stay home tonight." In the background, Cassie could hear her father ranting something about how her mother and the damned doctor had ruined all his plans.

"Should I come over?" Cassie sat down on the edge of the desk and examined the last of Amy's gifts, a red beaded clutch purse. She fiddled with the rhinestone latch, trying to figure out how to open it.

"No, sweetheart. He's fine. But if he goes to the party, all he'll do is talk business and Dr. Matheson doesn't think it's a good idea." This time Cassie heard exactly what her father thought of Doc Matheson. "Listen, dear, I need to go and calm him down. I'll talk to you later. Have fun at the party."

"Yeah, Mom. I will." Cassie hung up the phone. Maybe it was best if her father didn't come. If talking business didn't give him another heart attack, her outfit certainly would.

Frustrated with the entire evening so far, she yanked at the latch on the purse. It flipped open, spilling its contents all over the floor. Cassie looked down at the pile of red and black foil-covered condoms surrounding her high heels.

She laughed. "I'll get even with you if it's the last thing I do, Amy Walker." She squatted down and began to scoop the condoms back into her purse, heedless of her unladylike position.

A deep and very masculine cough had her teetering on her heels and almost falling backward on her butt. Grabbing on to the edge of the desk, she regained her balance and got to her feet. Although the sight that greeted her had her reaching out for the desk again.

A man stood by the Christmas tree in the foyer. Not a man really, more like a vision. The clear lights that twinkled around his dark head made him look like something straight out of a dream. A wet dream. Man, Elite Escorts had outdone themselves this time. This was no gangly college boy in an ill-fitting rental tux, but a mature man in a tuxedo that looked made-to-order for his tall, muscular frame.

Like James Bond right before he bopped a shapely beauty, his bow tie was undone and lay flat against the front pleats of the crisp white shirt that was unbuttoned at his tanned throat. He stood looking at Cassie with a slight smile on his firm lips and one brown brow arched over an eye that was the exact color of her aunt Wheezie's favorite Scotch.

Cassie forgot to breathe.

"Hi." The smile deepened, along with two dimples. "I didn't mean to spook you." When Cassie still didn't say anything, the smile dropped and both brows lifted. "Are you okay?"

He walked toward her, and she was reminded of the black panther at the Denver Zoo, his movements sleek and predatory. She swallowed and tried to get her mind off his hot body and back in her head. It was difficult, especially when this wonderful eye candy stood so close and when she and Amy had just been discussing how long it had been since she'd had sex. But hot or not, she needed to remember that this man was one of her employees. She dealt with men all day long. Alpha men. She could handle some pretty boy who worked for an escort service.

She plastered on a smile. "Yes, I'm fine. It's just that you're early."

The quizzical look remained, and he tugged up the sleeve of his jacket and glanced at a watch that looked an awful lot like her father's Rolex. "No, I'm right on time."

She waved him off. "It doesn't matter. You're here." She grabbed the car keys from the desk and brushed past him. He smelled really good, like hot spiced cider and primitive lust. Or was the primitive lust her?

"My truck's down in the parking garage." She kept talking as she headed toward the elevator. "We'll take it.

The party's at a house about thirty minutes away, so it's probably good you got here early." She pressed the button of the elevator, then turned to steal another peek.

He wasn't there. He still stood at the receptionist's desk, although his head had turned to follow her. Okay, so he looked great, but he was a little slow on the uptake. No wonder he worked for an escort service at his age. The elevator doors opened, and she pointed at them.

"Are you coming?"

He tipped his head to one side. "Who are you?"

Oh, so that was it. She just hadn't introduced herself. She laughed and held the door of the elevator. "I'm Cassie McPherson, your employer for the evening."

He didn't move. "My employer?"

Back to the mental deficiency theory. She tried talking slowly and clearly. "Yes, I called Elite Escorts and hired you for the evening to take me to my office Christmas party. I paid in advance, so I expect a little service here. Like maybe you getting a move on."

His whiskey eyes twinkled, but he still didn't move. "You're Cassie McPherson, the daughter of Al McPherson, and you called for a male escort?"

"Right. So are you coming or do I need to get a refund?"

"Your father's not here, I take it?"

"Not that it makes a difference, but no. He's at home."

He might be a simpleton, but, man, the flash of those white, even teeth and dimples was flat-out sexy. "Then I guess I'm all yours for the evening." He walked over and reached above her head to hold the elevator door. "Here"—he held up a foil-covered condom—"you forgot one."

Cassie jerked the condom out of his hand and then

nearly fell flat on her face as she stumbled over her feet on the way into the elevator. He reached out and steadied her.

"Easy there."

The door closed, and he pushed one of the buttons while she rubbed the warm imprint he had left on her arm. Her heart thumped wildly against the tight band of her push-up bra. And suddenly she worried if all her high-cholesterol lunches and lack of exercise were catching up to her and besides inheriting her father's bad disposition, she had also inherited his clogged arteries. She couldn't bring herself to believe that it had anything to do with the man who so casually leaned back against the rail that ran along the wall of the elevator. Cassie McPherson didn't go all weak-kneed over men. Even re-e-e-e-ally good-looking ones who belonged in magazine ads for expensive men's cologne.

She turned away from the hot picture he presented and took two deep breaths, willing her heart to resume its normal cadence. It was hard to do with those eyes pinned on her with such intensity. Hard, but not impossible. She wasn't called Cast-Iron Cassie for nothing. She never let emotions get in the way of business. And this was business.

Clearing her throat, she explained the terms of his employment. "So here's what I expect." She opened her clutch and dropped in her car keys and the condom. "Keep a low profile. Be attentive, but not clingy. And try not to talk. If you're asked a question about our relationship, simply say that we've just met."

His eyes narrowed, and one side of his mouth tipped up at the corner. Definitely not a smile, more of a smirk. "How about if I just say that I'm not the kind of man who kisses and tells."

Heat flooded her cheeks, but she held it together. "Just stick to the plan."

"It seems you have a lot of plans." He lifted an eyebrow in the direction of her purse. "I'm not sure I can keep up."

Cassie ignored the innuendo and stayed on track. "The old relatives are the worst. They'll try to get you to commit to family gatherings and such. Decline gracefully. Don't drink with my aunt Louise. She'll drink you under the table and then interrogate the hell out of you. She looks very sweet, but she's a barracuda."

The elevator doors slid open, but not at the parking garage. He stepped out and held the door.

"You pushed the wrong button." She punched L for the lower level. "I'm parked in the garage."

He took her arm and gently but firmly pulled her out. "I know, but I'm parked right out front. So we can take my car."

"I'd rather drive," she stated as she caught the elevator door before it closed.

"But then you'd be escorting me, and that's not what I'm getting paid for." He caressed the underside of her arm. The tingling sensation caused her to pull away.

She turned on him as the elevator door slid closed. "You're getting paid to follow my orders."

In her heels, Cassie was only a few inches shorter than he was. So she shouldn't feel intimidated by his size, not with four brothers who were just as tall, if not taller. Yet there was something about this man that had her taking a step back. She wasn't frightened, but she was smart enough to be wary.

"And I bet you're pretty good at giving orders." He tucked her hand in the crook of his arm and tugged her toward the glass doors. "But right now, it's my job to get you to a Christmas party, and I intend to do it. After that, you can order me around all you want to."

She tried to dig in her heels, but she wasn't exactly stable in the sky-high shoes. The slippery marble floor of the lobby didn't help.

"I like driving," she stated through clenched teeth as he pulled her along.

"No doubt." He reached for the large gold handle of the glass door. "But I'm kinda old-fashioned about that. When I take a woman out, I like to drive."

"You've got to be kidding."

He glanced down at her. "Nope. Not at all. I don't like women to pay, open doors, or drive." He shrugged. "Call it a character flaw." He pulled open the door.

"Obviously, one among many. Let's not forget arrogance and stubbornness." The toes of her shoes hit the threshold, and he was brought up short. "I want to drive."

"Ms. McPherson?"

They both turned and stared at the worried face of the security guard who had come up behind them. "Is everything all right?"

Cassie thought about saying no and getting her arrogant, stubborn escort tossed out on his ear. But then she wouldn't have a date for the evening and would have to suffer through all the wives feeling sorry for her and trying to hook her up with some desperate relative. Of course, how much more desperate could you get than hiring an escort for the evening?

She stopped pulling away. "Of course. Everything is fine, Scotty. How is that new baby of yours?"

The tension left Scotty's face, and he grinned. "As cute

as they come. Although he's not so cute when he keeps me up on my nights off."

"He'll outgrow it. My nieces and nephews all did."

"I hope so." Scotty moved over to the door. "Let me get that for you, sir."

"Thank you." Her escort flashed Scotty one of his megawatt smiles. "Merry Christmas."

"Merry Christmas, sir." Scotty nodded at her. "Ms. McPherson."

The frigid air hit Cassie like an ice-cold fist in the face. With it came the realization that she'd forgotten her coat. She stopped dead in her tracks. And her wallet. And her cell phone. The wallet she could live without, but she never went anywhere without her phone. It was her life-line. How could she have forgotten it?

She glanced at the man who turned to look at her, and a shiver that had nothing to do with the cold raced through her body. Great! Now, all because of some pretty face, she was freezing her posterior off with nothing in her purse but her car keys and a gross amount of condoms.

She tried to pull her hand away, and this time he re-leased it. "I forgot my—" Before she could finish her sentence a heat-infused tuxedo jacket slid over her shoul-ders, along with a very possessive arm. The warmth that enveloped her melted the rest of her resistance.

Maybe she could go one night without her cell phone.

"This way." He led her right out to the street, where a brand-new black Land Rover was parked in the no-parking zone. The locks clicked, and he opened the door and waited for her to slip inside. Once the door closed, Cassie was surrounded by the spicy scent that emanated from his jacket and overcome by a feeling that could be described only as…feminine.

Feminine? Cassie McPherson?

She shook her head to clear it. She needed to be careful. This guy was a bona fide gigolo who knew how to make a woman feel like a woman. A sexy, feminine woman. Which was why he could afford to drive a new Land Rover. The man probably had every wealthy housewife in Denver lined up with their wallets and legs wide open. Which brought up the next point. She waited until they had pulled away from the curb before broaching it.

"About sex."

The SUV swerved slightly, and she quickly glanced over at him. He didn't look shocked as much as amused.

"What about sex?"

She stared straight ahead and tried to keep her voice steady. "I don't want any."

"Ever?"

She looked back at him. "No, not ever. It's just that I don't have sex with escorts."

"Why not? You're paying for it."

Suddenly, her reasons for not having sex with escorts didn't seem valid anymore. Why shouldn't she have sex with an escort? Not just anyone, but this one. This tall, hot, arrogant, and slightly dumb escort who probably needed no sexual instruction at all, who probably could make her come just by looking at her.

An expert lover.

Which was the main reason she couldn't have sex with him. The guy had probably screwed half the female population of the city.

Lucky bitches.

"Because I don't want some nasty disease." She mentally kicked herself for blurting out the truth. "Not that you have some nasty disease, but just in case."

"Then why all the condoms?"

"Those are a joke."

"Too bad."

Her head swiveled around to look at him, but his gaze was pinned on the road. "So you hire escorts just for the company?"

"No, believe me. With my big family, I have plenty of company. I hire escorts to keep that big, loving—and sometimes smothering—family from matchmaking."

He glanced over at her. "That bad, huh?"

She laughed, relieved to be on a less intimate subject. "You don't know the half of it. I've been on so many blind dates, I could write a book on the dos and don'ts."

"But it must be nice to have a big family."

She sighed. "Yeah, sometimes. No, I take that back, most of the time. But it would be a lot nicer if I were married."

"And why aren't you?"

"I've been told I work too much. And I guess they're right." She turned in her seat and looked at his profile. He really was perfect. His features were strong and masculine, but not too prominent. "And what about you? And please don't tell me you have a wife and five kids at home."

He laughed. "I guess I've been told the same thing."

"You work too much?"

He tipped his head and winked at her. "A true workaholic."

Fall in Love with Forever Romance

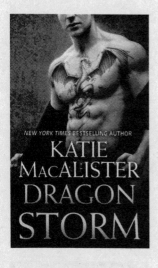

DRAGON STORM
by Katie MacAlister

In *New York Times* bestselling author Katie MacAlister's *Dragon Storm*, Constantine must choose: save his fellow dragons or the mortal woman he's grown to love.

HIS ALL NIGHT
by Elle Wright

In relationships, Calisa Harper has clear rules: no expectations, no commitments, no one gets hurt. She doesn't need a diamond ring to bring her happiness. She just needs Jared. Fine, fit, and ferocious in bed, Jared is Calisa's ideal combination of friend and lover. But the no-strings status they've shared for years is about to get very tangled...

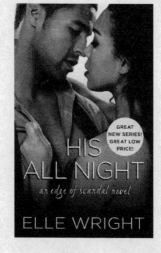

Fall in Love with Forever Romance

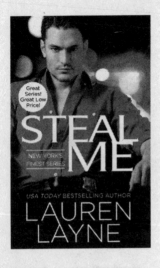

STEAL ME
by Lauren Layne

Faster than a New York minute, homicide detective Anthony Moretti and waitress Maggie Walker find themselves in a perilous pursuit that only gets hotter with each and every rule-breaking kiss.

A BILLIONAIRE
BETWEEN THE SHEETS
by Katie Lane

A commanding presence in the boardroom and the bedroom, Deacon Beaumont has come to save the failing company French Kiss. But one bold and beautiful woman dares to question his authority and everything he knows about love.

Fall in Love with Forever Romance

DUKES ARE FOREVER
by Anna Harrington

When Edward Westover takes possession of his rival's estate, everything that villain held dear—even his beautiful daughter—belongs to Edward. Will Kate Benton fall for the man who now owns everything she has come to know and love—including herself? Fans of Elizabeth Hoyt, Grace Burrowes, and Madeline Hunter will love this Regency–era romance.